You Better Knot Die

You Better Knot Die

BETTY HECHTMAN

BERKLEY PRIME CRIME, NEW YORK

THE BERKLEY PUBLISHING GROUP
Published by the Penguin Group
Penguin Group (USA) Inc.
375 Hudson Street, New York, New York 10014, USA
Penguin Group (Canada), 90 Eglinton Avenue East, Suite 700, Toronto, Ontario M4P 2Y3, Canada
(a division of Pearson Penguin Canada Inc.)
Penguin Books Ltd., 80 Strand, London WC2R 0RL, England
Penguin Group Ireland, 25 St. Stephen's Green, Dublin 2, Ireland (a division of Penguin Books Ltd.)
Penguin Group (Australia), 250 Camberwell Road, Camberwell, Victoria 3124, Australia
(a division of Pearson Australia Group Pty. Ltd.)
Penguin Books India Pvt. Ltd., 11 Community Centre, Panchsheel Park, New Delhi—110 017, India
Penguin Group (NZ), 67 Apollo Drive, Rosedale, North Shore 0632, New Zealand
(a division of Pearson New Zealand Ltd.)
Penguin Books (South Africa) (Pty.) Ltd., 24 Sturdee Avenue, Rosebank, Johannesburg 2196, South
Africa

Penguin Books Ltd., Registered Offices: 80 Strand, London WC2R 0RL, England

This book is an original publication of The Berkley Publishing Group.

Copyright © 2010 by Betty Hechtman.
Interior text design by Kristin del Rosario.

FIRST EDITION: November 2010

Library of Congress Cataloging-in-Publication Data

Hechtman, Betty, 1947–
    You better knot die / Betty Hechtman. —1st ed.
        p.   cm.
    ISBN 978-0-425-23693-2 (hardcover)
1. Crocheting—Fiction. 2. Murder—Investigation—Fiction. I. Title.
    PS3608.E288Y68   2010
    813'.6—dc22

                                                        2010028229

PRINTED IN THE UNITED STATES OF AMERICA

10 9 8 7 6 5 4 3 2 1

Acknowledgments

Sandy Harding is a wonderful editor, and I am so grateful to be working with her. A big thank you to Jessica Faust for helping make my dream come true. Thank you to Natalee Rosenstein for making Berkley Prime Crime such a great place to be. Once again the Berkley art department has given me a wonderful cover. Megan Swartz has been a great help with publicity.

I have to thank my team of experts for answering questions about all kinds of odd things. Financial information came from Steve Palley and Rich Scheiner. Howard Marx, M.D. took care of the medical questions. Los Angeles Police Officer and writer Kathy Bennett advised me on police procedures. Ken Sobel was my gambling consultant. With her crochet skill and eye for detail, Linda Hopkins was a great help with the crochet patterns.

A special thank you to Roberta Martia for all her support and crochet advice. Another special thank you to Judy Libby for her legal expertise and years of friendship going back to our college newspaper days.

Rene Biedermann, Connie Cabon, Alice Chiredjian, Terry Cohen, Clara Feeney, Pamela Feuer, Sonia Flaum, Lily Gillis, Winnie Hineson, Linda Hopkins, Reva Mallon and Elayne

Moschin are part of the Thursday crochet and knit group. Thanks for the friendship, support, sharing of patterns and knowledge, and fun. Paula Tesler keeps us stretching our yarn horizons.

Burl, Max and Samantha, you guys are the best. What else can I say?

You Better Knot Die

CHAPTER 1

"PINK, YOU'VE GOT A PROBLEM," ADELE ABRAMS said as she slowed her car in front of my house. I had been crocheting a snowflake—or trying to—while she drove, and it took me a moment to look up. But when I did—

Lots of strange things have gone on at my house, but the scene that greeted me beat anything I'd seen before. My mouth fell open and I dropped the silver hook and white thread I was holding.

I don't know what was the most shocking. Was it the line of police cruisers along the curb, the uniform stringing yellow crime scene tape across my front porch or the group of uniforms conferring on my front lawn? My house, a crime scene?

"What did you do this time?" Adele asked as she pulled to the curb in front of all the cruisers. Neighbors were drifting into the street and the kid who lived a few houses down had his video camera pointed at all the action.

I took a moment to glare at Adele. We had just spent two days together, which was about a day and a half too much. Adele and I worked together at Shedd & Royal Books and More and we were both part of the crochet group, the Tarzana Hookers, who met at the bookstore. I wouldn't call us friends exactly, more like family. You pick your friends—you get stuck with family. Instead of answering, I just shot her a withering look.

A black Crown Victoria roared into my driveway. The car had barely squeaked to a stop when the door flew open and a tall man in a suit jumped out. Before I could call out his name, Barry sprinted across the lawn, breaking through the yellow tape strung across the porch. He had some kind of tool in his hand. I heard the splintering of my front door and a moment later it flew open. I was out of the car by now, though I didn't get far. One of the uniforms stopped me and didn't seem to care when I said it was my house.

Adele was out of her side of the car in a flash, almost catching her jacket on the door. The jacket was part of what she called a more-subdued look. I wasn't sure what was subdued about it. She'd taken an electric blue ready-made boxy-style blazer and added kelly green and fuchsia crocheted trim around the neck, down the front and at the cuffs. "Pink, you dropped your snowflake." When I turned, she was holding out the ball of white thread, my steel hook and what appeared to be a tangle of the fine yarn. She glanced around. "Maybe I better stay here with you." I shook my head and gestured back toward the car. I didn't know what was going on, but I did know I didn't want to have Adele in the middle of it. She hung her head as I got my suitcase out of the trunk. "Pink, I've been your backup before. C'mon, let me be part of the action." When I pointed toward the car again, she went into a full pout, but she finally got back into the new Matrix station wagon and drove off.

Adele and I were just returning from our trip to San Diego, which Adele kept referring to as a yarn emergency. Since our crochet group, the Tarzana Hookers, had become so connected with the bookstore where I worked, one of the co-owners, Mrs. Shedd, had recently added a yarn department to the store. It was still a work-in-progress because Mrs. Shedd wanted the yarn we sold to be special and high-end rather than what was sold at the big craft stores. When she heard about a yarn store closing in San Diego and selling off their stock, Mrs. Shedd had sent us down there at the last minute.

It was just the high-end unusual stuff we were looking for, and we had packed the back of Adele's wagon solid with yarn. The rest was being UPSed up to us. Adding the new yarn section was good and bad. Good that we were getting all this wonderful yarn, and bad because everything at the bookstore was already on overdrive due to the upcoming holidays and our big launch event. Now we had more work than ever.

"Did you find the body?" one of the uniforms asked when Barry returned a few moments later.

Body?

I tried again to talk to the uniform, but he was impassive. That was when Barry saw me. When he's working, he usually has a neutral expression, but now his whole face relaxed and his breath came out in a gush as he crossed the space between us. Then his expression changed from relief to a mixture of surprise and annoyance.

Homicide Detective Barry Greenberg was my boyfriend. I thought boyfriend was a stupid title for a man in his fifties but had given up on finding a better one and finally gone with it.

"Molly, where were you?" Barry said, looking at the suitcase next to me.

"What body?" I said, ignoring his question. "What's going on?"

"It's okay, we'll get to that in a minute," he said. "You can't just disappear like that. So where were you?"

"Didn't you get my message?" I said. He shook his head. "I'm sure I left you a message." I stopped for a moment. I had left him a message, hadn't I? There had been so much to do when the trip came up and I had been in a hurry. "I know I meant to leave you a message." I thought when I explained my sudden trip was work related he'd understand. His work schedule was such that he often disappeared for days, sometimes with barely a word. I guess not. He just got more agitated as he asked why I hadn't returned any of his calls.

Cell phones are great as long as they're charged. I pulled out mine, which was completely dead. "Sorry. In my haste to leave, I forgot the charger. Now what about the body?"

By now all the cops were listening to our interchange. Barry refused to give out any details until I explained the details of my San Diego trip. He snorted when I mentioned it was a yarn emergency.

"Hey, Greenberg, we want to know about the body," an officer who seemed to be in charge finally said, getting impatient.

"It's *bodies* and they're in the attic," Barry said, reaching out to catch me as my legs went rubbery with the news. Still I pulled away and stumbled toward my house. As soon as I walked in the door, the smell of death was unmistakable. I covered my nose and went back outside.

It took a while to get everything sorted out. The gist was that the cops had been at my neighbor's taking a report.

Emily Perkins had called them, concerned that her husband Bradley had gone missing.

Coincidentally the gas meter reader was making his rounds and while reading my meter had noticed a bad smell coming from the bathroom window I'd left open a crack. Seeing the cops, he'd mentioned the smell. Well, woman with missing husband and dead smell coming from next door . . . The cops taking the report called out the cavalry. Barry heard the call and address and he hadn't been able to get in touch with me for a couple of days so he jumped to conclusions.

And the real source of the stink: I had a backyard full of orange trees that attracted all kinds of rodents who had started making side trips into my attic. I'd had all the entrances sealed up and some traps had been left for any stragglers. There had been three. As soon as the pest control people came by and removed the bodies, the smell disappeared.

I pulled off the last of the yellow tape that was still flapping on my front porch post as I finally dragged my suitcase inside. Barry was already on the phone calling the door contractor the cops used to repair mistakenly knocked down doors. In the meantime, he'd do a temporary fix. I had no doubt he'd be able to do it. Barry could fix anything, and besides, this wasn't the first time my door had been knocked in by mistake.

"You couldn't have used your key?" I said, looking at the light coming in through the broken door panel.

Barry made an uncomfortable face. "I guess I forgot about the key." He sighed as he checked out the battered door. When he turned back toward me, his face was full of emotion and he took me in his arms. "I heard body at your house and I lost it." He hugged me tighter. "I'm glad I was wrong."

"You and me both," I said. I apologized for not leaving him a message. "It's just that I've been so busy. The holidays are always busy at the bookstore. We stay open later and there are more customers. And now we're adding the yarn department. And there's the launch party to plan for. It's the Super Bowl of book events. I mean, how lucky can Shedd and Royal get? The Blood and Yarn series is the hottest of the hot." I caught a blank look on Barry's face. "You don't know about it, do you?" I barely waited for Barry to shake his head before continuing. "The books follow the life of a supersexy vampire who uses crochet to control his blood-lust issues. The latest, *Caught Under the Mistletoe*, comes out next week. The trucks are delivering the books at midnight to bookstores all over, but only Shedd and Royal will have the author, A. J. Kowalski. But here's the really exciting part: A. J. Kowalski is just a pseudonym and nobody knows who the author really is. It turns out he or she lives in Tarzana and has decided to reveal their true identity and sign books at the launch party. Do you realize what that means?" Barry nodded.

"I think it means you ought to take a breath or maybe two," he said. "You're starting to hyperventilate." He glanced back toward the living room as though looking for something, then his eyes grew concerned. "Where are the dogs?"

"And cats," I said, correcting him, referring to the newest residents. I explained that since my younger son, Samuel, owner of the cats, was on the road playing backup and I'd been in a hurry, I'd just boarded all of them. I took a few more breaths to make sure my breathing was back to normal. "So, how long has Bradley Perkins been missing?" I asked and felt his body stiffen.

"Look, babe, I know you like playing the amateur sleuth, but stay out of it."

"Play?" I said with a darkening expression. "I wouldn't call it play; I've solved a few murders."

Barry stepped back, shaking his head. "Here we go again. Okay, babe, you're not going to listen to me, but I'll say it anyway. I'm sure the officers who took the report are dealing with whatever needs to be done. Besides, with all you have to do, why take on anything else? I'd like to have dibs on any spare moments."

I didn't say anything in response. He knew what my silence meant. He sighed and said he had to get back to work. It isn't that I really planned to get involved. I just didn't want to say something I might end up not meaning. My phone was ringing as he went back to his Crown Victoria.

"Mother," my son Peter said. Only he could put so much disapproval in one word. My older son is a television agent, very ambitious and very concerned about his image. "What's going on?" Before I could answer, Peter told me that something had shown up on YouTube that featured me and a lot of cops. Apparently he had some kind of alert set up that notified him if anything came up about any of his clients or me. I explained quickly, but when I got to the part about Bradley Perkins being missing, I heard Peter's breathing change.

"Mother, you're not going to get involved, are you?" When he got dead air as an answer, he groaned. In the past, some of my sleuthing efforts had ended up on the news, causing him all sorts of embarrassment.

"Barry said the same thing," I said, finally. My son groaned again. Peter didn't like Barry. At first I had thought it was just the idea of my dating he objected to, but when Peter kept trying to push me together with an attorney he'd been dealing with, I realized Barry in particular was the problem. I don't know why I kept trying to smooth things over. It wasn't like Barry was going to be Peter's stepfather or anything.

When I got off the phone, I gave myself a few minutes to recover and then went back outside. The street was quiet and there was no hint of all the action that had been going on a short time earlier. The video camera kid was leaning against the wrought iron mailbox across the street. He looked up when I came out. He was at the end of his teens, and someday all his parts would probably fit together, but for now his features were too big for his face and his body was long and gangly. His black hair was tousled and deliberately cut to be uneven. When he saw me look toward the Perkins' house, he shook his head.

"Not home," he called. "She left right after the cops." I walked across the street to where he was standing. Though his family had lived down the block for years, I really didn't know them. I introduced myself and he stuck out his hand. "Ryder Lowenstein." I asked if he'd posted something on YouTube and he seemed pleased at the question. "Pretty cool, huh? I sent it to the channel three news, too, though since there wasn't a real body, I don't think they're going to use it."

"So what do you know about Bradley Perkins' disappearance?" I asked, glancing toward the neighboring yard. In the daylight the Santa's sleigh and reindeer was almost invisible. The lawn decoration was really just an outline with colored lights. Icicle lights ran across the front of the roof and then hung down to the ground next to several boxes with more lights. Someone had obviously been in the midst of putting them up. Some pots of crimson poinsettias were on the front porch. The holiday decorations seemed at odds with the thick green lawn and palm tree in the front yard. But this was the San Fernando Valley and winter was when everything was the most green and lush.

At one time the houses along the two-block stretch had all been similar, kind of like brothers and sisters. They were ranch-style with mullioned windows and pastel wood siding, but over time, between remodeling and additions, the houses were now barely even cousins. The Perkins' house had been given what I called a Mediterranean makeover. It had the trademark terra-cotta tile roof, flesh-colored stucco and an entrance porch that was too tall and too grand to be proportionate to the rest of the single-story house. The rectangular-divided pane windows had been replaced with tall arched ones.

"Not much. I tried interviewing the cops, but they blew me off. Something about not having press credentials." Ryder shrugged. "But right after Mrs. Perkins left, a black sedan pulled up," Ryder said. "A man and woman both dressed in suits went to the door. I don't think they were cops, but they looked official. They hung around for a few minutes, looking in the windows and stuff, but finally left." He looked up and down the street as if checking for any action and then turned back to me.

"Who was the cop in the suit?" Ryder asked. When I didn't respond right away, he pushed the question. "He hung around too long for it to be official."

Yikes, now I had a neighborhood busybody kid to answer to. I just used the boyfriend word, though for a moment I considered trying *relationship partner.*

"Boyfriend?" Ryder snickered.

"I couldn't agree more that it's a silly title, but what else can I call him?" Ryder nodded with understanding.

"It must be tough when you're old and dating. I suppose you're hoping he'll want to upgrade you to fiancée."

"Thanks for making me feel like I'm a hundred," I said with a tiny groan. "And no, I'm not looking for an upgrade in title." I made a move to go, but Ryder kept up with the questions. No doubt he was practicing his interviewing skills. The next thing I knew I was telling him how I'd been married to Charlie for twenty-five years when he died. And now I was enjoying being free. "Or as free as you can be with two sons, one living with you and the other constantly questioning every decision you make. And a mother who's a backup singer—scratch that, was a backup singer, and now is back with her singing group, The She La Las, and enjoying a second chance at a career. A mother who also might show up at any time. And that's not counting the two dogs and the two cats. It doesn't matter that one of the dogs officially belongs to the cop in the suit and just resides at my house or that the two cats really belong to my son." I looked Ryder in the eye. "And you know who really takes care of all of them."

Ryder was beginning to get the too-much-information look on his face, but I kept going. I got his attention back when I mentioned being part of the Tarzana Hookers. Once he heard that *hookers* referred to crochet, his eyes began to glaze over again. But when I mentioned my job at the bookstore, he nodded. "That's why you look familiar. I knew I recognized you from somewhere. You're the one who puts on the author events. I came to the one for that book *Keeping Your Balls in the Air.*" I smiled, uncomfortably remembering that evening. The book was about teaching yourself to juggle and the author had given a lesson. Let's just say it didn't go well. Imagine a bunch of people stumbling into each other while throwing balls around. "I have a tape of it, if you'd like to see," Ryder said. I declined. Going through my disasters once was enough.

"I'm coming to the vampire book launch party." He held up his tiny camera. "I bet my video will get a zillion hits.

If only I could get on the YouTube top ten." He gazed skyward with a dreamy look.

Then Ryder offered to show me his video portfolio, but I told him maybe later. Time was ticking away and I had to pick up the animals.

DRIVING ONTO THE CAMPUS OF WALTER BEASLEY Community College was like driving into the country. Calling it by its full name was really old school. These days everybody called it WBCC (pronounced *Wibk*). Did it really take so much longer to actually say the letters? I thought all this shortening things was due to texting, which I didn't get, either. Instead of all that typing, why not just call? It was easier, faster and less prone to misunderstanding. I guess that made me a dinosaur, though these days it was probably shortened to *dsaur*. The campus of WBCC was set on four hundred acres, most of which was set aside as an agricultural school. So there were fields of crops, livestock, barns and a farm store. I pulled into the parking lot close to the traditional classroom buildings, walked through a forest of tall pines trees to the bungalows and checked my watch. I'd timed it just right. As I stopped at the end bungalow, the door flew open and students flooded out. Dinah Lyons came out last, talking to a girl dressed in what was probably the current fashion, though to me it looked strictly bag lady. Dinah finished with the girl and rushed over to me. As always there was an aura of energy about her.

"Just a little longer, then I give them their finals and send them on their way and we all get to enjoy the holidays," she said with a happy smile. Dinah taught freshman English to what could best be called reluctant students. WBCC accepted everyone and Dinah got them raw from high school.

She had a reputation for turning newbies into real college students—if they survived the semester. She was also my best friend. "I've got news," Dinah said.

"Me, too," I said. There was a ministandoff as we each urged the other to go first. Dinah won and I told her about my homecoming.

"Geez, not again with your front door." Then she laughed and touched my arm. "It's lucky you have a sense of humor. Which I'm sure was sorely tested during your trip with Adele."

"That's the truth," I said with a laugh. Dinah knew all about the difficulties I had with her. Although Adele had been at the bookstore longer than me, and had coveted the job of event coordinator, Mrs. Shedd had hired me instead. Adele had tried to upend me many times. Just when it seemed Adele had finally accepted that I was the event co-ordinator, Mrs. Shedd decided to add the yarn department and asked me to oversee that as well. I'd be the first to say that Adele was much more qualified to run it than me. She had years more experience crocheting and knew much more than I did about yarn. There was just one stumbling block. Maybe calling it a stumbling mountain was more accurate.

Adele had a problem with knitters. It didn't matter that I now understood there was a real basis for it from her past. If Adele ran the department, there would be no needles, no knitting accessories or pattern books. No mention of the word knit. All swatches hanging on the yarn bins would be crocheted. Mrs. Shedd was a business woman and didn't want to leave out customers. So she put me in charge, with Adele as my assistant. "It's like when I'd first started working at the bookstore all over again," I said.

"I don't suppose Adele acknowledges there's a real reason Mrs. Shedd put you in charge of the new department," Dinah said.

I choked on a laugh. "Are you kidding? You know Adele; she just thinks she's gotten the shaft, again." We'd gotten to my car. Dinah was riding shotgun while I went to pick up the animals. Thanks to spending time with my pets, Dinah was finally becoming an animal person. Before, her idea of a pet had been maybe a goldfish.

"Do I know the neighbor who disappeared?" Dinah said as she pulled on her seat belt and I started the motor of the greenmobile. I called my Mercedes 190E that because of its rare blue-green color.

"You've met Emily Perkins. I brought her to a few Hookers' meetings when they first moved in. Then she realized she wasn't into handicrafts. Remember that green afghan I brought into the group last week? It belongs to her. She couldn't even tell if it was knitted or crocheted. Bradley Perkins is the original nice guy. The kind of guy who sees you pulling your garbage cans to the street on trash night and not only comes over to help, but insists on doing it for you. He doesn't seem like the kind of guy who would disappear."

"You're going to find out what happened, aren't you?" Dinah said as we headed toward the vet's.

"Barry told me to stay out of it," I said and Dinah laughed.

"Like that's stopped you before."

"I tried going over, but Emily wasn't there. I'll try again when I go home," I said. We pulled into the vet's parking lot and got out to retrieve the foursome. "Emily is probably a wreck."

Two dogs were a handful. Two dogs and two cats wasn't a job for one person. Dinah helped get the cat cases situated on the floor in the back. The small black mutt and the medium-size strawberry blond terrier mix got the backseat and Dinah's job was to make sure they didn't drift into the front and jump in my lap while I was driving.

Ryder was sitting on the curb when I pulled into my driveway. He got up and followed my car, pulling out his camera as we unloaded.

"Wow, dogs and cats," he said, stopping his filming long enough to ruffle Cosmo's black fur. "My brother's allergic so we could never have any pets." Ryder looked at Dinah and his eyes kind of bugged out.

"You," he said, pointing. "You're that teacher at Beasley. The one they call the . . ." He stopped himself and Dinah chuckled.

"I know they call me the terror." She gave Ryder the once-over. "Do you go to Beasley?"

Ryder held up his hand. "I've already taken English 101, with Mr. Fenster." He started telling Dinah about his You-Tube uploads and his plans for being a video journalist/documentary filmmaker. I watched with interest. Dinah might be known as the terror when dealing with students who slept in class or didn't do their assignments, but she had a way with kids. She listened to him and his plans and nodded at the end. "Too bad you've already taken English 101; I would have liked having you in my class."

"Really? Wow," Ryder said, standing a little taller. Then he turned toward me and gestured toward the house next door. "She came home. I tried to ask her some questions, but she blew me off like the cops. Told me not to be a pest. But you have to be a pest if you're going to get the story. Only thing I found out is she still hasn't heard from her husband."

Ryder gave us a good-bye nod, and the gangly figure sauntered back down the driveway.

"Nice kid," Dinah said. We got the dogs in the yard and took the cat carriers inside and opened them up. The cats popped out and promptly went to check out their food bowl.

When I went to call the dogs in, I kept glancing in the direction of the Perkins' house. The wall of greenery blocked the view. "You want to go over there, don't you?" Dinah said. When I nodded, she grabbed my arm. "I'll come with."

The Christmas decorations were still as they'd been in the morning. I nodded my head toward the box of icicle lights and Dinah replied, "Looks like somebody didn't get a chance to finish."

Emily Perkins opened the door and had a hopeful expression on her face until she saw it was us, and her face fell. Then she caught herself. "I didn't mean to make it look like I wasn't glad to see you." She had the potential to be very pretty, with her wavy dark hair, symmetrical features and angular face. All it would take was a little eyebrow shaping, maybe a stylish haircut and a little makeup and something more flattering than loose-fitting jeans and a sweatshirt.

"I wanted to make sure you were all right." I vaguely waved toward the street to imply all the activity of the morning. "What happened?" I said, touching her arm in a supportive gesture. I felt funny about coming out and asking her directly about Bradley's disappearance. Her brown eyes filled with water and she quickly blinked back her tears and glanced inside.

"Where are my manners? Come in," she said, stepping away to clear the entrance for us. We followed her into the living room and I expected her to start talking about Bradley, but instead she told us to sit and offered us tea. Nothing in the room gave a hint that anything was wrong. There was a serene quality to the sofa and chairs covered in fabric the color of unbleached muslin. I liked the paver tile floor with the Indian throw rugs. A large window looked out on the nicely landscaped backyard.

"It's some special soothing tea I picked up today. Nicholas recommended it." We declined, but she went to the kitchen to pick up her cup. Dinah and I immediately looked at each other. Nicholas Hartman was the proprietor of a lifestyle store that was next to the bookstore. It had everything from unusual clothes and decorator items for the house to spices, teas and coffees. If there was one thing everything had in common, it was each item was stylish and unusual. I knew what Dinah was thinking. What was Emily doing shopping when her husband was missing? I sat down on the couch but realized I'd sat on something. It turned out to be a cloth doll that no doubt belonged to one of Emily's girls. I went to set it on the bleached-wood table, but Dinah surprised me by picking it up. Generally she wasn't that much of a toy person. She commented on how, with the skirt and head wrap, it looked like it came from some island.

"More like an imitation island," I said, pointing to a tag on the doll's foot that said *Island Encounter in Las Vegas*. I was going to ask Dinah why she was suddenly so interested in dolls, but Emily came back in the room.

She slipped into a low easy chair, sniffed the tea and then took a sip. "The tea is called When the Going Gets Tough. Nicholas said it's some kind of cure-all. I hope he's right. I certainly need something to help me." Dinah and I nodded with understanding expressions but said nothing.

She turned to me. "I don't know if the officers told you, but Bradley has gone missing." She sat back and held on to the teacup, taking small sips.

"They might have mentioned something about it," I said.

"He went to the office yesterday like always. When he didn't show up at dinnertime, I called his cell phone and got his voice mail. I tried the office and just got voice mail there, too, since it was after hours. I kept thinking he'd show up, but he didn't. When he wasn't home by this morning, I called the police. I was much more worried before they came." She explained that one of the officers actually knew Bradley. "His daughter is on the girls' soccer team that Bradley coaches. He asked me a bunch of questions. Mostly he wanted to know if we'd been fighting." She sighed. "I wouldn't call it fighting exactly. You know what a nice guy Bradley is. Well, all of a sudden he seemed upset about everything. He fussed that the girls were making too much noise, he didn't like what I'd made for dinner. I can understand him being upset that his watch wasn't ready. It's the only thing he has left from his father. I forgot to take it in to be serviced until a couple of days ago. But to be upset about the afghan his sister gave us." Her gaze stopped on me. "That's the one I lent you. You said you wanted to figure out how it was made." She waited until I nodded with recognition before continuing. "When he made a fuss about me lending it out, that's when I knew he was upset about something else. If he cared so much about it, why keep it shoved away in a drawer? He probably only noticed it was missing because he was pulling out Christmas decorations."

The phone ringing cut into our conversation. She got up to answer it and came back a moment later, looking upset.

"Bad news?" I prodded.

"It's hard to keep covering for Bradley. You and the police are the only people who know the truth. The story I've given everyone else is that he had a last-minute business trip."

I got her back to talking about what the police officer

had told her. "He said Bradley probably just went some- where to cool off. He seemed sure that Brad would come back in a day or so. Of course, in the middle of it all the gas meter reader mentioned the smell at your house." She looked at me intently. "There wasn't really a body at your place, was there?"

I told her the real identity of the corpses and she rocked her head in sympathy. "And you ended up with your front door broken again. What a shame."

Suddenly we all looked at our watches. I had to get to work, Emily had to pick up her daughters from school, and Dinah had to get home.

Emily thanked us for coming over and we all stood up.

"Do you want the afghan back?" I offered. I certainly didn't want to be caught in the middle of their problems. I'd seen it when I came over with a package I'd taken in for them. Emily was cleaning out drawers and had left it sitting on the dining room table. I'd been enchanted with it at first glance. She, on the other hand, had no use for the green afghan with the scattered flowers. It reminded me of a meadow, but all she said was that it didn't go with their decor. I explained it was crocheted and asked if I could take it home to examine out how it had been made. When I couldn't figure out how the three-dimensional flowers were done, I had passed it on to Adele to figure out. I was going to tell Emily that Adele had it, but I realized she didn't care.

She shook her head and her mouth was set in anger. "I'm sure he could care less about it. He was just upset with everything I did. You said you wanted to figure out the pattern. Keep it until you're done and then give it to some charity. I never liked it, and after the way Bradley acted about it, I don't ever want to see it again."

As she walked us to the door, Emily gritted her teeth.

"At first I was worried about Bradley being gone—that something might have happened to him. Now, I'm just angry. How childish to run off because we had a fight. Why couldn't he just have told me straight out what was bothering him?"

I only had a shrug for an answer. I told her to let me know if I could do anything. For a second her anger returned to worry. "I know the officer said just to be patient and let Bradley show up on his own, but it would be great if you could find him."

"Branching off into locating missing persons?" Dinah asked as we crossed the lawn toward my place.

"All I said was that I would keep it in mind." A thought occurred to me and I stopped just before we got to my driveway.

"Don't you think it's odd that she told me to give away Bradley's afghan. It's as if she knows he's not coming back."

"And maybe she just reported him missing as a cover-up," Dinah said.

"And asking me to look for him is some kind of setup," I said, my voice rising in excitement. Then we both looked at each other and rolled our eyes. "Or maybe he really did just take off and we have crime on the brain."

We finally got to the greenmobile and I drove Dinah back to her car and then went on to the bookstore. It was only when I was walking into Shedd & Royal that I realized Dinah had never told me her news.

CHAPTER 2

WALKING INTO SHEDD & ROYAL BOOKS AND More was like going to my second home. The smell of books and coffee was comforting. Riding over the top was the scent of something chocolate, and I guessed Bob, our main barista and cookie baker, must have just taken some cookies out of the oven. As I crossed the front of the store, I looked in the café. A plate of brownies was sitting on the counter and the scent had drawn in some customers. One of the other counter people was waiting on them, while Bob sat at a table with his computer open. Whenever he had a break, he pulled out the computer and worked on his screenplay. He was secretive about the story. All any of us knew was that it was some kind of science-fiction piece. I stopped by Mrs. Shedd's office. She used to come in to do her work mostly when the bookstore was closed. But lately she'd been spending more and more time there when the store was open. And now that it was our busiest time of year, it was all hands on deck. Particularly since Adele and I had been gone for two days, checking out the yarn store in San Diego. I laughed at the framed poster on the wall. It said *I* and then had a big red valentine-shaped heart before the word *Vampires*. The poster was a hot item among readers since vampire books were white-hot. It had a different meaning for Mrs. Shedd. She wasn't a vampire lover. She loved what vampire books did for sales. We had a whole display set up for vampire books by different authors. They all did well, but for now the Anthony books were the star sellers and had their own table in the front.

Even though Mrs. Shedd had told me I could call her Pamela, it felt too strange. Kind of like calling your doctor by their first name. So, mostly I avoided calling her anything, but when I had to say something, it always came out as Mrs. Shedd. She was just clearing off her desk and shutting off her computer when I walked in.

I guessed she was somewhere in her late sixties, but her dark blond hair didn't have even a strand of gray, and I was sure it was natural. Something about the pageboy style seemed timeless. I was a little on the breathless side from rushing. My tote brushed her desk and the knitting needles clanged together. Mrs. Shedd wasn't into crafting, but she recognized the needles and chuckled.

"I'm glad you don't share Adele's obsession. She reacts to knitting needles like a vampire does to a stake." Mrs. Shedd glanced up at my face and looked suddenly concerned. "Molly, are you okay? You look a little frazzled."

In my rush to get to the bookstore, I'd forgotten to stop and check my appearance. Instinctively I reached up and touched my hair. I could tell by feel that it wasn't laying flat. I was still wearing the clothes I'd put on in the hotel in San Diego. The khaki slacks were wrinkle proof, but the white shirt was a little worse for wear from the car ride and the animal pick up. I pulled a vest out of my tote bag and put it over the shirt and tried to pat my hair into order while I detailed my arrival home.

Mrs. Shedd's eyes widened when I got to the part about the broken front door. "Molly, you certainly lead an interesting life." When I got to the real story, she listened with interest. "This neighbor that disappeared—is it anyone I know?"

"You might have seen him in the bookstore. His name is Bradley Perkins. He's on the tall side, reddish brown hair with a friendly smile," I said, expecting a dismissive nod.

"What do you mean Bradley Perkins disappeared?" Mrs. Shedd said abruptly.

"You know him?" I said, surprised.

"Yes, I do," she said. I waited for more details about how she knew him, but none came. I repeated what Emily had said about how he'd gone to work and just not come home.

Mrs. Shedd's placid expression had changed to agitated. "That's hardly a full story. Did she call his office to see if he showed up there? Was he there all day, or did he leave early?" I shrugged, realizing I didn't know. She seemed so concerned, I tried to calm her by telling her that it seemed most likely it was what the cop had said—he and his wife had had some kind of argument and he'd gone off to cool down. "I'd appreciate it if you'd keep me posted," Mrs. Shedd said as she gathered up her things. Mr. Royal stopped in the doorway and looked in.

"Ready, Pamela?" he said. I thought of Mr. Royal as the world's most interesting man. He'd been away for several years, and in that time, he seemed to have gone everywhere and done everything. Trekking through the Himalayas, driving a snowplow in Minnesota and training dolphins were only a few of the many adventures he'd had. He wore his charcoal gray hair long and I'd heard he cut it himself. I guessed he was close to Mrs. Shedd in age, but he moved with the agility of a young man. And now that he was back, he was lighting up Mrs. Shedd's life. It seemed funny now, but before his return, I had wondered if he really existed. I started to say I'd let her know if I heard any more about Bradley, but she gave her head a fast shake with a quick glance toward Mr. Royal. I didn't have to be a genius to figure out whatever connection she had with Bradley, she didn't want Joshua Royal to know about it.

"We're off to get a tree for the store. I was going to pull the artificial one out of the storeroom but Joshua convinced me we ought to have a live one. I was worried about it drying out and being a hazard, but leave it to Joshua to come up with a solution. We're going out to a Christmas-tree farm to get a truly fresh one."

I followed them back into the main part of the bookstore. They went on to the door and I stopped by the cashier stand. Our main cashier, Rayaad, had a couple of young men behind the counter with her and was showing them how to ring up books. Not that there was much to show anymore. The computer did all the work. I introduced myself to the new recruits.

"I'm going to be in the yarn department, if anything comes up," I said to Rayaad, then headed toward the back of the store. The store was quiet and it seemed like a good time to get some work done on the new department. We'd all agreed it was essential to have swatches of each of the yarns hanging on their bins. Some of us—as in me and Mrs. Shedd—had also agreed there should be both crocheted and knitted swatches. Adele had practically stamped her foot and had steam come out of her ears at the mere idea, but she was being ignored. The crocheted swatches were being done by both of us, but the knitted swatches were all in my court.

Adele would never admit it, but I was pretty sure she knew how to knit. Not that it mattered. No way was she going to pick up the needles. Luckily I had learned the basics while getting information during our creative retreat at Asilomar last fall. Knitting felt awkward and slow compared with crocheting, but I didn't want to alienate knitters, the way some yarn stores ignored crocheters.

Even though it was only partially completed, I loved the yarn area. The back wall had been outfitted with bins that were beginning to fill up with yarn. When we got everything put out from the store in San Diego, most of them would be filled. We were organizing them by color and the effect was beautiful.

Adele was already sitting at the table and looked up from her work as I approached. "It's about time, Pink." Her eyes narrowed. "What took you so long? Did you get arrested?" Adele stopped with her hook in the air over a strand of soft blue sport weight yarn.

I threw her my best don't-be-ridiculous expression and set my tote bag on the table. Now that we had the yarn department, the worktable stayed up all the time. Before I'd had to put it up and down every time the Hookers met. I heard Adele almost growl when I took out the needles attached to the beginning of a swatch of a thick off-white wool from Peru. In addition to the blue yarn Adele was working with, she had a ball of white thread and a fine steel hook. Next to it was a pile of limp snowflakes.

I started to repeat the story for the zillionth time. Just when I got to the part about the bodies, William Bearley walked up to the table and distracted Adele. She jumped up and hugged him and then made a whole production about straightening his jacket and knocking some lint off it. She told anyone who would listen that he was an important children's author, but never explained that he wrote the Koo Koo the Clown series about common childhood experiences like going to the dentist. When William did book signings or story time, he dressed up in a clown outfit complete with giant red shoes. But in his normal persona, he was bland looking and reserved. His receding sandy hair and pale skin appeared practically colorless next to Adele in her fuchsia-trimmed electric blue jacket.

"I'll be ready in a minute, honey," she said. Whatever his day job was, it didn't seem to require his red shoes. He wore a dress shirt, pressed jeans and some kind of tan tie shoes.

"Molly was just telling me about her house getting raided by the police." William regarded me with more interest, and I started to explain the real details. Adele didn't like losing the floor and interrupted me. "Her neighbor just jumped the gun about calling the cops. Her husband has only been gone a few hours."

"Bradley's been missing for more than a day," I said. "Though, from what Emily said, it sounds more like Bradley might have run away."

"Bradley who?" William said. When I said Perkins, his face showed recognition.

"You know Bradley, too?" Before I could ask for details, Adele stepped in.

"Of course William knows your neighbor. He brought his daughters in to all the Koo Koo events."

When Adele stopped talking, William asked what made me think Bradley had taken off. I told him about the cop getting it out of Emily that they'd been arguing and all. Adele intruded again. "I know what you're doing, William.

You're doing research for another book." She turned toward me. "William is always gathering information and ideas for his next book."

I smiled. "Right. It'll come in handy in case you decide to write *Koo Koo Goes Missing*." Both Adele and William seemed serious to the extreme about his books. Neither of them came close to cracking a smile at my comment. In fact, Adele seemed in a huff when she started gathering up her work. It only got worse when I picked up the knitting needles. She actually covered her face. Personally, I thought it was more for effect than any real horror at seeing me handle the tools of the other yarn craft. Eventually she took her hands down, though she still made a point to look away from them as she pushed the pile of finished snowflakes in my direction.

"Pink, these need to be starched and William and I have plans." It wasn't an unreasonable request. We were making them to decorate the bookstore, and in all fairness, she had made many more than me, but in typical Adele fashion, she came across as high-handed and annoying. Adele often acted as though she were in charge; however, the minute there was any kind of trouble, she would throw her arms around me and expect me to take care of everything. I gathered her thread creations up and put them in my tote bag.

When they left, I finally went to work on the swatch. I had learned the basics of knitting during the retreat but not enough to be comfortable. Casting on and doing rows of knit stitches felt awkward. The swatch didn't have to be that big, did it? As soon as I'd done ten rows, I laid down the swatch, anxious to crochet.

I thought of the discussion the group had had about making things to give to a shelter we supported. I pulled out the list of suggested items we'd come up with. My eyes stopped on toys. Yes, that was definitely what I wanted to work on. What could be better than making a holiday gift for a child? It would also be my first attempt at Amigurumi—small toys crocheted in the round using single crochet stitches.

I found a pattern for an elephant that was just a nice size for a child to hold. I checked the stash of yarn we had for our charity endeavors and found a skein of soft gray yarn. Within moments, I'd finished the first round. This was going to be fun.

My thoughts went back to Emily Perkins. How well did I really know her?

I wondered about the argument she'd mentioned. Was it real or made up? All I'd ever heard was their voices coming from their backyard, and they always sounded friendly. My pondering was interrupted when a young man stopped next to the table. I realized he was one of the holiday helpers our cashier Rayaad had been training.

"Mrs. Fazaha . . ." he faltered. I had trouble with Rayaad's last name and I'd known her for a while.

"We just go by first names around here, except for Mrs. Shedd and Mr. Royal."

The young man seemed relieved. "Okay, then Rayaad said to talk to you." Before he could finish two women had joined him. They were giggling and appeared a little embarrassed.

"It's about the Anthony books, the Blood and Yarn series. We wanted to get copies of *Caught By the Hook* and *Caught Up in Yarn* . . ." She let her voice trail off as if I was supposed to understand.

The clerk stepped in. "The display is empty. Are there any more books anywhere?"

"Oh, please say there are," the other woman said. "My

girlfriend had *Caught By the Hook* on CD and I heard the beginning in her car. We got stuck in traffic, but eventually I had to get out of the car. I need to find out what happens. When he picks up the hook for the first time," she said in a tremulous voice, "and when he realizes that he's found a way to control his lust for blood."

Her friend laughed. "But luckily not his lust for women. Whew. I hear there are some really hot scenes."

I left my work and followed them to the front of the store. A freestanding cardboard display had a blowup of the cover of *Caught By the Hook*. It featured a dark-haired man crocheting. There was just the slightest hint of a fang. Near it there was a cardboard cutout of Anthony holding a sprig of mistletoe in one hand and a woman in a trench coat in the other. Her head was thrown back with her neck exposed and he was leaning toward her with just a touch of fang showing. A banner across the middle announced the up-coming midnight launch of *Caught Under the Mistletoe* and the first public appearance of A. J. Kowalski. One of the women touched the poster with awe as she began to ask questions. Had I read the books, yes, and yes, I agreed Anthony was hot and, yes, I thought he had a heart even if he didn't have a real one beating in his chest. Then she leaned close and lowered her voice.

"You know who the author really is, don't you?"

I shook my head. "All I know is A. J. Kowalski lives in the area." She looked at me with the same disbelief I'd been getting a lot of lately. The two women started talking to each other about whether A. J. was a man or woman. Even though they both agreed that when people used initials it was usually a woman, one of the women kept insisting the author had to be a man.

"I don't think a woman could write a male character that

well." Her friend saved me the trouble and brought up J. K. Rowling, who did a great job with Harry Potter, and Stephanie Meyer, who pumped life into Edward Cullen.

I had a few books stashed in the office. When I handed them over, the women were so excited they almost tripped over themselves.

"I have to get this, too," one of the women said, seeing the sign for *Crocheting with the Vampire*. I had to explain the companion pattern book wasn't out yet but promised to let her know when it was. They seemed excited when I mentioned we were supposed to be getting Anthony action figures, along with a Colleen figure. She was the reporter who was bringing his story to the world and also the woman he'd fallen hopelessly in love with.

They wanted hooks, too, so I took them back to the yarn department and showed them our accessory display. One of the women picked up one of the golden K hooks and began stroking it. "Is this the kind *he* uses?"

"It could be," I said. "The author isn't exactly specific."

"I'm going to ask him about the hook at the launch party." She looked at me. "I'm sure it's a man." They had some discussion about whose credit card to put it on.

I watched them go to the cashier stand and suddenly I knew how I could help Emily find Bradley. That is if she was really looking for him.

CHAPTER 3

THE DAYS WERE SO SHORT AROUND THIS TIME OF year, it seemed liked midnight when I headed home, though it was more like eight. Some weather front had blown in and my light jacket didn't do much to keep out the cold damp air. My street was quiet and dark. The lights were on at the Perkins', but their lawn display was dark. I wondered if Emily'd had any more news about Bradley.

I pulled into my own driveway and left the car outside the garage. When I opened my back door, Cosmo flew past me into the yard. The small black mutt took off into the bushes. His long fur would no doubt be full of redwood bits when he came in. Blondie was probably sitting in her chair. The strawberry blond terrier was nothing like any other dog I'd had. Before I'd adopted her, she'd been in a shelter for a year and a half, and living in a kennel for all that time had left its mark. She was the only dog I'd ever had who didn't mind being boarded. It was like going home. The cats circled my legs with plaintiff meows as I walked in the kitchen. They were hungry and still considering whether I should be forgiven for leaving them at the vet's while I was gone.

As soon as all animals were fed, I called Emily. She still hadn't heard anything from Bradley and was thrilled to hear I had figured a way to locate him. I was going to tell her my idea on the phone, but she wanted me to come over.

I hated to go empty-handed, but there was no time to throw together a batch of cookies. I noticed the tin of fudge I'd picked up when Adele and I'd stopped on the way back from San Diego. In Emily's condition, she probably could really use some chocolate.

I crossed her front yard, being careful to avoid tripping over the dark holiday decorations, and barely had time to check out the huge hanging light fixture on the porch before she opened the door. Emily had all the lights burning inside. In the distance I heard the television and her daughters' voices.

"The girls still don't know," she said in a nervous voice. "They figured out something is wrong because we went out for pizza and I'm letting them watch a movie—two things I never do on a school night." I sensed she was telling me all this so I wouldn't think she was a bad mother. Far be it for me to judge anybody. I'd been known to eat ice cream for dinner. I handed her the fudge, which she gratefully accepted before bringing me into the living room. We sat down and she tore off the top of the fudge and took a piece. I was right about her needing some chocolate. She caught herself and apologized for not offering me a piece first. I passed and expected her to set the tin on the coffee table, but she kept hugging it. She really needed chocolate.

Curious about Mrs. Shedd's reaction when I mentioned Bradley, I asked Emily how he knew my boss.

"Bradley knows everybody. Leave him in a room with ten people, and in a few minutes, he'll have ten friends. He gets a lot of his business that way."

"What exactly does Bradley do?" I said, a little embarrassed that after having them as neighbors for a couple of years I wasn't clear on his profession.

"He's a financial advisor." When she said that, it jostled my memory and I recalled that when they'd first moved in, he'd said something about working in finance. I'd asked him a bunch of questions since it was shortly after Charlie had died and I was suddenly in charge of everything. I vaguely remembered he had seemed put off by all my questions and that was the end of it.

When I asked what exactly his title meant, she took a moment to collect her thoughts. "That's what he calls himself. But really what he does is invest money for people. He pools all the money and buys and sells securities. I don't know the exact details, but he has some special system. He always gets impatient when I ask any questions. I guess he thinks I won't understand. When he has me make bank deposits, he tells me what to do as if I'm a child. The same when I help with the monthly statements. But he's very good at what he does. Wherever I go, I run into clients of his and they always rave about Bradley's magic touch." Her face had brightened as she talked about her husband, but then her mood fizzled as she began to talk about how he'd acted the day before. "He's been short-tempered with me before, but never like that. I wish I knew what I did that set him off."

I put my hand on her shoulder in a consoling manner. "I'm sure it was more about him than anything you did."

"You said there was a way you thought I could find him," she said hopefully. "I'm mad at him for doing this to me, but I want to talk to him and find out what's really wrong. Running off isn't the way to deal with problems."

"Does he have a credit card?" I asked and she nodded. She also nodded when I asked if her name was on the account as well.

"We both have cards on the same account," she said. Then she began to get it. "And if I find out where he's charging . . ." Her voice trailed off as she went for her purse.

"I'd tell them you think there might be fraudulent charges on his card. They'll be more likely to give you more details." I mentioned that the women taking out their credit cards to buy the vampire books had been what made me think of it. "Not that there was any fraud going on with them." I told her about the run on Anthony books, trying to lighten up the mood. I was glad to see a smile show up on her face when I brought up the launch party. "All this with Bradley will be settled by then and you can come and have fun with the rest of us." I felt like I was on a teeter-totter. One minute the balance went toward her being involved in Bradley's disappearance and then, like now, the balance went the other way and it seemed like a ridiculous thought.

She said something about liking that as she dialed the number off the back of her credit card. She got stuck in voice-mail jail until she spoke the words *fraudulent charges* and the next moment I heard her talking to a customer service rep. Emily had a pencil and paper and began to scribble down information. Finally she thanked the customer service people and hung up.

"His last charge was for a one-way ticket on the seven P.M. Catalina Express yesterday."

I had a little experience with the island of Santa Catalina. The island was about nineteen miles off the coast, and in the spring, summer and fall, it was a big destination for tourists, and boats ran often. At this time of year, it was mostly just locals going back and forth and there were only a few boats a day.

"How can I thank you?" Emily said. She suddenly looked as if a heavy overcoat had been lifted off her shoulders. "I just felt so helpless before. As soon as I drop the girls off at school tomorrow morning, I'm going to catch the first boat I can and go over there. If I have to knock on every door, I'm going to find him."

Usually that would be a ridiculous statement, but in the case of Catalina, with one main town of only a few thousand residents, it was a doable challenge.

I admit I walked a little taller when I left. I'd done it. Problem solved. Bradley found. I walked across the dark lawn toward my house. As soon as I passed the row of trees that separated my property from the Perkins', I saw a car in my driveway. In the dark I couldn't make anything out beyond that it was a dark sedan. A figure started toward me. I recognized his walk and the outline of his solid build.

"Mason?" I said, going toward him. I was surprised to see the high-profile lawyer, and friend, at my home.

"I got worried when you didn't show up. And you didn't answer any of your phones. I went to the bookstore and there were a bunch of new cashiers who didn't know anything. So then I came here." He sucked in his breath when he saw the front door illuminated by the porch light. A piece of plywood covered the smashed part, but the door was obviously damaged. "What happened? Did somebody break in?"

I rolled my eyes and sighed. "Not exactly. Barry did it."

"The detective?" Mason said with a chuckle. "Didn't he wrangle a key from you with some story about having to take care of his dog?"

"It's a long story. He forgot he had a key." I peered at Mason in the darkness. "Was I supposed to meet you somewhere?" My life had become so busy lately, I was going to have to come up with a better organizational system than writing notes on scraps of paper and leaving them on the kitchen table for the cats to knock to the floor. I checked my cell phone and realized I'd forgotten to plug it into the charger when I got home. It was still dead.

Mason held out his hand and the moonlight reflected off something metal in his hand.

"We were going to have dinner and you were going to help me with Spike's sweater. Does that ring a bell?" he said in a fake hurt voice.

I sighed as my memory was jogged and it suddenly came back to me. Before the San Diego trip, I'd said I would have dinner with him and help him work on the dog sweater. He'd been anxious for us to get together because it was getting chilly and he didn't want the toy fox terrier shivering on his night walks. I wasn't sure how much dinner was about crocheting or just a convenient excuse to get together. It was hard to tell with Mason. Though he was a top criminal attorney known for keeping naughty celebrities out of jail, he was full of surprises. It was possible he really did want to learn how to crochet.

How to describe our relationship? At the very least we were friends—really good friends; Mason always came through with whatever I needed, whether it was background information on somebody or to catch me when I was about to fall. He was also always a willing ear. Did I mention that Mason wanted something more than friendship? We'd come close to that a few times, but something had always interfered.

"I'm sorry, I totally forgot," I said before rambling off all the obstacles that had clogged up my memory. Mason put up his hand to stop me before I got even halfway through.

"You're forgiven," he said with a gentle chuckle. "I'm just glad you're all right. So, what happened with the door?"

It had been a long day, an endless day by now, and all of it was beginning to kick in. How many times had I repeated the story? Somewhere in my busy day, I'd forgotten to eat. Mason heard my stomach growl.

"C'mon, we can skip the crochet lesson, but we both need dinner. You can tell me about the door when you've had some food." He took me by the hand and led me to his car. It sounded like a great idea to me.

It was late and a weeknight, but Mason knew exactly where to go. A valet relieved us of the car and we walked toward an island of activity amid all the closed businesses on Ventura Boulevard. I was doubtful about the outdoor seating at first. We'd been having unusually cold weather lately. The weatherman on channel three had even mumbled something about the possibility of a rare snow shower. But the chill was no problem as the café had plenty of patio heaters and Mason made sure we were seated close to several. The cuisine was Israeli and I let Mason order. Within moments the waiter arrived with so many small plates of different salads they covered the table. He finished by bringing a freshly made circle of soft flat bread.

I took some bread and dipped it in the creamy hummus dip before I was ready to talk. I finally got the whole story out about the door. I finished by telling Mason how I'd helped Emily locate her missing husband.

"Once she gets a chance to talk to Bradley, I'm sure they'll get whatever their problem is straightened out. I don't know the Perkins that well, but they seem like a pretty solid couple." When I mentioned Bradley's last name, Mason reacted.

"Do you know Bradley Perkins, too?" I said, surprised.

"Not personally, but I know of him. Somebody was telling me how Perkins had invested some money for them and they'd made a bundle. The guy is supposed to have some knack for making money grow." Mason seemed suddenly concerned. "You didn't invest any money with him, did you?"

"I wasn't even sure what he did for a living until a little while ago," I said. Mason seemed relieved.

"There are never big returns without big risks," he said as the waiter brought small portions of hot potatoes and falafel balls.

Mason delivered me home a short time later. He checked the front door to make sure it was secure. He wasn't a fix-it wizard like Barry, but he knew enough to make sure the lock worked right and that the panel across the broken part was secure. He did make some comment that if he'd damaged my door, he'd have gotten it replaced by now.

"You know you can always stay at my place," he said. Mason lived alone with his toy fox terrier, Spike, in a house in Encino that was big enough to accommodate a large family. "No strings attached," he added with a genuine smile. "I'm surprised Greenberg isn't standing guard." Mason's smile turned to a grin at the jab at Barry.

At last I hit the pillow, but as soon as I did, all my concerns about the upcoming unveiling of the vampire author began to surface. Who was he or she? Did I know them? What if it came out before the launch and took away all our steam? I had to untwist myself from the bedclothes several times before finally falling asleep. It was peaceful for a while, then a dog started barking in my dream. The noise was irritating and interfering with the story I was concocting. It didn't stop and I rose through the levels of sleep, finally realizing the barking was real.

Cosmo wasn't in his usual spot next to me. The longhaired black mutt generally slept nestled against my side with his feet in the air. The barking was coming from another room and I recognized it as his. There was something different about it, too. I heard an undercurrent of a growl.

By now I was wide awake and my heart was pounding big time. I heard something fall over and I sucked in my breath. Then suddenly relief washed over me. It was probably Barry and a late-night surprise visit. Still it seemed odd that Cosmo was making threatening sounds since he was more or less Barry's dog. The easy solution was to call Barry's cell phone. If I heard ringing, it would confirm it was him. I grabbed the phone next to me and punched in Barry's cell number, and as the call went through, I listened for ringing in the distance.

All I heard was something else fall over. Uh-oh.

A moment later, Barry answered in a sleepy voice, though he snapped to attention when I whispered, "Barry, I think there's somebody in my house."

I WAS HUDDLED IN THE FRONT YARD WHEN BARRY roared up in the Tahoe. He almost drove on the lawn. A police cruiser arrived a second later along with a helicopter. Barry's instructions had been for me to get out of the house immediately. It was only fear that gave me the guts to propel myself out the window and face the drop into the bushes. Now I wished I'd taken a moment to grab a shawl or robe before I went out. Even with the adrenaline rush, I felt shivery. The helicopter began to circle, bathing me and my front yard in its spotlight.

Barry waved for me to stay put as he ran toward the front door with his gun drawn—this time at least he used his key. The two uniforms went around to the back of the house. A few minutes later Barry came and got me and brought me inside.

"It's lucky Cosmo is staying with you. Blondie gets an F as a watchdog." He took me into the den. "I checked and nobody is in here now." The word *now* made me shudder. So somebody had been in there.

"Molly, first of all, this had nothing to do with your front door." He showed me the bathroom window I'd left open a crack. It was now wide open with the screen missing. "Here's where they came in." The outside door in the den was ajar. "Cosmo's barking must have scared them off." The two uniforms were searching the bushes in the backyard with the light from the helicopter. "Whoever it was is probably long gone." Barry said with a shrug. My backyard faced three others. All somebody had to do was go over my fence and exit through somebody else's yard. Barry called off the two officers and the helicopter.

I glanced around the den. The end table near the window had been knocked over, but other than that everything looked okay.

For the first time it sunk in that Barry was dressed in the suit he'd been wearing at his first stop of the day at my house. The shirt looked a little rumpled and his tie was pulled loose. His usually neat short dark hair was askew. Then I got it. He must have been asleep at his desk when I called.

Barry pulled an afghan off the arm of the couch and draped it over me, wrapping his arms around me at the same time. "Is there something you haven't told me?" he said with a little clench of his jaw. I had on occasion gotten involved in things that had gotten me into trouble.

I shrugged off his question as we headed to the kitchen. No way could I go back to sleep after all of this so I offered him breakfast. "All I did was tell Emily Perkins how to figure out where her husband was."

"And that was . . ." Barry said, following me as I turned on the lights. I told him about having her call the credit card company and his expression changed to admiration. "Good thinking, Sherlock. Though I still think you should mind your own business," he said. I started to pull out eggs and butter and waved Barry over to sit down at the table. It was still solid dark outside, but already almost five.

"I can't see how telling her that would lead to this," he conceded. "Is there anything else?" He didn't sit but instead came over to help me. Butter was melting in the frying pan and I was beating some eggs, adding some cream cheese and chives. Barry poured fresh coffee beans in the grinder and turned it on. "And don't hold back, okay?"

I stirred the eggs a last time and poured them in the pan. I popped some English muffins in the toaster as I debated whether to tell him everything. But Barry is a master at reading dead air. "C'mon, Molly, you can't fool me. There's something else, isn't there?"

"Okay, here goes," I said. "You know about the holiday party slash launch the bookstore is putting on for the latest Anthony book?" No recognition showed in his expression. "The vampire-with-a-heart books. I told you about it before," I said.

The no recognition was replaced with an oh-no look.

Barry wasn't into vampires and thought nobody else should be, either. "Our big reveal is who the author is. Mrs. Shedd thinks somebody is trying to scoop us. And some people might think that since I'm the event coordinator and this is a big event, that I already know who A. J. Kowalski really is and have the information here."

Barry started to dismiss the idea, but I interrupted him. "Think the Harry Potter books or the Twilight saga. We're talking a superstar author here. CNN is doing a live feed and all the entertainment shows are sending reporters. The local news stations are coming, too. The whole event would fizzle if somebody announced the author's identity before the launch. And whoever put out the news first would get a lot of attention."

Barry sat down at the table with an exhausted sigh. "Molly, you sure know how to fill a day."

CHAPTER 4

"NOPE, DOESN'T WORK," I SAID OUT LOUD AS I checked my image in the mirror. The makeup was supposed to cover up dark circles under your eyes. I'm afraid my lack of sleep was too big a challenge even for the self-proclaimed Miracle Circle Eraser. By the time Barry and I had finished breakfast, it was officially morning, though still dark. He checked all the windows and front door and then had to go home. It was his day to drive car pool. Barry was divorced and had his fourteen-year-old son living with him. Barry felt like a hero driving car pool. I don't think Jeffrey quite saw it that way. Nothing like having your cop dad talk to you like you were a kid in front of your fellow eighth graders to bust your image as the cool drama guy.

And me? I tried lying down, but I kept thinking I heard noises. Eventually I accepted that more sleep wasn't coming and decided to make better use of the time. I took the pile of thread snowflakes that Adele had made into the kitchen.

I poured some liquid starch in a plastic bag and dropped the snowflakes in the pearly liquid one at a time. They came out looking like hopeless clumps of thread. The magic was in the drying. I had already cut apart a cardboard box and covered it with wax paper. I laid the snowflakes and carefully stretched them into shape and held them in place with nonrusting pins. When I had them all done, I put them on the dining room table as dawn was breaking. In the half-light, the snowflakes looked almost real.

I had another cup of coffee and found the snowflake I'd been crocheting. I worked on it until the sunlight streamed in the kitchen. That's when I started with the makeup.

I was pulling out of my driveway on my way to work when I saw Emily standing beside her black Element in her driveway. I cut the motor and got out. I wanted to explain the middle-of-the-night commotion. When I saw her face, I realized we looked like no-sleep sisters.

I told her about the intruder and told her it was nothing for her to worry about. "I'm pretty sure it was all about somebody trying to find out about the author of the Anthony books." The flat look in her eyes came into focus and she surprised me by asking if I knew the author's real identity. Apparently Anthony was so hot, even a woman with a missing husband was interested. She mentioned that she'd read the first two books and couldn't wait for the third. We talked a few moments about vampires and I glanced at her car.

"I don't want to keep you. What time does your boat leave?"

Emily's demeanor changed to annoyance. "I changed my mind," she said. "I was so worried that something happened to him, but now that I know where he is, I'm not going to go running after him." She stopped and we stood for a moment looking at each other. Were we both thinking the same thing? *He might not be alone.*

"I've got errands to run and a life to lead," she said with a huff and she pulled open the SUV door.

As I headed back across my lawn, I saw Ryder standing across the street. He lowered his camera and headed back down the street toward his house. With no cop cars, I guess we weren't YouTube fodder. I wonder if he knew he'd missed the second round of action at my house.

The scent of real pine was the first thing I noticed when I walked in Shedd & Royal. A six-foot-tall fresh tree was standing adjacent to the cashier counter. I was instantly glad Mrs. Shedd had been talked into getting a real tree. More than a real tree, it was a live tree. It was sitting in a large pot of dirt. I stood next to the tree and inhaled deeply.

More of the wonderful fragrance was coming from the box of pine boughs on the ground next to the tree. Mrs. Shedd was going all out this year. I thought the credit really belonged to Mr. Royal. He had a zest for living and it seemed to be contagious. Joshua Royal walked out of the storage room, carrying a box of tiny clear lights. He brought it over to the tree and began stringing the lights on the graceful branches.

"Where should I put this?" a male voice said behind me. Nicholas Hartman, owner of the store next to the bookstore, caught up with me and held out a menorah. A table sat adjacent to the tree and I pointed to it. "Mind if I put a small sign next to it, saying it came from my store?" Nicholas asked.

Mr. Royal and I both said it was fine. As he stepped back to get a better view of the position of the menorah on the table, Nicholas knocked over the cardboard cutout for

Caught Under the Mistletoe. He viewed it with distaste as he picked it up. "The vampires are taking over."

Nicholas's store was called Luxe. It was best described as a lifestyle store and featured an eclectic array of items. I thought every item in the store had charisma, whether it was a scented candle in a silver cup or the brick red shirt with the crinkly texture that I'd gotten there. Nicholas was like the things he carried in his store—different. I didn't know all the details, but I'd heard he had a whole different life before the store. Now it appeared the store was his life. Talk about putting all your eggs in one basket. But the store seemed to be doing okay. All he needed was to get some young hip celeb to shop there and tell the paparazzi.

To me, Nicholas was all about the expression in his earthy brown eyes. They carried his smile and a little touch of uncertainty. His face was long and his brown hair had the ruffled and gelled look that seemed so popular. Once upon a time, it would have been considered messy.

No, I wasn't falling for Nicholas. But I liked him and I liked his store.

Once he'd gotten the okay for the menorah placement, he turned toward me. He viewed me with concern. "Hard night, huh? I have some tea that might help."

"Thanks, but I think I'll stick with a red-eye, though my neighbor said some tea you sold her really helped," I said.

"Who's that?" he said.

When I mentioned Emily, he nodded. "She was pretty upset. Has her husband showed up?"

I was surprised he knew. Hadn't Emily told me she'd only told the truth to me and the cops? He listened attentively as I went through the whole chain of events, along with the latest update. It was hard to read how he was taking the information. He seemed to be absorbing it, but not reacting.

One of the new Hookers, Rhoda Klein, came in and saw Nicholas. She was a gruff, opinionated person with dark short hair and a sharp jaw. But all her edges melted when Nicholas greeted her by name.

Sheila Altman rushed in the door and then screeched to a stop when she saw him. She pulled out a blanket from her tote bag. "Is this what you had in mind?" she asked.

Nicholas laid it on the table and looked it over. I was almost drooling. Sheila had outdone herself this time. She was known for making shawls and scarves that were mixtures of yarn textures and colors. She tended to stay with blues and greens and her pieces had an impressionist feeling about them. This one was a soft teal blue that mixed with lavender and then green. The yarn had a halo and looked like it would be cuddly to the touch.

Nicholas pronounced it as being just what he had in mind. They made arrangements for her to bring in a few more and negotiated the price. Sheila looked like she was waiting for a problem to show up. It was no wonder. She'd sold some of her work before through a local consignment store and been stiffed for some of the money owed her.

"Stop by if you change your mind about the tea," Nicholas said to me as he took the blanket and walked toward the door.

Sheila and I continued on to the yarn area. With the table always set up, our regular start-up time had gotten kind of soft around the edges. Translated—no matter how early I got there, there were always people already at the table.

As we got closer, I heard the conversation already in progress. Rhoda had only stopped in the front for a moment and then gone back to the crochet area. Her voice stood out above the others.

"You call that a vampire," she said in a voice that still carried a tinge of New York even after twenty or so years in L.A. "He's too foofie for me. Next they'll have him joining a group like us."

"Do you think he might actually join us?" Elise Belmont asked. She had a soft birdlike voice and was another new member.

"Who might join us, dear?" CeeCee Collins said, taking her seat at the head of the table. CeeCee was the unofficial leader of the group. Along with being a well-known actress and host of a reality show, she was a fabulous crocheter.

"That vampire, Anthony," Elise said in total sincerity. "Wouldn't we be the hottest group around if we had him as a member?"

Across the table Eduardo Linnares stifled a laugh. The cover model was amused but mannerly enough to hide it. Despite his large build and hands, he was an expert at delicate crochet. His grandmother had taught him well. The group was working on the gifts to be sent over to the women's shelter. Everyone was making something different, from baby blankets to scarves and shawls. I took out the gray yarn and began to add on to the rounds I'd already done, moving a stitch marker each time I reached the end of one round.

Of course, Adele jumped in to the conversation. "Elise, Anthony is only a fictional character. Vampires aren't real. Understand?" Without waiting for an answer, Adele continued. "I'm going to tell my boyfriend, William, he ought to do a vampire book. Maybe like *Koo Koo Interviews a Vampire*."

"But you just said vampires aren't real. I thought all of

Koo Koo's books were nonfiction, like *Koo Koo Goes to the Dentist*," Sheila said.

Adele glared at Sheila. "I was thinking William should branch out." I was surprised that she didn't get the words *my boyfriend* in the sentence. Adele rarely said his name without adding *my boyfriend*. I think she hoped William's next book would be *Koo Koo Gets Engaged*.

Elise gave a knowing nod. "That's what they want you to believe—that they're not real. Personally I think this A. J. Kowalski really is a vampire and the books are autobiographical."

Elise focused on me. "You know the author's real identity, don't you?" All eyes were glued to me. I noticed Adele had a look of horror, no doubt thinking it might be true and once again she'd been left out.

"No," I said. "Nobody but the publisher knows who A. J. is. And please spread the word that I am just as much in the dark as everyone else about who the author really is." I gave them a recap of what it was like waking to find an intruder in my house. Adele interrupted to talk about how my house had been a crime scene when we returned from San Diego.

"So, who's this neighbor of yours who took off?"

I said his name, expecting blank looks; instead, I heard a lot of sucked-in breaths of surprise.

Elise spoke first. "Bradley Perkins took off. That doesn't seem like him." Elise nodded to herself. "His wife must have done something really bad to make him that angry."

I asked Elise how she knew the Perkins. "We're what I'd call business friends," she said. "I wonder if Logan knows about Bradley. Logan thinks he's some kind of financial genius." Logan was Elise's husband and a member of the Tarzana Chamber of Commerce. He was one of the top real estate people in the area.

"That wife of his ought to thank her lucky stars for him," Rhoda interjected. "The way he just stepped in and acts like a father to her two girls."

"He's not their father?" I said, looking up from my work. The body was taking shape.

"You don't know?" Rhoda said, surprised. "They've only been married a couple of years. Emily's first husband died."

How odd that Emily had never mentioned either of these facts to me. Elise said Logan had sold them their house and he'd been taken from the beginning about what a great couple they were. "You have to give Bradley a lot of credit. He stepped right in as father to the girls. He even coaches their soccer team. I hear he's at every PTA meeting. He ran a booth at the spring carnival at Wilbur Avenue Elementary. Logan said he always comes to the chamber of commerce meetings. He's just this outgoing friendly guy. It's hard to imagine him having a big argument. Emily is kind of moody. I bet she started the fight and is just telling everyone it was him," Elise said.

So I wasn't the only one to wonder about Emily's story. All I had to go on was Emily's version, and as Barry kept telling me, people lied.

Dinah came in at the end. I was going to bring her up to speed, but when I saw she wasn't alone, I stopped.

All of a sudden I was pretty sure I knew what her news was.

Chapter 5

"Dinah, you didn't," I said as we headed to
the café. The crochet group had dispersed. I had held back
from saying anything until we were alone. My friend's dan-
gle earrings jangled as she hung her head.

"I know it sounds crazy, but I missed them, and what are
holidays without kids?"

She had a point about kids and holidays. Since my boys
had grown, I'd let the holidays go. We had always celebrated
everything so we'd made ornaments for our Christmas trees
and lit Hanukkah candles and made donuts and potato
pancakes. The last vestige had been our yearly Christmas
Eve party and I'd let that go when Charlie died. Decorations and events at the bookstore had become my only way
of acknowledging holidays lately.

Ashley-Angela told Bob she wanted hot chocolate and E.
Conner said he wanted hot cider. The almost five-year-old
fraternal twins were the children of Dinah's ex, Jeremy, and

his now ex-wife. If you were looking for a definition for irresponsible, Jeremy was it, although his newly exed wife was a close second. Dinah had ended up taking care of the kids a while back, and even though, if anything, she ought to resent them, she'd gotten attached. As she explained it, they were her son and daughter's half siblings. Jeremy had finally taken over their care, but the damage was done. Dinah worried about them, along with missing them. She had invited them to spend the holidays with her.

"Jeremy is such a snake. I'm sure he was relieved about not having to worry about buying them any presents." Dinah spoke in a low voice, so the kids off getting napkins wouldn't hear.

"What does Commander think about them?" I said. Dinah didn't say anything and I thought she hadn't heard me, but she finally answered.

"He doesn't exactly know yet."

Commander Blaine was Dinah's current male companion. Her choice of description. We were on the same page about the boyfriend term. I thought *male companion* sounded older than dust, which is why I didn't use it. He owned a local mail-it center that catered to the many people working out of their houses.

Their relationship almost hadn't happened. Dinah had found him too fussy about his clothes (think knife-sharp creases in his pants), too enthusiastic about everything, but his worst offense was that he was too obvious about liking her. She'd finally given him a chance, though I thought she was still having some trouble with the last part. She was the first to admit that she seemed to be attracted to jerks.

"But he does know Bradley Perkins," she added quickly. "I was going to tell him about the kids, but I stalled and started telling him about what happened at your house."

"What did Commander have to say about Bradley?" I asked.

Dinah scanned the area, then leaned a little closer. "You know how everybody keeps saying what a great guy Bradley is. Well, Commander didn't seem so sold." I was going to ask for specifics, but Adele sailed in the café and stopped at our table.

"Pink, where are the snowflakes I gave you to starch?" Adele didn't even give me a chance to explain that they were drying on my dining room table. "We need them now."

I looked out into the bookstore. Mr. Royal had finished putting the lights on the tree and had gotten on a ladder and started arranging the pine boughs around the windows—the big empty wall of windows where the snowflakes were supposed to hang. Mrs. Shedd joined us and Adele informed her I was the holdup in the snowflake department.

"Molly, I hate to ask you to do this, but could you go home and get them? Joshua is anxious to hang them up."

I looked at Dinah and she responded with an understanding nod. We'd catch up later. I grabbed my jacket and headed for my car.

Generally my street was quiet in the middle of day. The dog walkers and exercise people came out in the morning and evening. So when I turned the corner I was expecting a big nothing.

Not quite.

A fire department ambulance facing the wrong way was pulled up in front of the Perkins' house. The dark blue–uniformed paramedics were bending over a figure on the ground. I noticed a dark sedan facing the right way was parked behind the ambulance. A man and woman in business attire stood a little back from the scene.

I pulled into my driveway and ran across my lawn toward

the group. By now I could see the figure on the ground was Emily and one of the paramedics was helping her up. She looked shaky and pale.

"What happened?" I said to the group. The woman in the suit stepped toward me.

"She was at her mailbox and suddenly she just collapsed."

The man came forward. "It looked like she might have hit her head. We called nine-one-one."

I pointed to my house and explained I was a neighbor.

I approached Emily, who seemed dazed. Her eyes were locked in a stunned expression. When she saw me, she reached out for my hand.

"Bradley's dead."

CHAPTER 6

"HERE YOU ARE," BARRY SAID, WALKING INTO THE
yarn department. "Did you forget our plans?" I looked up
slightly dazed. The worktable was littered with yarn, hooks
and knitting needles. I had been switching between crocheting and knitting swatches, along with reading over
the plans for the two upcoming bookstore events. A ball of
thread along with a silver hook and a partially done snowflake was off to the side.

Barry appeared to have gotten some sleep and the jeans
and dark green pocket tee shirt with an open flannel shirt
over it were not his work clothes, and I recalled that he'd
had the day off. I didn't know what plans he was talking
about until he mentioned our parting remarks in the morning after I made him breakfast. "Remember we were going
to have dinner and . . . ?" The heat coming off his eyes made
it pretty clear what he meant by *and*. It seemed the distant
past now. Particularly after the events of the afternoon.

Barry suddenly realized I wasn't alone and he grunted as he saw my company. His irritated sound wasn't aimed at Sheila. Ever since the table had become a permanent fixture, so had she. Who could blame her? She lived in a rented room in a house in Woodland Hills. All his irritation was aimed at Mason, who was sitting next to Sheila and working on the red dog sweater for Spike.

"I thought you had the evening off," Barry said to me.

"I would have if it hadn't been for this afternoon," I said, sitting up and trying to stretch the kinks out of my back. Barry gave Mason a dark look, apparently assuming my afternoon's problems had involved him.

Mason put his hands up in innocence. "I had nothing to do with it. She forgot our plans, too."

Barry glowered at the last comment. "I called your cell a bunch of times but just got your voice mail. What's going on?"

"Really?" I said, fishing around for my cell phone. It had gone to silent, again. The screen flashed on and the message icon flashed. I put the phone on the table so I wouldn't miss any calls, but it was kind of like shutting the door after the chickens got out. I looked at Barry. "I'm sorry that I forgot our dinner plans." I nodded at Mason. "And I'm sorry I forgot I offered to help you with Spike's coat." I looked at both of them. "And I'm sorry I apparently made double plans. I'm sorry I didn't answer my cell phone, too." I let out a heavy sigh. "I'm tired," I said, bringing up my aborted night's sleep on top of a killer day on top of a two-day trip with Adele. "I thought I'd work through the afternoon and go home and crash. But life had other plans." The three of them had concern in their expressions by now. I sounded pretty close to cracking.

"Okay, what happened this afternoon that changed everything?" Barry said, leaning on the table.

I explained about going home in the middle of the day
to pick up the snowflakes, which as it turned out never got
picked up. I described the scene with Emily and the paramedics.

"She told me that Bradley was dead, and then as they
were loading her in the ambulance, she said her daughters
needed to be picked up from school."

"And you volunteered," Barry said.

"What else could I do—leave the girls stranded at
school? The couple in the suits certainly weren't going to do
it. They were already in their car."

"Who were they?" Mason asked. I didn't have an answer. They were gone before I had a chance to ask them and
Emily had a few other things going on.

"So, what happened to the Perkins guy?" Barry prodded.

"I didn't find out until later. I picked up her girls and
went by the hospital. Emily was ready to be released. They'd
determined she hadn't hit her head and had just passed out
from shock." I described driving them all home with a side
stop at a fast-food drive-thru.

"She told her daughters she'd taken a misstep off a ladder
while trying to finish putting up the Christmas lights. She
didn't say anything about Bradley to them, so I guess they
still thought he was away on a business trip. They bought
the story about the ladder and she got them to take their
merry meals into the den. When we were alone she dropped
the cheerful pretense and took a letter out of her pocket and
handed it to me. The torn envelope looked benign. It was
addressed to her and postmarked Long Beach. The letter
was anything but benign. Emily began to cry as I read it
over."

I took a deep breath, feeling my stomach clench at remembering the note. "It was a suicide note. He said by the

time she read it, he'd be gone. That's why he bought the one-way ticket on the Catalina Express. He knew it would be dark and not crowded and nobody would notice him go off the back of the boat. And why? He said he'd gotten in over his head with his business and this was the only honorable thing to do."

I described how helpless I felt watching her holding herself and rocking back and forth. How I wished there was something to say to comfort her. Charlie's death had been sudden and it had been hard to deal with, but he'd had a heart attack. Not the same as choosing to die.

"She had a momentary glimmer of hope. The note had said what he planned to do. Maybe he'd changed his mind. But when she checked her phone messages, there was one from the customer service people at the boat company. A wallet and cell phone had been found left on the evening boat the night before."

I told them that Emily called the police officer she knew. He was the one who'd been there when the meter reader had mentioned the smell coming from my house. Since he knew Bradley from his daughter's soccer team, she thought he could help her. I leaned back in my chair and tried to summon some energy. "I didn't get back to the bookstore until this evening." I didn't mention how I had doubted Emily's story before. Her reaction to the letter seemed genuine and the balance went toward believing her.

In my peripheral vision I noticed William had come up to the table.

"Somebody probably got in touch with the coast guard. I imagine they made a sweep," Barry said. "But after that amount of time, and that amount of ocean, and sharks . . ." Barry's shrug said it all. They wouldn't find anything. I was surprised when he offered to check it out to be sure. Mason didn't take that information well. I think he was happier when Barry told me to stay out of things and Mason got to be the ear I turned to and my source for information.

Barry pulled out his phone and went off into the corner. William was too polite to interrupt and only now, when there was a lull in the conversation, said hello.

"If you're looking for Adele, she isn't back here," I said.

"She'll probably show up here any minute," the clown author said with a knowing smile. "What's going on? I heard you say something about the coast guard."

I started to explain about Bradley, but as predicted Adele swept into the department and latched arms with his. I finally got it all out, even what was in the suicide note.

"That's terrible," William said.

"You're so right, honey," Adele added. "Those poor little girls, even if he wasn't their real father. He won't be there to take them to your next Koo Koo event." She gave William's arm a tug. "We better go if we're going to make our dinner reservation."

Barry returned just as they were walking away and said the coast guard had initiated a search by boat and aircraft for a possible person in the water and so far had found nothing. "There's nothing more for you to do."

Mason nodded in response to Barry's comment, though Barry was trying to ignore his presence. Sheila had stopped crocheting as she listened to the story and the tension showed in her eyes.

"How strange. I just heard somebody talking about Perkins this morning, Sunshine," Mason said. "I was getting a coffee to go at the French café and overheard two guys at one of the tables. One of them had funny hair and was telling the other one that Perkins had some magic system with investments. I remember thinking it sounded like the guy with funny hair worked for Perkins. You know, drumming up business."

Barry grimaced both at the nickname Mason called me and the information he was offering.

I sat back and looked at my elephant project. I'd started working on the head, but the last round was inconsistent. "That's it. Time to go. I can barely see straight and my stitches are horrible," I said. I packed up my yarn work to take with. Barry said he'd follow me. Mason claimed to be at a crucial spot with his dog sweater and said he needed help and asked if he could follow me, too. Sheila had a forlorn look as the three of us got ready to leave.

"Why don't you join us?" I said. Before I'd gotten *us* out, she was on her feet, stuffing her work in her bag.

A short time later the caravan of cars pulled in front of my house.

As soon as we all got inside, Barry made me sit down on the couch. Mason said he'd take care of dinner. Sheila volunteered to take care of the animals. The events of the past few days had caught up with me big time and I felt exhausted. The doorbell rang a short while later and I caught a glimpse of a delivery guy bringing in a box. The smell of hot food wafted across the living room and my stomach responded with a hungry gurgle.

Every time I started to get up to help, one of the three told me they had it covered. Mason had ordered from the local Thai restaurant. Sheila made up a plate of pad thai, curried rice, big noodles in gravy and yellow curry made with tofu and brought it to me. I wasn't used to being waited on but had to admit it felt good. Mason, Barry and Sheila joined me in the living room with plates of food. The conversation went back to Bradley.

"I don't know where Perkins got the idea killing himself

was the *honorable* thing to do," Barry said. "More like the coward's way out."

"I wonder if his wife realizes that whatever mess he made is probably going to fall in her lap," Mason said.

Sheila was quiet and I knew all this was stirring up her own issues. She'd been brought up by a grandmother who had died recently, leaving Sheila feeling abandoned. She always said the Tarzana Hookers were her family now. "Those poor little girls, losing their stepfather," she said finally.

Barry turned back toward me. "Fields is right. She is going to inherit the mess. I am going to say what I always say and you probably are going to ignore me, but, Molly, you don't want to be associated with it. It's great to be a nice neighbor, but you may find out you've just stepped into quicksand." He put up his hands in feigned capitulation. I was stunned. Had Barry just agreed with Mason?

Someone brought me a dish of ice cream after that, but my eyes started swimming before I tasted the first spoonful.

When I awoke I was laying on the couch. My shoes were off and a pillow was under my head and a moss green crocheted throw covered me. I glanced at the coffee table. Someone had cleared all the dishes. I thought back to the last few minutes of conversation before I'd nodded off. Maybe they were right about me not getting involved. But it was too late. I'd already agreed to go with Emily in the morning when she went to Long Beach to pick up Bradley's things.

CHAPTER 7

I REALLY DIDN'T HAVE THE TIME TO GO TO LONG Beach. I was behind in swatches and snowflakes, and there were the plans for our holiday event and the book launch. That didn't even count any personal preparations like sending out cards or shopping for gifts. But I couldn't let Emily go to Long Beach alone if for no other reason than she was too distracted to drive.

"Is there any family you can call to help you out? Or maybe some of your friends?" I said as we set out on our journey. She needed as much moral support as she could get.

"There's just my mother," she said. "But she's in South Carolina and we don't get along. She barely remembers my girls' birthdays." Emily said Bradley's parents were dead and the only reason she knew he had a sister was because she'd sent the afghan as a wedding present. "That was one of the things that drew Brad and me together. He said we were both alone in the world. I'll have to look through Bradley's things and see if I can find a phone number for his sister. I think her name is Madison."

"Then she didn't come to your wedding?" I asked.

Emily sighed. "It was just Bradley, me and the girls. He said the wedding didn't matter; it was about all of us being together. Isn't that romantic?" she said. I nodded, thinking his being romantic hardly seemed an issue under the circumstance.

"What about friends? You seem to have lots of those," I said.

Emily nodded, looking down. "All the people we know are part of Brad's investment fund. It might be awkward." She left it hanging and I understood. They were more likely to be concerned about how his death affected them than to be interested in being supportive to her. I reached over and gave her hand a sympathetic squeeze. She really was all alone in this.

I asked her about the couple in the suits.

"They're from the Securities and Exchange Commission. They wanted to talk to Bradley. They came to the house when they couldn't reach him at the office. They said something about needing to clear something up. I think they called it a friendly interview. Bradley never discussed his business with me," she said. "I mean I helped with bank deposits and I helped him send out statements, but he never told me what was going on . . . what he was doing. Whenever I asked any questions—you know trying to be the interested wife—he got impatient and said he didn't want to talk about it. If only he'd told me about whatever problem he got himself into, we could have worked it out."

I collected a ticket and pulled into the terminal parking lot. We left the greenmobile and walked across the street. The Spartan building had been strung with some colored lights and the counter had several tiny decorated pine trees in pots.

Emily seemed pretty shaky, so I handled things and told the woman behind the counter why we were there. After a moment a man in business attire came out of a back room and a woman in a dark pants suit got out of a seat and joined us. She introduced herself as Detective Brower from the county sheriff's department.

The man introduced himself and explained he was an executive with the ferry company as he led us into an office. Emily was looking more and more shaky as he invited us to sit. The detective told Emily the coast guard was continuing their search even as we talked. Then she asked Emily what Bradley had been wearing the last time she saw him. The wallet and cell phone were sitting on the desk. I saw Emily's eye go to them and then look away as her breath caught. The two items might be her last connection to her husband.

The man said they had tapes of people getting on and disembarking the ferry that the items had been found on. The resolution wasn't great and the picture was in black and white, but I heard Emily suck in her breath as she pointed to a figure in a light jacket walking onto the boat.

"That's him," she squealed as the figure disappeared from the tape frame.

The ferry executive stopped the video and began to play the one with passengers getting off in Catalina. She leaned forward, scrutinizing the people as they walked down the ramp off the boat. She pointed at a figure and said something. The man replayed the tape, froze it and enlarged the figure. But Emily slumped. False alarm—it wasn't Bradley. When the last person went down the ramp, the man shut off the tape.

He asked her if she was sure she hadn't seen anyone that

might have been Bradley. She shook her head sadly. "I'm sorry," he said. No one said it, but I think we all knew there was only one other way Bradley could have left the boat.

"What about his car?" I asked.

"I was just going to bring that up," Detective Brower said. There was just a hint of annoyance that I had beat her to the punch. The ferry executive offered to take us through the parking structure in a golf cart so Emily could check for Bradley's Suburban.

We found it on the second level. The doors were unlocked and the keys under the seat. Emily prepared to climb in, insisting she was fine to drive it home.

"You'll need the parking ticket to get out of the lot," the man said. Emily checked the dash, around the seats and even the glove box, but there was no ticket. "Not to worry," the man said. "I'll follow you to the cashier and tell her to waive the fee and let you out."

At that point I headed for the greenmobile. I needed to get back to Tarzana.

Before I went into the bookstore, I stopped by Dinah's. She and the kids were folding laundry. E. Conner and Ashley-Angela looked like they were having fun.

"Aunt Dinah, where does this go?" Ashley-Angela said, holding up a towel that was coming unfolded. Dinah pointed toward the hall closet she'd converted into a linen closet.

She leaned close and whispered that it didn't matter how perfect their job was; for now it was teaching them to take part in the chores of the house.

Dinah had just made coffee and gave me a cup that I sorely needed after the Long Beach trip. She told the kids to take a break and she and I sat down together, while they went off to the den to work on puzzles.

Dinah wanted to hear everything about everything and

I started by telling her about my company the night before. "It's about time those men waited on you," she said when I mentioned waking up on the couch. I reminded her that Mason was always doing stuff for me.

"I knew one of them needed to do something for you," she said in a remark pointed at Barry. I was never one of these people who insisted chores be divided down the middle. I knew that Barry was often so exhausted he could barely stand up. I was hardly going to ask him to load the dishwasher when he was in that condition. Besides I preferred the help to come like this, unsolicited.

When I told her about Bradley, she was shocked.

"He jumped off the Catalina ferry?" she said in surprise. "Not my first choice of suicide routes, but who can figure?" I filled her in on all the details, including how the coast guard was searching the whole area between Long Beach and Avalon Harbor on Catalina.

Finally I got to the part about finding Bradley's Suburban in the parking structure. "Something about it doesn't seem right," I said.

Dinah misunderstood and thought I was concerned that no one had noticed it was parked for so long, and she tried to explain. "People probably leave cars there for several days all the time when they stay over on Catalina."

"That's not it," I said. "It's about the parking ticket. It wasn't in the car."

Dinah shrugged. "He probably took it with him."

"That seems really odd," I said. "If you were going to get on a ferry and jump off somewhere, and you went to the trouble to leave your SUV unlocked and the keys under the seat, why would you take your parking ticket with you?"

Dinah started to speak and then realized she didn't have a pat answer. "Yeah, why would you?"

CHAPTER 8

"Molly," Mrs. Shedd said, grabbing me as I rushed into the bookstore. "What happened to you yesterday? You were supposed to bring in the crocheted snowflakes. When I left for the day, there was no you and no snowflakes."

"I did come back to the bookstore. I'm afraid I'd forgotten all about the snowflakes, but when you hear what happened, I'm sure you'll understand." I walked farther into the store and she seemed very agitated as she walked with me.

She gestured toward the entrance area. "I thought you were going to put up a sign for the holiday event and a countdown sheet for the book launch. We want to generate as much excitement as possible. It would be terrible if the trucks rolled in with the books and there was no one waiting for them."

I broke the news that I didn't have the snowflakes with me this time, either. Mrs. Shedd sighed in frustration, but before she had a chance to chastise me, I stepped close to her.

"It's about Bradley Perkins," I said and she let out a little yelp. Mr. Royal was watering the Christmas tree and looked up at the sound. She covered her mouth and seemed even more agitated.

"Tell me it's good news," she said. "I've been trying to call his office and all I get is his voice mail or a woman who offers to take a message."

I didn't know quite how to tell her what happened, so I went the direct route and told her about the suicide note and my trip to Long Beach. The color drained from her face and I pulled up a chair and had her sit.

"Oh, dear," she said, putting her face in her hands. She took a few deep breaths and sat upright. "You can't tell anyone about this. Joshua was against it, but Logan Belmont kept raving what a miracle man Bradley was with money. Other people had lots of good things to say about Bradley, too. It wasn't as if I was dealing with a stranger. Bradley lived in the area and everyone knew him. I kept hearing that he coached a kids' sports team, was active in the local school and chamber of commerce. I was sure Joshua was wrong. I just gave Bradley a little of my savings at first, but when I saw the kind of return I was getting on it, I turned over more money to him." She swallowed hard before she continued. "I used the store's credit line and borrowed one hundred thousand dollars to give to him. Then a few weeks ago, I heard someone say they were having trouble taking their money out of Bradley's fund. It made me nervous, so I called him last week and told him I wanted to pull all my money out. Bradley tried to talk me into waiting for a couple of months, but when I persisted, he said he'd need a little time. Something about his special method of investing made it impossible for him to pull out money at a moment's notice. It didn't seem right to me, but what could I do?"

I asked her who she'd overheard, but she didn't remember.

The store was getting crowded. Mr. Royal had left fiddling with the tree and was helping a customer. Mrs. Shedd stood up and said we needed to take care of the bookstore's business. Just before we parted she said, "Molly, you've done detective stuff before. Please find out what's going on. You understand that if I can't get at least the hundred thousand dollars back to pay off the bank, the bookstore might go under." There was something desperate about her farewell squeeze of my arm before she put on a brave smile and went to help a couple standing near the local history books.

"THAT SOUNDS BAD. WHAT DOES SHE EXPECT YOU to do?" Dinah asked me later as I sat down at the table at the bookstore café. Mrs. Shedd had asked me to keep everything she'd told me to myself, but telling Dinah didn't count. My friend had called about meeting and for once I actually noticed that my cell was ringing. Dinah said she needed my help with something.

But before I took a break, I made up the sign for the holiday event. We put it on every year to coincide with Santa Lucia Day.

The celebration was a carryover from Mrs. Shedd's childhood. She was Swedish and every December thirteenth, as the eldest daughter, she donned the traditional long white dress, red sash and crown of candles and served coffee and buns to her family. There were various interpretations to the origin of the holiday, but to Mrs. Shedd it kicked off the holiday season.

I made up the countdown sheets and attached them to the cardboard cutout of Anthony. Mrs. Shedd was right about it being a good idea. They attracted immediate attention. I waited on customers and, when there was a lull, went back to the yarn department and attached the completed swatches on the bins.

Bob was baking something with cinnamon and the air smelled delicious. He said he'd bring over our order when it was ready.

"Mrs. Shedd didn't say exactly, but I think what she really wants me to do is to get her money back. I can't see where Emily will be much help. She kept telling me that she didn't know about Bradley's business," I said with a sigh. I smiled at Ashley-Angela and E. Conner, who were sitting at the bistro table with Dinah. They were sharing a box of crayons and drawing. It was amazing to see how they'd calmed down compared to their first visit, thanks to the Dinah effect. She'd worked the same wonders on the kids that she did with her students.

"But I came here to help you out," I said. "What's the problem?"

"Molly, Dinah, hi," a chirpy voice said before Dinah could answer. Our fellow Hooker, Elise Belmont, passed by, carrying a shopping bag from Nicholas's store. She walked over to a corner table, where I noticed that her husband Logan had set up his portable office. He had his papers, his cell phone and minicomputer set out on the table. Logan was the go-to guy for real estate in Tarzana and Woodland Hills. The bookstore café and Le Grande Fromage were favorite spots to hang out among the Tarzanians who worked out of their houses.

Bob brought over Dinah's order. He handed me a red-eye and a container of fruit and cheese the café had just started carrying. Dinah had a café au lait and a bagel and cream cheese, which she cut up for the kids. Bob gave them each a mug of steamed milk and honey. I mouthed a thank-you to Dinah. As usual she'd ordered right. But I was more interested in Logan than the food.

"Mrs. Shedd kept mentioning Logan and how he was the one who'd turned her on to investing with Bradley." I watched the action at the corner table for a moment. Logan appeared upbeat as his wife pulled out a chair and I had a feeling he didn't know about Bradley. "I'm going to go talk to them," I said, getting up.

"Go for it, Molly," Dinah said.

I greeted Elise and Logan when I reached their table. I thought I'd begin with a little small talk, but Elise took care of that.

"I think I figured out who A. J. Kowalski is," she said with her eyes so bright they practically sparkled. "I know you said you won't tell, but if I guess right, you could blink twice. That wouldn't be telling."

I was beginning to realize it was useless to keep repeating that I didn't know who the vampire author was, so I just listened and let her think whatever she wanted based on what she thought my eyes did.

"It's Adele's boyfriend, isn't it? All that stuff she said was just a cover. Pretty smart of me, huh?" She turned toward her husband as he worked on his computer. "Logan said William took a lease with an option to buy on a nice little house over in College Acres."

Elise was staring at my eyes, trying to count blinks, while I restrained a laugh. Koo Koo as the vampire author? Right. He reminded me of a glass of warm milk. I couldn't picture him writing the smoldering undercurrent that surrounded the Anthony character. Even the way An-

thony stroked a crochet hook as he drew it through a loop
was sensual.

Logan nodded in agreement. "Bearley's writing career
must be going well. His big concern was finding a house
that had a room for a writing studio that he could keep
separate from the rest of the house."

Since Logan seemed to be in the know about William/
Koo Koo, I asked if he knew what his day job was.

"He teaches English at a private school and does a lot of
tutoring. He dropped a few hints that he might be making
some changes in his life soon."

"Sounds like he might be getting married," Elise said,
and I suddenly had an image of Adele as a bride. No question, with her sense of style she wouldn't be wearing a white
dress. More likely purple or magenta.

Logan shrugged. "I listen, but I don't ask."

"You didn't blink twice, did you?" Elise said, her voice
heavy with disappointment, for a second, anyway. Her mind
started working again and her eyes brightened. "What
about Nicholas?" She focused on my face, trying to keep
track of my blinks again, while I tried to change the subject. I noticed something black and white was overflowing
from her project bag on the chair next to her.

"What are you making?" I asked, touching it.

She pulled it out and displayed it on the table. "It's a
vampire scarf." When I didn't get it, she explained. The
white stripes were pale and chalky like a vampire's complexion, the black ones were for their color of choice for clothes.
Anthony was big on black turtlenecks and black fine wool
slacks. Even the half double crochet stitches looked like tiny
fangs, she said, indicating the pointy edges of the stitches.
She was going to add pointy edging with a fanglike shape
at the ends of the scarf and the final touch—a red tassel.

She didn't have to tell me why anything scarlet reminded her of vampires.

"And think of it," she said, "what is the most vampire-centric part of the body? The neck," she said, stroking hers in an exaggerated manner.

I'd gotten sidetracked from my real purpose. I'd already thought it out and decided to ask questions first, because once I told Logan about Bradley's suicide, I didn't think he'd be interested in answering.

Logan was on the short side, with an aura of cheerfulness, which worked well for being in real estate. He had a weird hairline that made it look like he was wearing a cap. It was a little touchy figuring out how to mention Bradley without bringing up the suicide, but at the same time not making it sound like he was alive. I finally just said, "You know Bradley Perkins, don't you?" Then instead of continuing, I let it hang in the air.

"Know him?" Logan said with a laugh. "You could say so. He's the best thing that happened to us." He smiled at his wife and she nodded in agreement. "You joined his fund, didn't you?" When I said I hadn't, he seemed surprised. "If you want, I can help you get in. The investment club has become so popular Bradley had to limit who he would let join."

I mumbled something about having to think about it. Logan took my comment to mean I didn't know enough about the fund to want to put my money in and he began what seemed like a sales pitch.

"I met Bradley and Emily when I sold them their house," Logan said. He detailed how he and Bradley had gotten talking and Bradley had mentioned making a lot of money on stocks. "The guy has a knack for buying and selling securities. It's amazing. He has some secret system. He calls it Strike and Split." Logan let the comment sink in before continuing on. "I don't remember exactly how it came up, but I asked him if he'd be interested in letting me put some money in with his." Logan said Bradley had been hesitant at first, but then thought it was a good idea. "I just threw in a little money and in a few months he gave me a check that covered just the profit on my money. It was a nice hunk of change," Logan said. He turned to his wife. "That's what we used to remodel the kitchen, remember?"

"Like I would forget. It's not every day you get your dream kitchen. Thank you, Bradley," she said before taking a bite of Logan's cheese plate.

"So, then I gave him more of our money and I'd told some other people about Bradley and they wanted in, too. He started calling it a club and it seemed like everybody wanted in. Finally, he made up some rules about whose money he would take. I'm always hearing from somebody around here, asking me to put in a good word for them."

"Wow, I had no idea," I said when he finished. Who would have guessed, looking at the Perkins' house? It was nice and all, but hardly fitting someone who was that successful. Logan said that was part of Bradley's appeal.

"Bradley charges a small fee for handling the fund—just enough to cover his expenses. He doesn't go in for fancy offices and an extravagant lifestyle. He's one of us."

Now I'd come to the hard part. It was obvious Logan was done giving out information and I had to break the news about Bradley. "When was the last time you talked to Bradley?" I asked.

Logan thought a moment. "I don't know, maybe a week ago."

"Did you know that he went missing a few days ago?"

Logan made a dismissive shrug. "Elise mentioned something. She heard he and Emily had some kind of argument and he'd taken off for a few days. I was going to call him, but I decided it was best to stay out of it. I was kind of surprised, though. They are such a perfect couple. I can't imagine them having that big a fight."

I swallowed hard. "So, if something were to happen to Bradley, who would take over this fund you were talking about?"

"Interesting question," Logan said. "Well, Bradley is the club, so no one could take his place. I suppose all the stocks in the fund would be sold and the money divided up to the members. I'm glad you brought that up. I'm going to talk to Bradley about it. He's a young guy in good health, but it's a good idea to have all bases covered."

"It might be too late." The words slipped out before I could stop them and Logan's head jutted forward.

"What do you mean?" he demanded.

Suddenly I didn't want to say any more. I knew he wasn't going to react well. "Maybe you should talk to Emily and get the exact wording in his note."

"What kind of note?" Logan asked. It was like a shade had been pulled over his upbeat demeanor.

I just repeated that he ought to talk to Emily as I excused myself. He grabbed his cell phone, and as I headed back to my table, I saw him start running his hand over his hair as if he was trying to soothe himself and I realized Logan must have been who Mason overheard. What had Mason said—that it sounded like the guy was working for Bradley. Hmm.

CHAPTER 9

"Mission accomplished," I said as I slid back in my chair. There was no joy in my voice. I looked across the bookstore café toward Logan. He was still on the phone and I could tell by his expression he'd heard the bad news. He'd lost his golden goose and there'd be no more golden eggs. I told Dinah what Logan had said he thought would happen in the event of Bradley being out of the picture. "It might take a while since no doubt there will be lawyers involved, but Mrs. Shedd should get her money. At least some of it," I said. "Bradley mentioned some business problems in his note. I'm guessing it means his special system didn't work and he made some bad investments." Dinah seemed preoccupied as I spoke and grabbed my wrist when I'd finished.

"You have to be my wingman." Dinah's gaze darted toward the door and then back to me. She straightened Ashley-Angela's blue shirt and fluffed E. Conner's golden blond hair. "It's Commander," she said. Dinah, who could practically make her freshmen cry with just a look, was not her usual confident self.

"You never told him about Ashley-Angela and E. Conner, did you?" I said.

Dinah slumped forward and shook her head. "I was going to tell him all about them before I invited them, but there was one thing and then another . . ." She glanced over toward the kids, who were happily drawing and eating mini-croissants with Swiss cheese. "Okay, I just didn't. And now it's really awkward."

"Showtime," I said under my breath as the door to the café opened and Commander Blaine hesitated in the doorway. When he saw Dinah, his face lit up like a three-hundred-watt halogen bulb, and with a buzz of energy in his step, he headed toward our table. Commander was a nickname leftover from childhood. His real name was Sylvester, which Dinah thought sounded like some kind of synthetic yarn. I guess that's what happens when you have yarn on the brain, you see everything in terms of it.

He crossed the space in a few steps and leaned down to give Dinah a greeting kiss before pulling up a chair from a nearby table and sitting down. Commander had thick white hair, which made his complexion appear even ruddier. He had a wiry build that seemed unaffected by his age, which I guessed to be in his late fifties. It was obvious that it wasn't occurring to him that the kids sitting at the table were with Dinah.

He and Dinah's gazes met and simultaneously, they both said they had a surprise for the other. I attempted to make my exit, but Dinah had grabbed my wrist and wouldn't let go until I sank back into my seat.

"You go first," Dinah said, taking the chance to stall. Commander looked at Dinah's hand on my wrist.

"Molly seems to want to leave," he said as if he thought Dinah wasn't aware of this.

"No, she doesn't," Dinah said, still holding on to me. "In fact, she wants to ask you about somebody." I felt her knee nudge me. Okay, telling your male companion that you were hosting your ex's kids might seem a little hard to understand, but I thought she was making more out of it than necessary. Though as owner of the local mailing center, he did seem to be in the middle of the information flow and she had mentioned that he knew Bradley Perkins.

Commander seemed a little disappointed when I stayed. I'm sure he thought the kids would have left with me. But he knew Dinah well enough to just go along with it. So he forged ahead and brought out some sheets he'd printed off the Internet and laid them out on the table. "My business is at a standstill around the holidays. It's an easy time for me to take some time off. You and me on a Christmas trip up to Pacific Grove to see the monarch butterflies. No conference center this time," he said, referring to the place we'd held our retreat. "We'd stay at a cozy inn I know. Fireplaces in every room. How about it?"

Dinah squirmed and nudged me again. "Molly, didn't you want to ask Commander about Bradley Perkins?"

"Uh, I was just wondering if you knew him," I said as she nudged me again. I was definitely earning the title of wingman because I was certainly winging it.

Commander seemed disappointed not to have gotten a more enthusiastic response to his trip idea, but he nodded at me. "Someone else was asking about him."

"Who?" I asked. Answering a question with a question was an old investigative standby I'd learned from Barry— not because he meant to teach it to me, but because he'd used it on me.

Commander Blaine took a moment to collect his thoughts. "It was a couple of investigators from the Securities and Exchange Commission. Perkins used to rent a post office box from me. I offer the advantage of a real address instead of just a post office box number," he said with a certain amount of pride in his voice. For some reason the kids looked up at his comment as if they'd noticed him for the first time and then in typical kid fashion figured whatever he was talking about was boring and went back to their coloring. If Commander noticed them staring at him, he didn't let on.

I asked if it was a man and woman in suits and he nodded. Obviously the same people I'd seen.

"What did you tell them?" I asked.

Commander leveled his gaze. "Exactly what I knew directly about his business—nothing. Bradley's a great guy. Friendly with lots of personality. Even after he stopped renting the box, he'd drop by and we talked about sports scores and how the soccer team was doing. I'm one of the sponsors, you know," he said with a certain amount of pride. "But that's it. He never discussed his work other than to say things were going really well." Commander saw Logan and Elise heading toward the door.

"Now, Logan was always trying to sell me on Bradley's business. He'd go on and on about what a genius Perkins was and I ought to think of investing some money with him. I never bothered with exact details of what Perkins was doing, but Logan said he'd made a bundle with him. Logan was like a one-man advertising campaign for the guy. You'd think he was making a commission or something." I just nodded and listened.

"Then you didn't join the investment club?"

Commander looked at me like I had asked him an absurd question.

"Nope. Call me an old fool, but when it comes to money, I'm conservative. Federally insured savings accounts are the way I go."

I told Commander about Bradley's suicide and his expression grew grave.

When I mentioned the note saying he'd gotten into some kind of trouble, Commander looked even graver.

"Makes me glad I never let Logan talk me into anything. Who knows what happened to all that money. I know what's what with mine, which is why I can easily afford this trip." He nudged the papers in Dinah's direction again.

Before I could find out how my friend was going to answer, our cashier Rayaad came in from the bookstore and interrupted. The UPS guy was there with a delivery and needed a signature. I didn't get a chance to see Commander's expression when I walked away and the kids stayed behind.

The UPS guy was shifting his weight and glancing toward his truck. He swatted his electronic signing pad against his leg. A dolly with a stack of brown boxes stood next to him. He smiled expectantly as I approached and held out the pad for me to sign.

"What is all this?" I said, eyeing the boxes. Rayaad shrugged and said that was why she'd gotten me. She wasn't going to take the responsibility for signing for them. I looked at the return address on the boxes and hesitated. Mrs. Shedd and Mr. Royal had left without mentioning a delivery. I was considering what to do when Joshua Royal came back into the store. He saw the boxes and his face broke into a happy expression.

"Good, the things I ordered have come," he said. The UPS guy straightened and handed him the signing thing. No hesitation here; Mr. Royal signed quickly and the UPS guy pulled the dolly out from under the boxes and left.

Mr. Royal lifted the back of his leather jacket, exposing a knife holder hanging from his belt. I stifled a gasp as he pulled the knife out of the case. I wasn't expecting anything so long and lethal looking. I suppose it was a leftover from all his adventuring.

"Would you clear off that table," he said, pointing to the best seller table that was adjacent to the display of Anthony books. Rayaad and I did as he asked, while he used the knife to split open the box tops.

I was surprised to see the content was all Anthony accessories. "Does Mrs. Shedd know about these?" I asked, lining up the Anthony action figures. I had to admit they were appealing and very detailed. The figure wore Anthony's trademark black turtleneck top and black slacks and had a crochet hook in one hand and a ball of yarn in his pocket.

"I don't need her approval," Mr. Royal said. I listened to see if there was an edge in his voice, as if to say he could do whatever he pleased, but there wasn't any. I took it to mean that they were really partners. Apparently his days of being the silent one were over. The other boxes had mugs, tote bags, key chains and tee shirts—all with Anthony likenesses. There was still some space on the table when we finished putting everything out. He gestured toward the back of the store and the yarn department. "Why don't we bring some crochet hooks up here and a few balls of yarn. Let's do some cross marketing," he said. There was something charismatic and fun about him and we all headed toward the back.

As we were setting up a selection of crochet hooks and skeins of yarn next to the action figures, I mentioned Elise's vampire scarf to Mr. Royal.

"Do you suppose we could offer copies of her scarf pattern? Complimentary, of course," he said. He held up a female action figure wearing a trench coat and carrying a laptop bag. "Who is she supposed to be—another vampire?"

"That's Colleen. She's a reporter—a human reporter. She's been bringing Anthony's story to the world since he decided to go mainstream in the first book," I said. Rayaad obviously hadn't read the books, nor cared to. The little shake of her head was filled with distaste, and she headed back to her domain at the cashier stand.

"Mainstream?" Mr. Royal said, holding up an Anthony doll. "Please elaborate." Apparently Mr. Royal had no idea of the story line. I had to explain that vampires were supposed to stay in the shadows, out of the public eye, and when Anthony decided to become part of the regular world, it caused a stir among the humans and stirred up trouble with the vampires.

"You see, Anthony wants to do something for mankind during his immortality. He's stopped drinking human blood ever since he began to crochet. Now he gets by on blood products from a hospital supply place and fills in with animal blood."

Mr. Royal made a face.

"You eat meat, don't you?" I said and he nodded. "Anthony just takes out the middleman. But the blood stuff isn't that important in the story line. It's really a love story. See Anthony has fallen for Colleen, though to her he's just a story. You do know that vampires are always very, very sexy and incredibly attractive, don't you?"

Mr. Royal said he wasn't familiar enough with vampires to know that and smiled good-naturedly while I continued.

"It's not that Colleen hasn't noticed him, she's just keeping him at arm's length. There's a really hot scene in the first book. He's telling her that learning how to crochet has changed his existence and she says she wishes she knew how to crochet. So, he teaches her, but not the usual way by demonstrating. He stands behind her, molding his body to hers, with his arms against hers, guiding her hands with his. Kind of like that scene in *Ghost* where Patrick Swayze helps Demi Moore with her clay piece." I looked at Mr. Royal for some kind of recognition. He remembered the movie scene.

"So Anthony has made crochet sexy," he said, and I nodded.

"The promotional material for *Caught Under the Mistletoe* gives the setup for the book. Colleen takes Anthony home to her family's house in Connecticut for the holidays. It's the first time he's celebrating Christmas since he was turned into a vampire, so it's a big deal."

"I get it and he's hoping to catch her under the mistletoe and wow her with his hot kisses."

"Something like that," I said. "Oh, and the other vampires are upset with Anthony and they're supposed to show up at Colleen's and cause trouble. Did I mention that her family doesn't know Anthony is a vampire?"

"Thanks for bringing me up to speed," Mr. Royal said, handing me the Anthony doll. "Since you seem to be an expert, why don't you finish the display." He started to walk away and then stopped. "I heard that neighbor of yours who was missing turned out to be a suicide. Do you know why Pamela was so upset about it?"

What could I tell him? Certainly not the truth, but I didn't like lying, either. I was struggling for an answer when Dinah saved me by walking up and interrupting.

"Well, I told him," Dinah said. She seemed oblivious to Mr. Royal standing there and after a moment I noticed he'd disappeared. "I don't think Commander would mind the kids—if their father was someone else. He was kind of quiet after I explained who they were." Dinah looked down. "I hope this doesn't turn out to be a deal breaker."

I did my best to reassure her and said he probably just needed a little time to process. I hoped what I was saying was true. Dinah noticed the display. I told her Mr. Royal had ordered all the action figures without even knowing the story line.

"Or so he says," Dinah said with a knowing nod. "Did you ever think that he was A. J. Kowalski?"

"Wow," I said. "I hadn't thought about him." I looked in the direction he'd gone. He was helping a customer in the travel section. "Maybe he was just pretending not to know the story line. Having me bring him up to speed was just a cover," I said as Dinah steered the kids toward the children's department.

When Mrs. Shedd returned, her face clouded when she saw the display. That is until I explained whose idea it was. Then she smiled and pronounced it brilliant.

"I found out some information about Bradley's business," I said, checking that no one was in earshot. I told her what Logan had said about the stocks being sold and the money divided up among the investors.

"Molly, I don't find that very reassuring," she said. "Or the complete story. Who is handling the business right now? Who is going to sell the stock and divide up the money?"

"I don't know," I said. An image of the man and woman in the suits I'd seen at the Perkins' came to mind. In all that had gone on, I'd forgotten about them. I repeated what Emily had said about them being from the Securities and Exchange Commission. Mrs. Shedd seemed even more upset when I mentioned they had wanted to have a friendly interview with Bradley before he disappeared.

"What they call a friendly interview is an investigation,

Molly. Bradley must have known and that's why . . ." She let her voice trail off as she wrung her hands.

Of course what she said made sense. I didn't know that much about high finance. I was pretty much on the same page as Commander and had all my money in CDs. But the people showing up from the SEC might have been what pushed Bradley over the edge. Mrs. Shedd looked around the store and then at the time.

"We have to do something," she said. "I told you if I don't get back the money I gave him, the bookstore is in trouble. We're all in trouble." She sighed deeply and shook her head. "Someone is answering his office phone and taking messages. They must know something. It's pretty quiet for the moment around here. You know how to do sleuthing. Why don't you go to Perkins' office right now and see what you can find out."

CHAPTER 10

THE ADDRESS MRS. SHEDD GAVE ME TURNED OUT to be a high-rise in the Warner Center area of Woodland Hills. I'd often admired the way the all-glass high-rises reflected the sky. The directory gave a suite number on the seventh floor for Perkins Financial. This place looked like high rent to me.

A woman sat behind a counter in front of a wall of windows with a clear view of the Santa Susana Mountains. I was glad she was on the phone since I didn't know what I was going to say and it gave me time to think. I wasn't there just for Mrs. Shedd. I had a personal reason to find her money. I loved my job at the bookstore and didn't want to lose it.

The woman went to another phone line. "Pearson Productions, please hold," she said. A moment later, I heard her answer, "Higgins Insurance." I stood up, thinking I was in the wrong office, but she answered the phone again and this time she said "Perkins Financial." I listened while she asked their identity and put them on hold while she contacted somebody and announced the caller. A moment later, she went back to the caller and said she would have to take a message. I thought it was some kind of scam until I realized it was one of those office suite arrangements where you get some office space and services like having someone answer the phone. But even better, I figured out that someone from Perkins Financial was there. The woman clicked off after she'd written down a message. She glanced in my direction and asked if she could help me.

I didn't want to tell her I wanted to talk to somebody from Perkins Financial and have her announce me and take the chance of being turned away. Then I had an inspiration. Instead of telling her the truth, I said I was looking for an office.

"Oh," the woman said, brightening. She took out a brochure and began to describe what they offered. I tried to appear interested and nonchalantly asked if I could look around. I said I was really checking it out for my husband. Her phone started ringing again and she gestured toward the hallway with a nod. I was in!

I walked down the corridor and looked in the first open door. The office was so small as to be claustrophobic with the door closed, which ended up working to my advantage. The doors to most of the offices were open. Halfway down the hallway, I caught a glimpse of Emily and the couple in the suits in one of the offices. Before any of them could see me, I took a step back and slipped into the office behind them. The clear desk and empty shelves made it obvious it didn't belong to anybody. At least I didn't have to worry about someone coming in and wondering why I was in their space.

The walls between the offices were paper-thin, and with

the door open, it was easy to hear what was going on in the next office.

"I realize this is a very difficult time for you and we appreciate you cooperating with this informal investigation, but there have to be more records than this," the man said. "We received a tip from one of your husband's clients that they were having trouble taking their money out of this investment club. All you've shown us is checking account statements and canceled checks. What accounting firm did your husband use? And where did he keep the physical securities he bought for his clients?"

"I don't know," Emily said. Her voice sounded strained. "I helped him with bank deposits and sending out quarterly statements, but that's it. Who complained?"

"That's confidential," the man said. Emily said something about a box of files that Bradley had taken back and forth to the office with him, but she didn't know where they were now. The woman asked if they could take an image of Bradley's computer. Emily gave them her permission.

"What do you know about these checks?" the man said. "They're all written to casinos." Emily sounded confused as she said she knew nothing about them. She insisted she'd never seen Bradley gamble or even heard him talk about gambling. She finally excused herself to go to the restroom. I slid behind the door until she'd passed.

With her gone, the SEC pair began to talk. Their investigation was by no means finished, but they'd come to several conclusions. Even though it was questionable that there was no body, they believed that Bradley was really dead because there was still fifty thousand dollars in his checking account. They reasoned that if Bradley had been trying to fake his death, he would have cleaned out the account. The second part made me shudder. The couple, who

I now knew were a lawyer and a forensic accountant, were going to investigate further, but they thought Bradley had committed a blatant fraud and never bought any securities with the money his clients had given him. Instead he had used the money to gamble. Judging from all the checks written to the casinos and the lack of deposits back into the account, they guessed he'd lost all the money.

Poor Mrs. Shedd. Poor all of us.

"Do you think the wife was an accomplice in the fraud?" the woman said.

"Hard to say. It's not as if he left her a hunk of money," the man said.

"That we know about," the woman added.

"And the whole episode of fainting at the mailbox could have been staged to buy time so she could hide whatever she did have." The man paused. "Still, I tend to think she was just another of his victims. Everything she has is going to end up being seized. Too bad since it's around the holidays."

I waited until Emily came back from her bathroom stop and then slipped out of the empty office. The receptionist had a hopeful expression, which I quickly dashed when I told her the office wasn't quite what my husband was look-ing for.

Mrs. Shedd was pacing across the front of the bookstore when I returned. "Well?" she said. I think my expression gave away the fact that I didn't have good news. I put my hand on her shoulder for support and then told her the SEC people thought Bradley had gambled all the money away.

"Oh, no," she said as the color drained from her face and she slumped against one of the bookcases. "We can make it through the holidays, but after the first of the year I have to pay the bank back." She glanced around the bookstore and her eyes grew watery. She loved the store and didn't want to lose it. "Let's try to make the holiday season our best ever, since it might be our last." We hugged on it.

I didn't tell her, but I wasn't giving up. There had to be something I could do to save the bookstore.

It was dark when I headed home. The bookstore had gotten crowded and I'd spent the rest of the evening help-ing people choose gift books. There hadn't even been time to go back to the yarn department. I patted the tote bag on the passenger seat. It overflowed with yarn that needed swatches and the elephant in progress. I was also hoping to make some more snowflakes to add to the ones Adele had made that were still sitting on my dining room table. At least my street was quiet, the way it was supposed to be. As I drove past the Perkins', I automatically looked over, wondering about Emily. What a day she'd had—from the morning in Long Beach, seeing Bradley alive for the last time as he got on the ferry to being grilled in the so-called friendly interview with the SEC people.

Her driveway was long like mine and at the end curved toward her garage door. The motion-sensor light came on and I noticed a gray cat running across the driveway. Then something else caught my eye. A wheel or a portion of one showed beyond the bush that obscured the area in front of the garage. Before I could make out what it was, the light went off.

My only excuse was extreme nosiness, but all things con-sidered I wondered what was in her driveway, particularly since it seemed hidden. After pulling into my own drive-way, I cut across my lawn toward her place. I didn't want my nosiness to be obvious, so I crept up the edge of the drive-way, hoping to stay out of the range of the motion sensor.

My best of intentions failed and I got in the path of the sensor and the light flipped on. I dropped next to the bush to avoid being seen. The light stayed on long enough for me to get a good look at what was behind the bush. A motorcycle? Emily hated motorcycles. She'd said more than once that she thought they should be banned from the road. So what was one doing hidden in her driveway? Or more importantly, who did it belong to?

Enough sleuthing, I thought as I backed down the driveway. The light didn't go on again, and I was just about to step onto the street when a hand grabbed my shoulder and I jumped straight up.

CHAPTER 11

"HEY, WHAT ARE YOU UP TO?" RYDER LOWESTEIN, the kid neighbor from down the street, said. He peered at me as my breath came out in a ragged gasp; it felt something like when you jump into water that's too cold.

"You could have given me a heart attack," I said.

"Sorry, MP. I forgot I was dealing with someone older. You know you really can frighten someone to death. Something about the vagus nerve. I read about it—"

"MP?" I said interrupting. Then I got it. Everything was down to abbreviations—even me.

He nodded toward the driveway. "You doing some kind of reconnaissance?"

It was too embarrassing to admit that I'd been snooping, even if Mr. YouTube was as nosey as I was. Instead of answering I asked him if he knew who the motorcycle belonged to. He couldn't see it in the darkness, but I assured him it was there. Then I asked him what he was doing wandering around in the dark.

He pointed down the street with his video camera in his hand. He'd been taping the holiday decorations at the different houses. He was going to sync it up to some music and give it to his parents to use as a holiday greeting on their Facebook page.

We finally parted company and I watched him saunter off with his slightly shuffling walk.

I retrieved my tote bag and purse from my car and walked into my dark yard. Something brushed against my leg and my breath immediately went back to that jumping-into-too-cold-water mode. It only got worse when more something touched me. Moving things with fur. I looked ahead toward my kitchen door, which only had a worse effect on my breath. Even in the dark, I could see it was ajar.

I rushed ahead and reached inside the door and used the switch on the wall to turn on the yard lights. I saw that what I'd felt was the two cats making figure eights around my legs. They knew they weren't supposed to be out alone at night and they were freaking out. Cosmo charged out of the bushes and started barking, which seemed kind of after the fact. Even Blondie had come outside and was sitting on a chaise lounge. She regarded all of the action with her usual calm expression.

I took out my cell phone and called Barry. Within minutes a helicopter was circling overhead with its rhythmic *thwack* sound, bathing my yard and the bushes that marked the border with its spotlight. Barry arrived at the same time, along with two uniforms in a cruiser. They all went inside while the animals and I stayed in the yard.

"Molly, you've got to stop leaving windows open," Barry said in a frustrated tone when he came back outside. Whoever had been there was gone. There was no sign of forced entry and whoever had broken in had used the door to exit like before. "Why bother to break in when you practically put out the welcome mat for them?" Barry said, throwing up his hands.

I didn't know what he was talking about until he took me inside and pointed out the open windows in Samuel's room. Mr. Detective hadn't noticed the suitcases or the note on the bed announcing that Samuel was back from the road and had gone out to meet up with some friends. He said he'd opened the windows to get out the smell of the cat throw up and would I close them when I got home. There was a post script asking what happened to the front door.

Barry led me to my craft room. All the grocery bags had been dumped on the floor. Everything on the shelves pulled out. And the containers holding the finished pieces for holiday gifts had been dumped.

"Ugh," I said when we got to the den. All the cabinets were open and the contents pulled out. "It was probably the same person as before," I said. I tripped over a book, and when I picked it up, saw that it was *Caught By the Hook*. I showed it to Barry. "See, I told you someone thinks that I am hiding the identity of A. J. Kowalski here. They must have thought I kept it in here or with my crochet stuff."

"You must have some idea who it is," Barry said, putting the box of photos back in the built-in cabinet.

"Whoever it is obviously knows Cosmo is all noise and no bite," I said as the black mop of fur raced through the den and stopped at Barry's feet.

Barry grunted, as if the comment about his dog was aimed at him. I couldn't help but think Ryder showing up was just a little too coincidental. He probably figured he'd find out who the author was and then confront him or her, tape them and stick it on YouTube ahead of the book launch. Ryder had said he was looking for something that would make a splash on YouTube. I suppose he thought anything was okay in pursuit of a story. What did they call them? Gonzo journalists or something. I'd have to have a little talk with him. Barry read my silence.

"Okay, who are you thinking about?" he said in his best cajoling voice.

"No one," I said too quickly for it to sound real.

"Molly," Barry said, shaking his head. "Someone coming into your house is serious, even if all they're after is some author's real name."

If I mentioned Ryder, I knew Barry would go after him like gangbusters. Much better for me to handle it in my own way. I agreed that it was serious but held my ground and didn't give up a name.

"You should be more upset," he said. "You should look pale and have a pounding heart."

"Gee, thanks for the good wishes," I said. "By now I'm immune. First you thought there was a dead body in my house and broke the door down. Then somebody was creeping around when I was asleep. Someone just going in the window and throwing around my yarn seems like no big deal."

The helicopter was long gone and the cruiser had left, too. The den was picked up, but I said the mess in the crochet room was too much to tackle. Barry had pulled his tie loose and taken off his suit jacket. "Maybe I should stay awhile and help you calm down," he said, putting an arm around my shoulder. "There's no rush. Jeffrey is at a friend's. I don't have to drive car pool."

I pointed toward my tote bag. "Yes, but I have stuff I have to take care of. I need to get those swatches done and make more snowflakes or Christmas will be over before we even get them hung."

He tried to say he wouldn't interfere with my work, but I gave him a look of total disbelief. And I mentioned that Samuel might show up any minute. Barry finally left but not before giving me the speech that my sons were both adults and should certainly be able to deal with their mother having a boyfriend. He reminded me that while he'd been protective of his son Jeffrey at first, not wanting him to meet me unless we were at least engaged, he'd finally relented. "Jeffrey loves you," Barry said. "I realize that isn't going to happen between me and your boys, but they have to accept me."

He had a point, but it wasn't just about Samuel and Peter. I'd been married a long time and this was like a second chapter of my life. I was hanging on to my freedom. I hated to admit it, but I was using my sons as an excuse to keep Barry from getting too close.

I glanced in the crochet room again and sighed. The morning would be fine to start clearing it up. Through the window I saw the lights of the Perkins' front porch. I thought of Emily. With everything she'd been through lately, her nerves must be shot. The helicopter and cop car must have sent her into freak-out mode. I ought to at least tell her what was going on, though I doubted she had to worry about my burglar branching out. And maybe I could find out about the mysterious motorcycle.

Emily peeked out the window before opening the door. She looked wan and preoccupied, which under the circumstances seemed appropriate. She said the cops had knocked at her door and already filled her in on my break-in.

I gave her my theory about what they were after and she barely reacted. She had only opened the door halfway and hadn't invited me in. "Sorry, you probably have company." I gestured toward the driveway. "The motorcycle."

For a moment she stared at me. "Motorcycle?"

I fibbed a little. I left out going up her driveway and made it sound like I'd seen it from the street. She appeared perplexed and led me out the front door. We went across the lawn. "Where did you see it?"

I pointed at the spot behind the bush as the motion-sensor light illuminated the area, but now the spot was empty.

"See, there's nothing there," she said. "You must have just thought you saw a motorcycle."

Okay, she was lying. I wasn't crazy. There had been a motorcycle there and she knew it.

CHAPTER 12

"So you still haven't seen Ryder?" Dinah asked. We were standing outside the entrance to the bookstore. The sun had peeked through and added a little warmth to the damp air. Several days had gone by with no further break-ins at my place. I had forgotten another dinner Mason had set up so I could help him with the dog sweater. Barry was either sulking or had picked up a homicide because I'd heard nothing from him. Not that I had time to notice. Once I cleared up the crochet room, I finished the elephant, which was adorable, if I said so myself, and was going to brighten up some little kid's Christmas. I was so pleased with how the toy turned out, I started on another—this time I was making a snow owl. In between I worked on snowflakes and swatches. I had discovered it was best to work on the knit swatches at home. I couldn't take Adele's endless grumbling when I tried doing them at the bookstore. Not that I'd had time there anyway now that the store was crowded with holiday shoppers needing help.

"No. But when I do I'm going to have a little talk with him. I know he probably thinks that's the way to be a real journalist. The ends justify the means and all that. If he's willing to stop sneaking into my house, I'm willing to drop it."

Dinah considered what I'd said. "You better be firm," she said, going into her teacher mode. "If you want I can be your wingman when you talk to him. I'll get the message across to him. No more sneaking in windows or else. The secret is in the tone you use when you say the 'or else.' You have to fire up his imagination, which is much scarier than anything real you could threaten him with." The kids weren't with her and when I asked about them, she said she was meeting Commander later and she didn't want to push the kids in his face. Conveniently her neighbor had invited them over for a play date.

I pushed the needles out of sight in my tote bag as we walked into the bookstore. The rest of the bag was filled with completed swatches. All done in the garter stitch, which meant knit only, no purl. The snowflakes I'd completed were starched and drying on my dining room table. I had finally brought in the ones Adele had made, but when Mrs. Shedd saw how few there were, she said it wasn't worth hanging them until we had more.

I was looking forward to some crochet time with the Hookers. As we headed to the back of the store I saw that most of them were already at the table. CeeCee was at the head of the table and even at a distance I could see she was talking enthusiastically about something. Sheila had several blankets on the table next to her and was just beginning another. She seemed totally devoted to her work. Eduardo was sitting next to someone I didn't recognize. A new recruit perhaps. He was showing her something that she didn't seem to get. I almost choked when I saw what he did next. He got up and stood behind her, guiding her hands. Okay, it wasn't a hot scene with him molding his body to hers or anything, but it did remind me of the scene in the first Anthony book, *Caught By the Hook*. I watched him for a moment. Eduardo had been on the cover of a lot of romance novels. Maybe he decided to write some. The Blood and Yarn series really were more or less romances, weren't they?

Dinah saw me staring at Eduardo.

"What's up?" I reminded her of the scene in the first book and her eyes lit up. "Wouldn't it be something if Eduardo is A. J.?"

Before I could answer, Adele came bustling out of the children's area. Just when I thought Adele couldn't possibly top herself, she managed to. Story time had featured *The Rag Doll Chronicles* and Adele had dressed up as the chief rag doll, Clarissa, from the red yarn wig to the loose denim overalls with the giant yellow flower. Adele didn't stop with just the clothes. She had blush circles on her cheeks and lots of eye makeup—the eye makeup wasn't really part of the doll look, just her touch. Adele had finished with bright red lip color applied so it appeared she had large bow-shaped lips.

We all knew that Adele didn't love kids and the only positive of being stuck with story time was that she had met William, but she didn't usually look this discombobulated. "Pink, those kids are little hoodlums. Look what I confiscated from one of them." She pulled out a black metal gun and started waving it around. I gasped and threw myself in front of Dinah to protect her.

"Relax, ladies, it's a toy—a cap gun," Adele said, looking

at me with consternation. I tried to get it away from her, but Adele pulled away too fast, and to prove her point, she squeezed the trigger. I pulled Dinah with me as I darted behind the "New in Nonfiction" bookcase. There were a bunch of pops and that unmistakable smell of caps. Everyone in the bookstore froze at the sound. Even Bob ran in from the café, shouting should he call 911. I didn't even want to think of a bunch of cops running in to find Adele in that getup, waving the gun. I made sure he knew there was no emergency.

Adele looked around at the stir she caused and laughed. "Looks pretty real, doesn't it? It just shoots caps," she said, showing the red strip hanging out of the gun. Everyone stayed put and she made a move toward a couple crouched behind the "Great Gifts for the Holidays" table. They backed toward the door and ran out. I hooked my arm in Adele's and pulled her toward the office.

"Yes, it does look real. So real it's scaring everyone," I said. "Please stop shooting it and put it away before somebody looks in the window and thinks you're robbing the place. In fact, don't put it in the office; someone may see it there and freak out. Put it in your car," I said. "And don't go waving it around in the parking lot, either."

We also debated about whether or not she was going to give it back to the owner. Adele stuck to no. "I told them no video games, whoopee cushions or toy guns. And I made it clear they would be confiscated and not returned. How will they learn if I give it back?"

She had a point and I decided that if the irate parent showed up I was going to sic them on Adele.

It took a few minutes for everyone to calm down after Adele's Annie Oakley routine. When Dinah and I joined the others at the table I introduced myself to the new person and made sure to explain what had just happened wasn't typical of the bookstore.

"Dears, you missed my news," CeeCee said to Dinah and me. "I was just telling everyone I got my Christmas present early. I'm finally going to be back where I belong." She sat a little straighter. I knew her reality show had finished shooting and was on hiatus. She'd mentioned she was being considered for something else, but hadn't wanted to jinx it by talking about it. "You know they're making a movie out of the first Anthony book, *Caught By the Hook*? I got the part of Ophelia, Anthony's neighbor and confidant," she said with a proud shake of her head.

"Yes, I'm back in the movies." CeeCee tried to give Dinah and me high-fives, but we didn't realize what she was doing and there was an awkward missing of hands.

"Who's playing Anthony?" Sheila asked.

"Hugh Jackman," CeeCee said in an offhand manner.

"Hugh Jackman?" Rhoda said with a snort. "He's too foofie for a vampire. But then Anthony is too foofie for a vampire. If I was casting the part, I'd give it to Quentin Tarantino."

"He's a director," CeeCee said with a hopeless roll of her eyes.

Rhoda seemed unconcerned. "He could direct himself in the part."

Surprisingly Elise never looked up but was intent on crocheting the black-and-white scarf. She seemed close to being finished and I noticed she'd already made a scarlet tassel to put on the end.

Rhoda looked at Elise. "Hey, how come you aren't saying anything? Usually you're in the middle of anything about the foofie vampire."

Elise looked up with a slightly vague expression. "Sorry,

I've been a little preoccupied." She turned toward me. "That neighbor of yours—he's the worst thing that ever happened to us," she said with disgust in her voice. How strange. The last time she'd been talking about Bradley, her husband had been saying Bradley was the best thing that ever happened to them. Elise told the group about Bradley being presumed dead and how word of it had spread around Tarzana. Everyone who had been part of Bradley's investment club had tried calling Bradley's office, and when they got nowhere, tried the Perkins' house. All they got there was a voice mailbox so full it wouldn't take any more messages.

"They all started calling Logan and expected him to take care of everything. They seemed to think Logan and Bradley were joined at the hip or something. Our life has become a living hell," she said.

Sheila had a blank look. "Did I miss something? What happened? Last I heard Molly's neighbor was just missing."

Rhoda made a noise between clearing her throat and a snort. "My Harold thinks he pulled off a Ponzi scheme. The way it worked was Bradley kept collecting money he was supposedly going to invest. Only he never invested any of it. He used the money he was taking from new people to pay anyone who wanted their dividends or to give people their money back if they wanted out. But he was so smooth and made it look like his investments were making such huge profits, most of the investors left their dividends in the fund to make even more money." Rhoda looked at Sheila. "Are you getting it honey?" Sheila nodded.

"Harold said he heard Perkins started gambling with the money and eventually lost it all."

"Personally, I think it's a little strange how he supposedly dies, but there's no body," CeeCee said. "What kind of money are we talking—thousands? Millions?"

"Logan figures it's millions. And there's no body because Bradley jumped in the ocean in the middle of the channel," Elise said. "It might still wash up." Elise spoke to the group. "Logan feels terrible because he got all these people to put money in. The records are such a mess. Logan's trying to help the SEC make a list of all the investors." Her gaze swept the group. "Were any of you in the investment club?"

CeeCee spoke first. "My late husband lost all my money and I had to start over from scratch. He made foolish investments. I never would."

Rhoda made another one of her snort sounds before she answered. "My Harold always says if something is too good to be true, it usually is—not true."

Sheila put her hands up in a hopeless manner. "With what money?" Dinah and I both shook our heads. The new woman said she'd just moved to the area and didn't even understand what we were talking about.

Everyone turned to Eduardo. His chiseled face was solemn and he finally nodded. He never talked much and I often wondered if he just tuned out all our chatter. He always did at least his share of any charity projects the group took on and generally seemed pleasant.

His eyes looked angry and he was holding a plastic size Q hook. He turned to Rhoda. "Your husband is right. I wish I had thought of that instead of being taken in by Bradley." Eduardo said that men had a bigger window of time as models, but it didn't last forever even for them. "I've been exploring other avenues," he said. "I thought if I could grow my savings, I'd have a stake to start my own business." His face grew impassioned. "I think what that guy did was terrible. It wasn't my life savings, but I bet for some others it was. He deserves to be dead." There was a loud snap and

Eduardo seemed as surprised as the rest of us when we saw that he'd snapped the thick hook in half.

"But what if he isn't really dead?" Rhoda said. I considered bringing up what I'd overheard the SEC lawyer say about believing that Bradley was really dead, but mentioning it would no doubt bring up questions about why I was investigating since I hadn't invested any money. Questions that might lead to Mrs. Shedd and I'd promised to not tell anyone she'd been in Bradley's club.

Elise pondered the thought for a moment.

"It happens," Dinah said. "There was a guy who tried to fake his own death by bailing out of the plane he was flying. He figured the plane would crash and everyone would think he died in the crash."

"So?" Rhoda said. "What happened?"

"He got caught. Somehow they figured out the plane was flying empty."

Adele came up to the table. She was back in street clothes, but she hadn't been able to get off all the makeup.

Rhoda handed Adele a shopping bag. "Here's the afghan. Thanks for letting me look at it. You're right, though, somebody doesn't know about symmetry. I mean, if you're going to put on tassels, you either just have one on one corner for accent or you put one on each corner. And if you're going to scatter flowers on it, they ought to be balanced. You don't crowd flowers on one square and then have none in the next. "

Adele peeked inside the bag. "That's exactly what I told William. Don't give it to me. Give it to Pink. It belongs to her neighbor."

"I think it's lovely," I said, pulling part of the blanket out to examine it. The green background was such a nice contrast to the different-colored flowers scattered over it.

"Whatever, Pink. I did what you asked and wrote down the directions for how to make one of the squares and how to do surface crochet." She handed me a sheet of paper.

At my puzzled look, she pointed to the flowers. "That's how they were done. With surface crochet, you anchor your yarn on the top and do chain stitches into the top. Once you finish the chain stitches, it's just crochet as usual."

I took the blanket all the way out of the bag and passed it around the table. Across the table, Rhoda shrugged. "One guy's opinion of lovely is someone else's of mishmash." I explained that when I hadn't been able to decipher the pattern, I'd passed it on to Adele to look at. It wasn't the squares that had given me a problem. They were just single crochet, but I couldn't figure out how the varied colored flowers had been crocheted on top of the background. After everyone admired it, I folded it up and brought it over to CeeCee. "Emily doesn't want it back. She said to give it to a charity sale. Isn't Hearts and Barks having some kind of holiday bazaar?"

"Yes, dear. I'm sure they'd be glad to add the afghan to the auction." CeeCee repacked it in the paper bag and put it under the table.

"Finished," Elise said, holding up the black-and-white scarf. The scarlet tassel flopped back and forth as she waved it.

"So what's that about?" Rhoda said, catching the end as it swung over her head.

"It's a vampire scarf," I said, remembering what Joshua Royal had said. I asked Elise if she could write down the directions and if I could borrow it to put in the front with the Anthony accessory display.

She was breathless. "You want to put my scarf on display and call it an Anthony scarf?" She hugged it to herself as if she was hugging the handsome vampire in person. "Of course, you can use it. I'd be honored. I'll type up the directions and bring them to you."

"A vampire scarf? What does that mean?" Rhoda said, examining it.

Elise seemed to have forgotten all about her money troubles and explained the significance of the colors and pointed out the fang-shaped stitches. Elise swung the tassel that hung from a corner. "You must know what the scarlet is for."

Rhoda rolled her eyes. "The foofie vampire barely even drinks blood."

The conversation never went back to Bradley and I never got a chance to bring up the question I'd had before. Why would someone who was planning to kill himself take his parking ticket with him?

CHAPTER 13

WHEN THE GROUP BROKE UP, SHEILA STAYED AT the table, her hook flying through three strands of the mohairlike yarn. She looked up for a moment and seemed surprised that only Dinah and I were still there. She leaned back in her chair and dropped the hook on the table. She closed her eyes and began massaging her temples.

"I promised Nicholas I'd finish his order by today." She sounded close to tears and the way her shoulders were hunched, I knew she was on the verge of an anxiety attack. It didn't help that both Dinah and I said Nicholas would understand if she was one short.

"I know. That's what makes it worse. He's so nice, I don't want to let him down."

She checked her watch and said she didn't have to be back at the gym for her receptionist job until late in the afternoon. She picked up the hook and muttered something about if she pushed herself maybe she could finish.

I stopped her hands. "Dinah and I will go with you to Luxe and explain the delay to Nicholas. Then you're coming to get food with us. I bet you haven't been eating."

Sheila tried to argue, but when I pressed her, she admitted that maybe she had missed a few meals.

A hunk of downtown Tarzana was in the process of being rebuilt. The old Brown center had been demolished with the movie theaters and odd little stores and was being replaced by something called the Village Walk; I kept telling myself change was good. Along with reminding myself it was going to happen whether I liked it or not, anyway.

The bookstore, Le Grande Fromage and Luxe were in the old section of interesting low buildings. Nicholas had done wonders with the storefront when he created Luxe. He'd added a large fountain on one wall that spread good ions around the store. The mixture of soap by the slice, a selection of unisex colognes and the exotic spices in the food section gave the store a wonderful signature scent. The merchandise was equally enticing. It was an eclectic mixture of things, and the only thing they had in common was they all seemed to have style. Nicholas said he sold only what he particularly liked.

We set off a bell when we came in and he walked through a door from the back. He was as appealing as his store. He seemed to give off good ions like the fountain. Though just for a moment I wondered if he was really as he seemed. He was almost too nice, too concerned, too compassionate. It made me wonder if it was all a front and that big back area he kept so private was really full of dead bodies.

"Don't worry about the other blanket," he said, once I'd explained that Sheila was upset about being short one. He took the ones she'd completed and insisted on paying her even for the one she was short. While they conducted business, Dinah and I browsed the store.

We were admiring a hand-painted pasta bowl on a table when I looked out the front window. We were directly across from Tarzana Jewelers. Emily Perkins had just parked her SUV in front of it and was walking toward the store. I nudged Dinah. "It seems like a strange time to go jewelry shopping."

Nicholas saw us peering out the window. "Anything interesting?" he said, standing next to us.

I pointed out Emily as she went in the store.

He watched for a moment before saying anything. "I don't want this to sound like I'm gossiping. I'm only telling you because you're her neighbor, but she came in here earlier. She wanted to return some things she bought last week." He pointed out a silver hairbrush and comb set and a basket with bathroom accessories sitting on the table that served as a checkout.

"Was something wrong with them?" I said, examining the bathroom basket. Along with soap and some special organic bath salts, there was a selection of washcloths that I realized were crocheted. Sheila joined us. She was surprised to see the washcloths and said she'd almost forgotten that she made them. For a moment the conversation turned to crochet, and she said she'd made them in no time. They were all done in organic cotton in a creamy beige and sage green. "I can't believe she'd return either of these; like everything else in the store, they're great," I said.

"It wasn't because there was anything wrong with them," Nicholas said. "She didn't want the money put back on her credit card. She wanted cash. Normally I wouldn't do that, but she seemed pretty close to the edge, if you know what I mean."

He knew all about her situation. What she hadn't told him, he'd heard on the street. "Suicide, missing money—it's the topic of conversation wherever you go."

"So then you weren't part of Bradley's investment club," I asked.

He nodded with a joyless half laugh. "I got taken along with everybody else. After hearing Logan Belmont go on and on about what a magician Bradley was and talking about the remodel he'd done on his house with some money he'd made—you felt like a fool if you didn't put some money in the fund, if you could get in. Logan had to put in a good word for me." Nicholas did the mirthless laugh again. "I felt like a winner when Perkins took my money. Everybody knew Bradley. Who wouldn't trust him?"

"I wonder why Bradley never tried to get me to join his fund," I said.

"Under the circumstances I wouldn't complain." Nicholas sighed. "I'm trying to let it go and move on. It's much worse for Emily. Anything Bradley left will get split up among the investors. They may take everything she has, too." He mentioned how Ruth Madoff had to leave her apartment with nothing but her purse because of the huge Ponzi scam her husband had pulled off. Some customers came in and Nicholas left us to wait on them.

We watched Emily come out of the store carrying one of the jewelry store's signature tiny shopping bags.

I turned to Dinah. "Didn't you say you wanted to look for some cuff links for Commander?" She picked up on my drift and we told Sheila we'd be back in a few minutes.

Dinah and I put together our story as we went across the street. She'd ask about the cuff links while I worked on getting information about Emily. If they thought we were real customers, they would be more likely to talk.

"I really do want to get him some cuff links." Dinah shook her head as if she couldn't believe what she was saying. "How did I end up with someone who likes French cuffs?" Dinah was still having some difficulty dealing with what she considered Commander's over-the-top fastidiousness. Whether it was the creases in his casual pants you could cut butter with or the tassels on his polished loafers, she thought he was a little too meticulous for her taste. But she liked him well enough in other ways that she was trying to adjust. "Maybe if I say the kid's picked them out, he'll feel a little better toward them."

As soon as we walked into the jewelry store, a salesman in a well-fitted dark suit stepped forward and offered his assistance. I wasn't particularly into fine jewelry and hadn't been in this store for years. I liked silver and stones with colors like turquoise or amethyst. When it came to watches, my only requirement was that it kept time. This store was filled with gold and diamonds and watches where keeping time was only a side benefit.

The salesman was pleased to bring out trays of cuff links for Dinah.

"I thought I saw Emily Perkins come in here," I said, looking around with a innocent face.

A woman at the next counter looked up. "You just missed her."

"She has such good taste. What did she buy this time?" I said, hoping they'd think I was implying I might buy the same thing.

The man showed Dinah some gold cuff links with onyx inserts. I heard Dinah choking when she glanced at the price ticket. He directed his attention my way momentarily. "She was picking up," he said.

"Picking up?" I said, surprised.

"She brought in her husband's watch to be cleaned and serviced," the woman said.

"Really?" I said, trying to keep the surprise down in my voice. I asked if they'd heard about what happened to him. The man glanced toward the woman and they both nodded.

"I thought under the circumstances she'd want to sell the watch. It's a Bond Submariner Rolex," he said as if I was supposed to understand what that meant. "But when I offered to buy it from her, she said no without the slightest hesitation. She just paid for the service and asked if she could use the phone." He sighed. "I really was hoping she would sell it. I've been trying to find one of those watches for a long time."

Dinah kept looking at cuff links while I processed what he'd just told me. Or tried to. It simply didn't make sense. She'd made it clear to Nicholas she was short of money. The watch sounded like it would have gotten her a hefty hunk of money. Was it sentimental value that was making her hang on to it or something else?

CHAPTER 14

"I SURE HOPE COMMANDER APPRECIATES THE GIFT," I said as we headed toward Le Grande Fromage. Sheila had already gotten a table and was looking over the menu when we walked in.

"I still can't believe I'm encouraging his fussiness by buying him cuff links. I should have bought him a sweatshirt with the arms cut off to help loosen him up," Dinah said, eyeing the tiny shopping bag with the elegantly wrapped box.

The café was busy and there was a line at the counter waiting to place their orders. Logan was sitting at the back table with his portable office setup. He wasn't alone. Two men were standing over the table, with their hands resting on it. It appeared they were trying to keep their conversation private. And judging from the expression on Logan's face, whatever they were talking about wasn't happy.

Pretending to be bothered by the closeness of the door

to our table, I suggested we move. I chose the table next to Logan's, but made sure to appear not to even notice him. Then I made a big deal about looking over the menu. Of course, it was all a ruse while I leaned back in my chair and tried to hear.

"I'm in the same boat with everyone else," Logan said.

"You better take some responsibility. The only reason I turned over our money to Bradley was because of you," one of the men growled.

"Everyone's saying he must have given you some kind of commission," the other man said.

Logan neither confirmed nor denied it but tried to convince them that he was in no way Bradley's partner or involved with the stock dealing. He insisted he'd been duped by Bradley as much as everyone else. Both men objected and seemed convinced that Logan was more involved with Bradley's business than he was letting on. Their voices flared as they both reminded Logan that just saying he didn't know anything didn't let him off the hook as far as they were concerned. Logan told them what Elise had told us—that he was helping the SEC people sort things out. The men didn't seem to care. They were just angry that they'd lost all their money and they were looking for somebody to blame. Logan was that guy. The degree of their anger made my heart palpitate. I was afraid a fight might erupt. I was relieved when the men walked away. When Logan was alone, he banged on the table as he packed up his stuff and mumbled something about being ruined. Then in a voice that gave me a chill he said, "If Bradley wasn't already dead, I'd kill him."

"There you are, Pink," Adele said when I got back to the bookstore. She stepped in front of me and put her arms on my shoulders, pushing me back toward the front door. "You have to do me a favor."

I chuckled to myself. "You could say please."

"Huh?" Adele said. Her confusion was real, definitely not faked. She had no sense about how to deal with people.

The favor involved helping her do a favor for William. He'd had a new dishwasher installed and the city permit guy was on his way to check it over. There was some complicated story about William's car being in the shop and Adele letting him use her new car. She must really care for the guy to let him actually drive her Matrix. She would barely let me operate the windows. I offered her the use of my car, but she said she'd become too used to driving a new car and probably would strip the gears or something if she tried to drive the greenmobile. I resented her calling it an antique.

Adele made a face as she opened the passenger door. Maybe it did squeak a little bit, but I thought it was entitled. The 1993 190E Mercedes ran beautifully but was beginning to show its age in little malfunctions and weird noises. Adele got in as if she thought the car might crumble.

Technically this was supposed to be my day off, but I'd come in for the Hookers meeting, so helping Adele out wasn't really a problem.

William's house was in a Woodland Hills area called College Acres. The name came from its proximity to Walter Beasley Community College, I mean WBCC. I really needed to get my abbreviations down. Was I ever really going to start saying OMG and LOL out loud?

The streets around William's house went by a different name at this time of year. I didn't know when or how it started, but all the houses in the area went into decoration overload for the holidays. Everyone knew the area as Candy Cane Lane.

I had lots of memories driving through it when Peter and Samuel were young. Everybody turned off their cars' headlights and crept through the streets with parking lights. I glanced up and down the street. The decorations were in the process of going up in the yards on either side. It seemed to me in the old days it went from right after Thanksgiving to New Years, but over the past years, it seemed to have been funneled down into a few weeks before Christmas until New Years.

Who could blame them? I thought of the congestion on the street. Heaven help anyone who lived in the area and wanted to pull out of their driveway after dark.

"Does Koo Koo know what he got into?" I said to Adele as we pulled into the driveway of William's house. Next door two men were carrying a giant animatronic Santa into the center of the yard. I watched as they placed it on the lawn and plugged it in. The giant red-clothed figure began to wave and shout "Ho, ho, ho." Adele let out a loud *harrumph* and told me to follow her. She fished the keys out of her purse, and although she tried to act as if they were hers, the note attached to them said "spare set."

The house was appealing from the outside, with its white-wood siding and green shutters. She struggled with the lock, one more indication she hadn't done a lot of coming and going on her own. As much as she tried to give the impression that she and William were on their way to a permanent relationship, I began to wonder if it was mostly in her imagination.

Inside, the house smelled of fresh paint and new carpet. My first impression was of lots of light and very little furniture. I followed Adele down a short hall and through the service porch into the garage.

"Pink, William not only knows about the area, he's all

set with his own decorations," Adele said as she flipped on the light. I stepped back and almost tripped over a bike. A giant wooden cutout of Koo Koo dressed as Santa was in my face staring back. The trademark giant red shoes showed from underneath the Santa suit. A freestanding toy bag sat next to the figure. I laughed when I saw what was showing out of the top. Apparently William had large mock-ups of all the Koo Koo books made and then positioned so they showed above the bag. Underneath the quiet exterior, William was apparently quite the marketer.

The doorbell rang and Adele said it must be the inspector. She started giving me some speech about how William asking her to handle the city inspector meant he thought of her as more than just a girlfriend. "A girlfriend with a future," she said, touching the door in a possessive sort of way.

Adele took the inspector into the kitchen and I took the opportunity to look around, curious to see how William lived. The living room did nothing to change my initial impression of him as very orderly and on the austere side.

I wandered toward the bedrooms. The smallest one was completely empty of furniture. There were just three pairs of the giant red shoes. He seemed to be using the next bedroom to sleep in, which was odd since it was clearly not the master bedroom.

I understood why when I got to the master. It was his writing studio. A computer sat in the middle of a glass desk. The walls were covered with framed book covers of his books and some awards he'd gotten, along with reviews. One whole wall was a bookcase. He had an interesting combination of children's books and reference books. There were books on the history of dentistry, ciphers and codes, and an encyclopedia of animals. He had a whole set of different kinds of dictionaries and even a whole section devoted to myths, angels and fairies. I was surprised to find a copy of *Caught By the Hook* sitting on a table next to a comfortable-looking chair.

A large table sat against the wall. I was just checking out what was on it when Adele stopped in the doorway.

"Pink, you shouldn't be in here."

I didn't move and she glanced around the room from her vantage point as it came out that William had never allowed her in the room. "He calls it his man cave and said it was strictly private. The door is always closed."

"It was open this time," I said with a shrug. "It just looks like a workroom to me." I said, laughing at the man cave name. It was so light and bright, calling it any kind of cave seemed ridiculous.

"You're right." She took a tentative step into the room. I guess she went along with the in-for-a-penny-in for-a-pound approach. Once she'd stepped into the room, she must have figured why not check everything out. She went to his desk first and picked up an electronic frame and watched as it flipped through the photos.

"None of me?" she said in a disappointed voice. "He probably just doesn't have any." She moved over to the table and did a double take when she saw its contents.

"What's he doing with crochet hooks and yarn?" she said, touching the selection of hooks and yarn that were scattered across the table. I looked over Adele's shoulder as she checked out a stack of books.

"This is one of mine," Adele said, picking up the top book and waving it about. "William asked if he could borrow it for someone at his school." She looked at the ones underneath. They were instructional volumes and had crochet patterns in them.

"Maybe William took your suggestion and is planning to do a *Koo Koo Crochets* book."

Adele set the book back down and looked over the things on the table. She seemed concerned when she saw a sheet of green paper on the floor.

"I guess this must have fallen out of the book he borrowed." She scooped it up and waved the sheet in front of me. It had a drawing of something with squares and lots of notes all over it. "It's just the notes I made about your neighbor's afghan. I must have used it as a bookmark." She appeared flustered—something I'd never seen before. "Did you happen to notice where it was in the book?" When I shrugged helplessly, she took a deep breath and stuck it in the middle. "William is very into details. I don't want him to figure someone was in here."

She looked around the room again. "I wonder why he's being so secretive. I could write the crochet book with him."

I didn't want to say that might be the exact reason he was being secretive. I knew what it was like working with Adele. She seemed deep in thought as she moved around the room. She checked out the chair and books next to it. She looked at the bookcase and examined the titles and all of a sudden she screamed. "Pink, I know why he's being so secretive."

She had pulled out a book and held it for me to see. It was an old book with a dark worn binding. There was no dust jacket; instead, it had paper plate on the cover. In gothic-looking type was the title—*Vampire Legends*. When I didn't respond, she yelled at me.

"Don't you get it, Pink, he's not writing an instructional book. Vampires and crochet research. William is A. J. Kowalski." Adele's excitement bubbled over into her jumping up and down. "It makes sense. He wouldn't want to write the Anthony books under his own name because then people would expect them to be kids books." She stopped jumping and put her hand on her hip. "You know people do that. Like Nora Roberts calls herself J. D. Robb when she writes mysteries."

She grabbed my hand and pulled me out of the room and shut the door behind us. "I'm A. J. Kowalski's girlfriend," she said, dropping my hand and letting it sink in. "Pink, we can't tell anybody." She said, "wow" a bunch of times and then grabbed my arm. "I have to make him one of those vampire scarves. Thank you, Pink. If you hadn't been so nosey, I'd never have found out."

Adele had a way with compliments.

CHAPTER 15

WE WENT BACK TO THE BOOKSTORE. MRS. SHEDD was with a customer, and as soon as they left, her smile faded. I took the opportunity to tell her the latest developments in the Bradley Perkins situation. Mostly I wanted to tell her about the SEC people not knowing who all the investors were. I suggested she might want to let them know she belonged on the list. I couldn't tell if she planned to or not.

The store was bustling with customers, many of whom seemed as if they needed assistance. Day off or not, I stowed my purse and went to help out. Mrs. Shedd looked over and her eyes softened and she mouthed a thank-you.

There was a lull later in the afternoon and I slipped back to the yarn department. I managed to complete one crocheted swatch. I really got the point of the swatches when I looked at the finished little piece. The ball of yarn was pretty with its shades of blue and purple, but nothing compared to how the yarn looked when it was crocheted. The swatches were going to help sell a lot of yarn—if I ever got them finished.

There was a surge of business in the late afternoon and I went back to waiting on customers. When I finally left I was determined to work on snowflakes all evening to add to the stock. I promised myself I'd only do a couple of rounds on the owl. I loved the sparkling white yarn I'd chosen to use instead of the plain white in the pattern. Our last holiday event before the launch party was coming up and we all agreed the snowflakes needed to be hung by then. I pushed away any thoughts that it might be our last bookstore holiday event altogether. It was too sad to consider.

People always thought of Southern California as being warm in the winter, and maybe compared to the Midwest it was. However, the Valley occasionally got frost in the middle of the night. It wasn't enough to kill anything but the most fragile of flowers, but the grass and leaves on the orange trees would have bits of ice in the morning. It felt like it was going to be one of those nights when I walked outside. There was a sharpness to the cold and it cut right through my fleece hoodie. The days were almost at their shortest and it had already been dark for so long it felt very late, though it was only seven. Before I turned into my driveway, the car's headlights washed over the tall gangly figure of Ryder. He was sitting on the curb. His face was illuminated by the bluish glow that came off his video camera as he watched something he'd taped.

I pulled in quickly and hit the brakes, making the car squeak to a stop. I cut the motor and jumped out of the car and marched toward him. Something in the way I was walking must have scared him because he stood up quickly and took a defensive pose. I couldn't say I blamed him. I had a bit of the crazy-lady thing going by then.

"What's up, M?" he said.

"I'll tell you what's up," I said, getting so close to him, he stumbled back. "I know you are all focused on your career in journalism or reality TV or being the YouTube king and you probably think the ends justify the means and all that trash talk. But you sneak in my house one more time and throw everything around, and I'm giving you up to the cops."

"W-what?" he stammered. "Why would I be sneaking in your house?"

"We both know why. You want to scoop everybody and find out who the vampire book author is. You think I know who it is and have the information hidden in my bags of yarn."

"Wow, do you? Know who it is, I mean?"

"No," I said firmly.

"You have to believe me. I wasn't in your house," he said. "I do want to be a journalist, and I know you have to walk that extra mile to get a story sometimes, but I didn't. I mean, I wouldn't—"

My crazy-lady demeanor began to diminish. As much as I didn't want to believe him, I did begin to think he was telling the truth. But if he wasn't breaking into my house, who was?

Ryder and I had just about finished conducting our business when Barry's Tahoe pulled into the driveway and stopped near the street. Barry and his son, Jeffrey, got out. Barry zeroed in on me, and Jeffrey walked up to Ryder.

"Hey, weren't you Curly in the junior production of *Carousel*?" Ryder said.

Thanks to the floodlight on my garage that illuminated the end of the driveway, I saw Jeffrey's surprised expression. When Jeffrey nodded with a confident toss of his head, Ryder held out a hand to high-five him. "Hey, man dude, you done good."

"Man dude?" I said, looking at Ryder.

"I'm trying to start a new phrase. You like it? I want to include it in my next YouTube piece and maybe start a trend."

"You put stuff on YouTube?" Jeffrey said, impressed.

"All the time, Columbia," Ryder said. I heard Barry groan. He hated that Jeffrey wanted to be an actor and even more that he'd decided to go by Columbia. What Columbia/Jeffrey said next made Barry choke.

"I think Columbia is too long. I'm considering shortening it to Cgreen," Jeffrey said. Ryder mulled it over and proclaimed it very contemporary.

"Or you can change it altogether and sound like one of those rappers and go by Ice Berg," I said. Jeffrey, Ryder and Barry all glared at me.

"Sorry. I should have added an LOL at the end. I was just joking."

The two boys stepped away and Barry stopped next to me. He was glaring at Ryder. "He's the guy, isn't he?"

I tried playing stupid, but that only convinced Barry more that Ryder was the one I thought was breaking into my house. "I think I'll have a little talk with him." Barry made a move toward Ryder, but I grabbed his arm.

"I already took care of it and he said it wasn't him."

"And you believe him? Wake up and smell the coffee, Molly. People lie. The people I see lie twenty-four, seven unless you know how to get at the truth." He seemed disappointed when I wouldn't let him interrogate Ryder. Barry said he'd stopped over to check that his temporary repair to my front door was still secure. There was a delay with getting the new door, he explained.

Samuel's jeep stopped in front of the house. He got out and crossed the lawn. "Hey," he said, nodding a greeting to Ryder and Jeffrey. The nod he gave to Barry was only marginally cordial. While Samuel wasn't as bad as my other son, Peter, there was always a certain level of tension between him and Barry. Peter didn't like Barry, but with Samuel, it was more about the problem he had with me dating. Dating? That was as out of place as calling Barry a boyfriend. Dating implied Saturday night movie dates followed by a hamburger somewhere. Barry showed up whenever. I usually cooked something, after which he fell asleep sitting on the couch while insisting he wasn't tired.

Samuel moved on to me. "I'm just here long enough to change. I got a gig," he said before giving the details. Samuel could play a bunch of instruments, but this job called for him to play piano at a hotel bar in Woodland Hills.

"How about I go with," Ryder suggested. "I'll video one of your songs. I'm a wiz at editing on my computer. By the time I post it on YouTube, it'll look like a real music video."

"As long as you don't cause any problems," Samuel said.

"I could go, too," Jeffrey said, stepping next to Ryder. I saw Barry's jaw clench and he put his hand on his son's shoulder. He didn't even have to say it, just the shake of Barry's head got the message and Jeffrey slumped with disappointment.

A dark sedan pulled behind the jeep. It was too dark to make out what kind of car or who got out until he was halfway across the lawn. What was Mason doing here?

Barry apparently wondered the same thing and said as much.

"Don't tell me you forgot again," Mason said, taking his crochet project out of the bag.

Mason saw Samuel and they slapped hands. Samuel had no problem with Mason. Mason had helped him get his musical career going and I think he viewed him just as a family friend as opposed to someone I was involved with.

By now it was getting pretty chilly and Samuel and Jeffrey didn't have jackets on. What could I do, but invite everyone inside?

Samuel looked at the crowd moving into the backyard. "Mom, you ought to start having the Christmas Eve party again." I was surprised at his comment. The party had been a yearly tradition until Charlie died. It wasn't that any of us made a decision to stop having parties, it had just sort of happened. The fact that Samuel was suggesting it meant he was finally beginning to move on. I certainly wouldn't have any trouble finding guests. The group followed me in, and all RSVPed on the spot.

I offered everyone dinner if they'd take potluck. I hadn't managed to get to the grocery store lately and had resorted to eating whatever I could scrounge.

"Not a problem," Mason said, taking out his cell phone. "Everybody likes Italian, right?" There was a chorus of yeses, except Barry, who didn't appear pleased that Mason was handling the food again. In an effort to make up for it, Barry made a big deal about going to check on the door.

I said I'd make salad and Mason left to pick up the order. I reminded Samuel to take care of his cats and Jeffrey fed the dogs and took them out into the yard to play. Ryder made a video of me making salad. He was very interested in all the ingredients and interviewed me as I mixed a bag of herb salad with some wild rocket lettuce. I added grated carrots, kalamata olives, cucumber, fresh tomatoes and sun-dried tomatoes. I made my own salad dressing. It was really just olive oil and balsamic vinegar, but it was the way I did it. I poured the olive oil on first and tossed the salad. Then I sprinkled on the garlic powder and seasoning salt before shaking on the vinegar. I never measured, but it always seemed to work out. I finished the salad by adding gorgonzola cheese and walnuts.

Dinner was a big success, though over quickly. Samuel had to get to his gig. Ryder tagged along with him. Jeffrey had some homework. Barry hesitated while Mason situated himself on the couch with the dog sweater. But finally he couldn't stall any longer and left with a reminder to be sure to keep everything locked up.

I took a ball of iridescent-flecked white bedspread-weight thread and a steel hook into the living room along with the instructions for a snowflake Adele had given me. Hers were more elaborate, but she said she was doing me a favor by giving me something more basic to make. There was probably a slap at my skill in there somewhere but by now I'd learned to just let it go. Mason moved next to me, saying something about it was a better arrangement if he needed help. He watched as I struggled to make a slipknot with the fine thread and do the beginning circle. My hook slipped and the yarn was hard to see. It always took me a little while to adjust to working so small.

Mason took out the partially completed dog sweater and something else.

"Is that for me?" I said, looking at the gift-wrapped package.

Mason handed it to me and I commented that it was kind of early for a Christmas present.

"No, this just something I think you really need. I had something grander in mind for a holiday gift. Open it," he said.

"Wow," I said as the paper fell, revealing a box that said *BlackBerry*. Mason took it out and told me about all the features. He had even charged it up. He took out his own and called someone. After a few minutes of punching in some codes to the BlackBerry, he had activated it and it was now my phone.

He showed me the calendar and said if I put stuff in, it would pop up as a reminder. "So no more missing our crochet evenings," he said with a grin before he demonstrated how to use the camera feature. I got in a mind muddle after that. The BlackBerry just did too many things to take in all at once. I hugged him a thank-you and when I looked up he was looking back at me. The usual smile in his eyes was replaced by something else. What was it? Longing maybe. I pulled away and he returned to his usual self.

I pointed to the dog sweater he'd laid beside him as I went back to my snowflake. "We better get crocheting." He nodded in agreement and picked up his hook.

"Too bad the detective hasn't taken up crochet. It would do him good." Mason worked a few stitches. "I suppose he doesn't think it's manly enough." Mason paused a beat. "I've always thought real men don't have to keep proving themselves."

"Different strokes for different folks," I said vaguely, not wanting to get sucked into their competition. I changed the subject and brought up Emily and the break-ins. Mason was always a good sounding board. This was the first chance I had to put together all the discordant pieces and try to make sense of them.

"If this kid wasn't the one sneaking in your house, then

who was?" Mason said. He seemed doubtful about someone going to so much trouble to find out the identity of an
author.

"You don't know how people are about the Anthony
books. It would certainly take the thunder out of our launch
party if somebody disclosed the real identity of A. J. Kowalski first," I said.

The snowflake began to come together quite quickly,
though the limp white stitches were hardly impressive
looking. Starching them was what did the magic.

Mason asked the obvious question. Did I know the vam-
pire author's real identity? And I gave him the same answer
I'd given everybody else. No. No matter what I'd seen with
Adele, the jury was still out on whether it was William.

"Maybe you know, but you don't know that you know,"
Mason said, chuckling at his own tongue twister. He
gestured toward the tote bag I'd been carrying back and
forth. A file stuck out that had *Holiday Events* written on it.
"What's in there?"

I pulled it out and showed him. Everything was about
our multicultural holiday party. "See, there's nothing in
here."

He suggested maybe it was something I'd brought home
a while ago. We looked over my desk and there was nothing there. I took him in the crochet room and I heard him
chuckling behind me. "Someone ransacked this room,
right?" He bent down and pulled a plastic grocery bag off
his foot that had caught there. I explained I'd cleaned it up
since then. This was normal.

"You're into crochet now, so you should understand
this is how we roll." I picked up the bag, looked inside,
and pulled out a half-finished pale green shrug made out
of some bamboo mix yarn. I put it with the pile of need-

to-be-finished items while I explained he could look at them two ways, either as UFOs—unfinished objects—or as WIPs—works-in-progress.

As we were leaving the room, Mason saw me glance out the window toward the Perkins' house and asked what the latest was with my neighbor. I told Mason about Emily needing money, which didn't surprise him. He was surprised when I mentioned her picking up the watch, particularly when he heard how she could have turned it into cash. I also mentioned the disappearing motorcycle. However I didn't mention the situation with Mrs. Shedd's money and the fragile financial state the bookstore was in, partly because I'd given Mrs. Shedd my word to keep it quiet and partly because it was too upsetting to think about.

"Maybe the watch has some kind of sentimental value. She wants it to remember Bradley by," Mason said.

"I don't buy that. I've been thinking about it all day. I remembered something Emily had said when she thought Bradley was just missing. He'd been upset with her about a lot of things and one of them was that she hadn't picked up his watch. It's some kind of James Bond Rolex. What if Bradley isn't really dead and he wants his watch?"

I mentioned what the SEC guy had said about them being tipped off before Bradley disappeared. "Bradley must have known he was going to get caught." I told Mason about the money left in the checking account and that was what made the SEC guy believe Bradley was dead. "He thought Bradley would have cleaned out everything if he was planning to disappear. But maybe he deliberately left the money in the account because he knew that was what it would look like."

I thought back to how oddly Emily had acted the night

I saw the disappearing motorcycle in her driveway. "And maybe Emily knows he's not dead."

Mason and I went back into the living room and started to brainstorm with the facts. We came up with scenarios that had Bradley dead or alive. The dead scenario had Bradley mailing the suicide note on the way to Long Beach, leaving his car in the terminal parking lot where it wouldn't be noticed because people often left cars there for a number of days, then getting on the boat with his one-way ticket and, somewhere in the middle of the journey, leaving his cell phone and wallet on a seat before jumping off the boat.

We also came up with a faked-death scenario. In that one Bradley leaves his car but has some other mode of transportation. His Suburban was big enough to fit a motorcycle in the back. He gets on the boat with his one-way ticket. Somewhere during the trip, he leaves his wallet and cell phone on a bench. He gets off the boat in Catalina and then buys a ticket with cash and goes back to Long Beach. He takes the motorcycle and leaves the car. By the time Emily gets the suicide note, he's long gone.

I mentioned my parking-ticket issue. It worked with the not-dead scenario. He would have used the parking ticket to get out of the lot when he left on the motorcycle. I brought up Emily viewing the tape and not seeing him disembarking. That was an easy obstacle to overcome. He could have disguised himself or she could be his accomplice and merely said she didn't see him. Mason asked me if I'd been watching the tape.

"Yeah, but not that closely. I was looking for a guy in dress clothes. Suppose he brought along a change of clothes? If he put on jeans and a puffy jacket and a hat, I wouldn't have recognized his form.

"This is what I love about you, Sunshine, never dull conversation." He sat forward, his eyes bright as he considered what I'd said. "Emily could have been an accomplice from the start. All of her talk about not really knowing much about her husband's business might be a cover-up."

I was doubtful and he read my expression. "Or not."

It was fun being able to shoot ideas back and forth with Mason. Whenever I tried with Barry, I got the same response. "Stay out of it." He wasn't even interested in conjecture. I told Mason that Emily had seemed too convincing in her reaction to Bradley being missing for it to be fake. "Her emotions seemed to be on a roller coaster. First she was worried, then angry. I think if it were an act, she would have stuck with worried."

"But what if she didn't know from the start, but found out later when he contacted her about the watch?" Mason offered.

I slumped back on the couch. "But would he take the chance of hanging around for a watch, even if it was a collector-quality Rolex?" I glanced in the direction of my neighbor's house. "Do you think he's there now?"

Mason grinned. "As your lawyer, I'm suggesting you don't do anything illegal."

"But as my friend?" I said, matching his grin.

"Probably the same," he said, getting up. He put the dog sweater and yarn back in his bag. He'd done maybe two rows. At this rate, it wouldn't be ready until summer. I walked him to the back door and was concerned to find it open. No break-ins this time, break-outs. The dogs had let themselves and the cats out. Cosmo and Blondie came in without problem. Cat Woman came in with the promise of some beef jerky, but Holstein was nowhere to be found.

I explained that we only let the cats out during the day

and kept them in the yard. There were raccoons, skunks, rabbits and other critters in the yard at night that we worried the cats would mess with and be the worse for it. I heard a meow coming from somewhere.

"There he is," Mason said, trying to reassure me.

"Yes, but where?" I said, turning around to see where the sound was coming from. Both Mason and I got it at the same time. It sounded like it was coming from the Perkins' yard.

I was going to go alone, but Mason insisted on coming with. I thought if we stood on the bench near the fence to their yard, we might be able to see the cat and maybe get him to come to us. It was easy to forget Mason was in his fifties and a high-powered attorney when he got a Tom Sawyer kind of expression on his broad face. He pushed the lock of gray-flecked hair that had fallen across his forehead and seemed unconcerned that he was wearing wool slacks and a cashmere pullover. I led him to the white bench that was almost against the ivy-covered fence between our properties. He climbed on it first and gave me a hand. Neither of us saw the cat, but we did notice there was a low shed just on the other side of the fence.

"What's your advice now?" I whispered. Mason let out a low chuckle.

"You're just trying to get your cat. As your lawyer, I think I should go along." He reached toward the roof of the shed and used it to balance himself as he stood on the fence. He looked down into the Perkins' yard and stepped on something a little lower than the fence. He waited until I got on the fence and saw where he'd stepped before leaving his perch. It turned out to be a hose holder and I held on to the fence as I jumped off it.

It felt strange to be inside my neighbor's yard. I heard

another meow and we thought the sound was coming from across the yard. The lights were on in the house. I knew the den faced the backyard and had a sliding glass door. It was obvious by the amount of light shining on the patio that the curtains were open.

We stayed low and checked the driveway. No motorcycle tonight. We moved on and peeked in the window of the garage. Mason conveniently had an LED light hooked to his key chain. The bluish light didn't illuminate very well, but it was enough to see Emily's black Element and Bradley's Suburban she'd driven home in the garage.

I made a move back toward the fence, but then I heard muffled voices coming from inside.

We kept to the back of the yard, hoping to blend in with the ivy growing along the fence. When we got in line with the sliding glass door, we stopped and looked. Emily was pacing across the paver tile floor and another woman sat on the rust-colored couch. Her hands were moving, and when I looked closer, I saw that she seemed to be crocheting. The shopping bag from the jewelers was sitting on the bleached-wood side table. I waited a moment to see if anyone else would come into view, but it was clear it was just the two of them.

I heard another meow and whispered Holstein's name. Dogs are easier to retrieve. They're more likely to stay put or come to you. Cats? They completely follow their own drummer. Holstein stuck his head out of the bushes, took one look at us and ran across the yard. I heard a rustle in the bushes, followed by claws on chain link.

Mason and I were a little giggly now from our escapade as we slipped back across the yard. I climbed on the hose box, held on to the roof of the small shed and, with Mason close behind, I stepped over the fence and felt for the bench.

Moments later I was standing on the bench and Mason came over and joined me on it.

As I began to turn around the sound of someone behind me clearing their throat made me jump. Barry was standing in the shadow. He was speechless. Mason saw him and gave him a little salute.

Barry had come back to make sure everything was okay. Translated that meant he wanted to make sure Mason and I were only crocheting. "I saw the back door open and nobody home . . ."

He left the sentence hanging.

"Our girl and I were looking for the cat," Mason said, clearly enjoying Barry's consternation at the fact that we'd had some adventure together and that I had been referred to as their girl. I wasn't so sure about being called "our girl," either. As far as I was concerned I was strictly my own girl.

"Really," Barry said. I couldn't see the expression of his eyes in the dark, but by the tone of his voice, I had a pretty good idea they had a bit of a glare. He pointed back toward my house and we all stepped closer. When we got near the French doors leading to the dining room, Holstein and Cat Woman were clearly visible lying on the cat tree. They both were sound asleep.

CHAPTER 16

"I WISH I COULD HAVE SEEN BARRY'S FACE WHEN you climbed over the fence," Dinah said. Ashley-Angela and E. Conner were flanking her sides as we walked through the bookstore to the Hookers' table. Dinah set them up at the end of the table with a shoe box of art supplies. She was a firm believer in getting kids to use their imagination instead of providing all kinds of electronic doodads. It seemed to be a good plan because the fraternal twins got busy with the shoe box as soon as they sat down. They took out piles of colored paper strips and a jar of paste and started making a chain.

I set my red-eye on the table along with the box of thread snowflakes. After Barry and Mason had left together, I'd finished the one I'd started and made another. I'd starched and shaped them, letting them dry overnight. Even with the addition of the two, the amount was still light. I looked at the orb of pink cashmere yarn I was supposed to use to make a swatch. The yarn was beautiful but not easy to work with. Instead I pulled out the skein of white yarn with flecks of silver. I'd messed up on the increases for the owl head and unraveled it. This time I was going to get it right.

Dinah showed off the scarf for our shelter collection she'd almost finished. Seeing it reminded me of the importance of the swatches. The ball of worsted multicolored yarn she was working with didn't look like much, but when it was knitted or crocheted, it automatically made stripes. Momentarily I felt guilty for not doing the pink cashmere swatch, but my owl was much more interesting to work on.

"Barry didn't look happy," I said. Then I laughed. "I kind of see his point. Mason and I were having way too much fun."

"So Mason thinks Bradley might be alive because of the watch," Dinah said.

"I can't think of any other reason Emily would have kept the Rolex. The clerk offered to buy it and we know she needs money. But we both wondered if he'd risk coming back to their house to get it," I said. Glancing at my owl, I saw that instead of being round, the head was taking on the shape of a cucumber. Obviously I couldn't keep track of when a round ended and talk at the same time, so I set down my work and instead took out my BlackBerry to show it to Dinah.

"Mason gave you this? How thoughtful. How'd Barry take it?" she asked, checking out all the icons. When I didn't answer, she laughed. "You didn't tell Barry, did you?"

"No," I said. "It just would have stirred up more trouble."

"Trouble?" Rhoda said, pulling out a chair. "Who's in trouble?"

"Me, if I don't get these swatches done," I said, successfully changing the subject. Eduardo joined us next. He'd been a Hooker longer than Rhoda, but she still always gave him a strange look when he pulled out his hooks and yarn. He glanced around furtively.

"Here, take these before Adele gets here," he said, pushing a small pile of snowflakes across the table. He said he'd heard her harassing me about not making enough snowflakes.

"Why does she have to hide them from Adele?" Rhoda asked. Before I could answer, Adele appeared from out of nowhere and wanted to know what was being hidden from her. For the moment everyone forgot about the snowflakes and stared at Adele's sweater. She was known for wild getups, but the sweater was priceless. The background was black, with white trim around the end of the sleeves and the neckline and down the front. Maybe it was incorrect to call it a sweater. It was more like a canvas she covered with holiday decorations. The back had a Christmas tree, a couple of elves and a lot of thread snowflakes. Candy canes hung off the shoulders, along with icicles and dreidels. The front had Santa and Mrs. Claus, more dreidels, gold circles to signify Hanukkah coins, some weird brown things that might have been potato latkes, cookies with Christmas designs, holly and mistletoe. When she moved, everything swung.

"Quite a jacket," Rhoda said. Her tone said it wasn't a compliment, but as usual Adele didn't get it and took it the way she wanted to hear it.

"Great, isn't it?" Adele said as she turned, modeling the sweater for Rhoda. Adele explained she'd made the sweater years ago and then started adding new holiday things each year. I hadn't noticed the little vampire with the sprig of holly on his black suit until Eduardo touched it. Adele gave me a knowing smile.

"Elise is going to love that," I said.

"I should add a little black-and-white scarf," Adele said

when she stopped doing her modeling thing. She finally sat down and saw the stack of snowflakes on the table.

"Pink, you didn't make these, did you?" Adele said, picking up the top one. "Your picot stitches are always twisted. Who is the detective now?" Adele said with a triumphant jiggle of her head. Eduardo had done a fabulous job as usual. Nobody said anything.

"Pink, I think you should tell Mrs. Shedd that you've bitten off more than you can handle." She pointed to the wall of windows that faced Ventura Boulevard. "The So Many Traditions event is just a few days away and we have barely enough snowflakes for a snow drizzle. We need something more along the lines of a blizzard."

CeeCee arrived at the head of the table. She'd overheard the whole exchange and had a suggestion. "I think you're going to have to settle for something in between. I have a pattern for a simple snowflake. If we all pitch in, Molly will have enough for a nice display."

CeeCee passed around the snowflake pattern she had and everyone agreed to make some. I went off to make more copies. When I came back, Sheila had arrived and Adele was just taking out balls of black and white. They were attached to something, and I realized she was making Elise's vampire scarf. She announced she was making it for her boyfriend, William.

Rhoda couldn't contain herself. "Enough with repeating that Koo Koo is your boyfriend. We get it."

CeeCee reached over and picked up Adele's work and examined it. "I think I'll make one for Hugh," she said. She didn't need to add *Jackman* for us to get she meant her costar—or at least that's how she described her role. "You know, sort of a nice-to-work-with-you gift." She paused as something occurred to her. "How could I have missed this?" She pulled out her cell phone. "I'm going to call my agent and tell him to offer my services to teach Hugh how to crochet for the part. Even if they have a stand-in do the actual crocheting, I'm sure he'll want to learn so it'll look authentic when he's holding his hook."

"What kind of vampire crochets?" Rhoda said under her breath. Then she answered her own question. "A foofie one."

We all kept looking toward the front, but Elise never showed up. But someone else did. Emily and the women I'd seen in her den the night before walked into the yarn area. Everyone looked up automatically when someone entered our yarn area, even though I'd tried to get the group to be a little less territorial. One of these days some knitters were going to come in during our meeting and I didn't want a scene.

I introduced Emily to everyone and she turned to the woman with her. "This is Bradley's sister, Madison. She crochets, too." Now that I knew who she was, I saw the resemblance. She had the same reddish hair and lean shape. But she didn't have same magnetic personality of her brother, although from what I'd been learning, having his outgoing nature wasn't necessarily a positive.

Everyone knew about Bradley's suicide and they offered their condolences to the pair. Adele added something extra. She wanted to know if Madison was the one who'd made the afghan, and when she nodded, Adele laid into her.

"It was a good idea, but I think you made a lot of mistakes," Adele said.

Madison seemed surprised by Adele's comments and said she'd actually made another version of the afghan. Adele wanted to see it and Madison went to the car and got it. She laid it out on the table. I knew right away that it was what she was working on the night before at Emily's house.

It was green like the other one but made in one piece and the flowers were bigger and fewer.

It took a moment for Madison to recognize CeeCee. She got all flustered and said she was a big fan of CeeCee's reality show, *Making Amends*. CeeCee was used to getting that kind of reaction and was very gracious, even inviting them to join us. They declined. Madison was just looking for yarn.

"There are supposed to be swatches on all the bins," Adele said before offering to help her.

Madison said she knew what she wanted and went over to a bin of royal blue wool she said she wanted for felting. CeeCee complimented Madison on her choice and said it had worked for her.

Once the pair left, the group went back to work. I kept looking for Elise, but she never showed. When we finally broke up, I got ready to walk Dinah and the kids outside.

"Here, Aunt Molly," Ashley-Angela said, holding out the chain she and her brother had made. "You could put it in the window till you get all the snowflakes you need."

I hadn't realized they were listening. I was touched and said I'd find a special place to display it.

The sky definitely said winter with its leaden gray color. The kids pulled on their hoodies and zipped them up. I smelled moisture in the air as we walked to Dinah's car and wondered if it was going to rain. This was our season for it. She was parked next to a black Element, and as soon as I saw the bumper sticker about being citizen of the month at Wilbur Avenue Elementary, I thought it was probably Emily's. I glanced at it as Ashley-Angela got in Dinah's car and saw something sitting on the driver's seat. It was the shopping bag from the jeweler's. I called Dinah and pointed it out to her.

"It's strange that she'd be driving around with it," I said.

"Maybe she's giving it to his sister," Dinah said.

"And in exchange the sister is giving her a hastily made afghan that barely resembles one she gave away and didn't like to begin with," I said.

"Where's my truck?" E. Conner said, tugging on Dinah's sleeve. I said it was probably still on the table and offered to get it.

I went in the store and found the truck. On the way back, I looked in the café. Emily and Madison were sitting at a table. There were drinks on the table, but only Madison seemed interested in hers. They weren't talking or even looking at each other. Emily was holding her wrist and kept checking her watch. Suddenly I got it and rushed back to the car.

"I think I know why the watch is in the car. What if they're planning to meet someone and that someone happens to be Bradley?" I said as I handed E. Conner his truck. "No way would he show up here. They have to be going to him."

"What should we do?" Dinah asked.

"We could follow them," I said. Dinah hesitated a minute, looking at the kids. I knew she was concerned for their safety.

"They'll be fine. It's not like we're going to shoot it out with Bradley if we find him." I bent down closer to the kids' level and asked if they wanted to go for a ride. No surprise, they said yes.

Dinah's silver Honda blended in with all the other silver cars and was perfect to follow someone in, unlike the green-mobile, which blended in with nothing.

"I've got to tell Mrs. Shedd," I said. I rushed back into the bookstore and found my boss. She was straightening up the Anthony area. More books had come in and she had taken some more things from the yarn area and added them to the table. There was also a small sign saying there was more of Anthony's favorite yarn in our new yarn department.

"Do you think the sign's too much? I wouldn't want to upset the author. I'm sure he'll see it when he comes in," she said.

"You said *when he comes in.* You know who A. J. Kowalski is, don't you?" I said, for the moment forgetting why I'd run back inside.

"I have an idea. I'm sure you have someone you think it is, too. In my case it's a he, so that's how I'm referring to him until I know otherwise." Two women came up to the display and Mrs. Shedd smiled as they picked up two copies of the books and, after looking at the sign, headed toward the back of the store.

When I looked up I saw Dinah standing outside her car waving her arms and it brought back why I was there. "I need to leave for a while," I said in a gush.

Mrs. Shedd's face clouded with concern. "This isn't the best time. Could you wait a—" I was shaking my head before she finished.

"I think Bradley Perkins might be alive. I'm trying to find out or sure," I said, getting right to the point.

"By all means, go then," she said. Adele had just stepped next to Mrs. Shedd.

"Where's Pink going?" Adele said as I walked toward the door without looking back. I was out the door, when she caught up.

Dinah's waving had gotten more frantic by the time I got outside. She'd moved the car away from Emily's Element and was pointing toward it. Emily and Madison were in the process of getting in. I sprinted toward Dinah's car with Adele hanging on to my purse strap.

I pulled open the passenger door and got in quickly. Adele stood by the car a second before Dinah and I both yelled at her to get in the backseat.

Adele hadn't quite gotten the door closed before Dinah put the car in gear. Emily had already backed out and was almost to the driveway that went onto Ventura Boulevard. I heard something like a yelp of surprise coming from the backseat and I twisted to see what was going on.

Adele had just realized Ashley-Angela and E. Conner were in the backseat with her. She might run story time, but Adele's basic opinion about children was that they were from an alien planet. We were stuck in the line of cars waiting to exit onto the street and I offered Adele the chance to change her mind now that she saw who her seat companions were, but she declined, saying Mrs. Shedd had wanted her to go with me.

"She did?" I said. "Why?" The car was on Ventura now and Dinah was frantically trying to get close to the Element. Up ahead I could see the SUV had its right turn signal on.

Even Adele seemed a little surprised Mrs. Shedd wanted her to go. "One second she was telling me I absolutely couldn't go with you and that you were on some secret mission for her. Then Mr. Royal came up to her and wanted to know what the secret mission was. I started to say it had something to do with your neighbor, but before I could even say all of it, she started to walk me toward the door and said I ought to go with. She's acting very weird," Adele said. "She said whatever I learned while I was with you, I better keep it to myself or else." Adele jiggled her head in disbelief. "She ought to know I'm the picture of discretion." Dinah made a sharp turn and we were all a little thrown around.

"So what's going on? What are we doing?" Adele leaned

toward the front and stuck her head between the seats. "We're the three musketeers again," she said, referring to what she'd called us during an earlier adventure. I told her that I thought Emily and Madison might be going to meet Bradley.

"And we're following them?" Adele pointed vaguely toward the traffic.

"Right," I said, hoping to end it there.

"So, Pink, what are you going to do if you find the dead guy alive?" Adele was still leaning on the seat. I swallowed. I hated to admit it, but she'd brought up a valid point and one I hadn't considered.

"I-I am going to do something," I said. Adele stuck her face closer.

"What?" Adele demanded.

I pulled out my new BlackBerry. "I'll take a picture of him." As I said it, I started pushing buttons and clicking on things, trying to find the camera feature. The next thing I knew I'd taken a picture of my knee.

Adele took the BlackBerry out of my hand and looked it over. She demonstrated how to get to the camera and how to take a picture. Unfortunately she did it so fast I didn't get a chance to make note of it. She fiddled with it some more and when she handed it back, I saw I had the picture she'd taken of herself as my wallpaper. She sat back mumbling something about how it was lucky for us she'd come. "I have to call my boyfriend, Koo Koo, I mean William. If he comes by the bookstore and I'm not there, he'll get worried," she said.

A moment later she was telling him she was off to help me track down my supposedly dead neighbor. William must have said something because Adele started telling him about the watch and the afghan, which was followed by an exasperated sound and then she said something about a wild-goose chase. She ended the call with a few icky loud kisses. She was doing her best to ignore the kids, but they were staring at her.

"You know Koo Koo?" Ashley-Angela said in an awe-struck voice.

"Of course. He's my boyfriend," Adele said in a self-important tone. I wanted to scream that we got it that he was her boyfriend and she didn't have to keep repeating it. But I kept quiet. Now that the kids were looking at her with such high regard because she knew Mr. Red Shoes, Adele suddenly seemed better about sharing the backseat with them.

"Hey," Adele said sharply as Ashley-Angela reached out and touched a yarn candy cane on her sleeve. The little girl let go of the cane but kept staring at Adele's sweater.

"That's the beautifulest sweater I've ever seen," Ashley-Angela said.

Dinah corrected the little girl's grammar and an-nounced Emily was headed for the Ventura Freeway. She made a sharp left, zooming through a yellow arrow to stay behind them. There was a car between us and the SUV as we headed up the incline to the west-bound 101. Dinah's driving maneuvers got my attention away from the backseat temporarily. Ashley-Angela's compliment apparently made an impression on Adele. More than an impression, it had blasted through her usual reaction to kids. When I looked back Adele was telling Ashley-Angela about the sweater. She was not only letting both kids touch all the objects hanging off the sweater, she was telling them about why they were connected to the holidays. It was actually kind of interesting. Who knew that candy canes were supposed to symbolize a shepherd's staff? Though she got a little carried away when she started talking about mistletoe and Druids and people using it to ward off witches.

E. Conner reached over to check out the dreidel and Adele told him about a game that could be played with a real one. "If you come to holiday night, I'll show you how."

I did a double take. Was this the Adele I knew and was constantly annoyed by?

The SUV got off at Topanga Canyon Boulevard and went north. Dinah was good at keeping us a couple of cars behind. When I saw Emily's turn signal go on, I realized where they were going.

"They're going to the mall?" I said, feeling dismay. It wasn't the kind of clandestine meeting place I'd imagined. "I must have been wrong."

"Don't be so sure," Dinah said. "Think about it. Crowds of holiday shoppers. It would be easy for him to get lost in the crowd. Who'd notice him?"

"While you two go looking for the dead guy, I'm going to Sephora. I need some purple eye shadow," Adele announced. It took some wrangling to convince Adele that none of us were going shopping and to get her to take off the sweater. She argued everybody loved it and that people even stopped to look at it and tell her how great it was.

"That's the point. We don't want to be the center of attention," I said. Finally she took it off, but she told me I was depriving the shoppers of seeing a treat.

Dinah stayed close to the SUV until they parked and then she pulled into a space nearby. Topanga Mall had recently expanded and now was a huge sprawling shopping extravaganza with everything from Target to Tiffany's. By the time we got everybody out of the car, Emily and Madison were almost to the entrance to the mall. We rushed to catch up. Emily had the shopping bag from the jewelry store. I was surprised to note that Madison carried a plastic grocery bag. The afghan she'd shown us was peeking out of the top.

Dinah had to drag the kids past the indoor carousel and I held on to Adele to make sure she didn't take any shopping side trips.

Emily and Madison turned into the area they called the Canyon that ran between the old mall and the new addition. There was a whole Santa Claus setup, with a little house and the man in red on a throne.

As we followed at a distance, the kids started jumping up and down and waving at Santa. This wasn't good. They were drawing attention to us. Emily and Madison had stopped and seemed to be waiting for something. I pulled Adele next to me and we acted as a wall as Dinah calmed the kids. I was winging it. Nothing in my sleuthing bible, *The Average Joe's Guide to Criminal Investigation*, had covered doing surveillance with an entourage.

The two women kept shifting their weight and it was obvious they were waiting for somebody and impatient for them to get there. I kept checking the crowd for any signs of Bradley, but all I saw was a sea of faces. When I checked the pair again, a woman had stopped in front of them and some kind of interchange was going on.

Dinah looked around me and saw what was going on. "Is that Bradley in drag?"

"What? Who's in drag?" Adele said, swiveling her head frantically.

"Nobody and can you keep it down. The point is for us to blend in," I said. I laughed at myself. Adele blending in? Like that was ever going to happen.

The woman gestured and pointed at the crowd before handing Emily a piece of paper. Emily looked at it and grabbed Madison's arm and they started retracing their steps.

"We're moving," I said to our little group. We let them get ahead and then took up their trail.

They went back to Emily's Element and we rushed to Dinah's Honda. Adele tried to talk me into letting her have the front seat. What a surprise. I held firm as she went through her list of reasons, starting with that she was better at tracking Emily's Element than I was. As a last-ditch effort she said something about getting carsick and throwing up on the kids. I said we'd take the chance.

As we trailed the Element to the mall exit, I said I bet the note was telling them to go somewhere else.

We followed the black SUV to another mall in the east Valley. This one was smaller and the crowd was a little thinner and I worried the women might notice they were being followed. Dinah came up with a solution. Whenever we stopped, the whole group of us would turn and pretend to be admiring a store window. It got a little weird when we stopped in front of the storefront of the mall office and ended up staring at a security guard eating his lunch.

They stopped at the Santa area again. Emily still had the jeweler's shopping bag and Madison clutched the grocery bag. When we got too near them, I pushed the group behind a sign advertising the food court. A tall elf stood next to the counter with an ad touting photos with Santa. He ignored the line of kids and surveyed the crowd. His gaze landed on Emily and Madison before he walked over to them.

I had the BlackBerry in my hand. Was the elf Bradley in disguise? Nope. He said something to them but didn't pick up the packages. Emily looked annoyed as she turned away. Madison's posture sagged as she followed. I turned to gather up our group, but they weren't behind the food court sign. I did a three-sixty and still didn't see them. I did notice that Emily and Madison had already been swallowed up by the crowd.

"Sorry," Dinah said, squeezing between two teenage girls. The kids were holding hands and hanging on to her. "Bathroom stop."

Adele appeared about the same time holding a bag from a women's store. "We were just standing around," she said by means of explaining. "I saw the perfect dress to wear to the book launch. I was just going to wear something I had, but that was before . . ." She winked at me.

I threw up my hands at her wink and rushed ahead toward the parking lot. But when I got to the spot where Emily's SUV had been parked, it was empty.

"We lost them," I announced when the rest of them caught up with me a few moments later. Dinah put her head down and apologized again and then we turned toward Adele.

"Am I supposed to say I'm sorry, too?" she asked. We all nodded—even the kids. Adele seemed perplexed by the answer. "Okay, if it makes you feel better, Pink, I'm sorry you lost them." She glanced back to the mall. "As long as we're not in a hurry, there were some shoes that matched the dress." Dinah shook her head in annoyance at Adele and told her if she didn't watch it, we'd lose her.

"Don't move," I ordered Adele. I told them all to get in the car and wait. I had an idea.

I rushed back inside and retraced my steps to the Santa house. I checked elves until I found the right one. He was easy to pick out since he was kind of beefy and seemed more like Santa's bodyguard than his helper. Under the makeup, he had a five o'clock shadow. There was something rough around the edges about him and I bet there were tattoos under the elf suit.

I mentioned seeing him talking to Emily and asked him what it was about.

"Who are you, the elf police?" he said in a grumpy voice. "You want to know anything, you have to get your picture taken. Or let's just say you had your picture taken, if you get my drift." He held out his green-gloved hand. I fumbled in my purse and pulled out a five and he shook his head. I found a ten and his shrug said that was acceptable, but barely. He looked over my shoulder at some kid sitting on Santa's lap. "Hey, kid, I saw that. No pinching Santa. Do it again and you're gonna get a sack of coal." He turned back to me. "Kids ain't what they used to be. Santa, either. He's got a script now, you know. No more promising anything thanks to some idiot Joe suing the mall. Now it's just he'll see what he can do." I asked him again about what he'd said to Emily.

"All I said was 'The Grove.' Whatever that means. I thought the guy who asked me to relay the message said Grover, like the Sesame Street character. You know, since he was talking to an elf and all. But he said no in an annoyed voice and made me repeat what I was supposed to say. Then he said he'd be watching to make sure I did it."

"He did?" I said excited. "Is he still here?" I looked around and the elf did, too, but then he put up his green hands.

"Naw. Don't see him." I asked for a description, but the elf was getting impatient.

"Hey, lady, I didn't really look at him. I was more interested in the fifty-dollar bill he laid on me. He was a guy, that's all. I think he had on a baseball cap," he said before walking away.

Dinah had managed to keep everyone in the car. I prom-

ised everyone snacks at the next stop no matter what. I told
Dinah and Adele about my conversation with the elf and
the message Emily had gotten.

"The Grove," Dinah said with a exasperated sigh. "That's
all the way over the hill into the city and it's rush hour. He
couldn't have picked another shopping area in the Valley."

"All I could get out of the elf was that it was a guy
maybe wearing a baseball cap who gave him the message
for Emily. It could be Bradley," I said as Dinah peeled out of
the parking lot, heading for the 101. The most direct route
was to take the freeway to the Laurel Canyon off-ramp and
take the canyon into the city.

Traffic was thick as we started up the steep grade on
Laurel Canyon Boulevard. At the top the road turned curvy
as it threaded through the Santa Monica Mountains. The
traffic clogged to a crawl as we passed Sunset Boulevard.

"I can't believe Mrs. Shedd let you leave the bookstore
to chase after your neighbor," Adele said. I didn't say anything, hoping she would drop it. I should have known—
Adele never dropped anything. I heard a big *aha* come from
the backseat.

"Mrs. Shedd was in Perkins' investment club, wasn't
she?" Adele didn't wait for a confirmation. "Yes, that's it."
She prattled on, wondering how much Mrs. Shedd had lost
and then I heard her suck in her breath. "She didn't lose
the bookstore, did she?" When I didn't say anything, Adele
took it as an affirmative answer and got panicky. "Pink,
you've got to do something," she said. She glanced around
as if the pieces were falling into place. "Mr. Royal doesn't
know, does he? Who's the great detective now? Well, thank
heavens William and I don't keep secrets from each other."

I guess she forgot about not being allowed in his writing
room and his not mentioning anything about being A. J.

Kowalski. By the time we turned off Fairfax Avenue into the shopping center driveway, Adele had forgotten her panic over the bookstore's future.

"This is my fav shopping center," Adele squealed as Dinah pulled into the entrance of the parking structure. "It's like a little town," she said to the rest of us as if we'd never been here. "The decorations must be amazing. The Nordstrom here is the best. You know this is where all the celebrities come to shop now."

"No stopping until I say it's okay," I snapped.

Parking at The Grove was much more of a production than at either of the Valley malls. There were tickets to be had and a lot of levels and people directing cars to the level with open spots.

I figured that Emily and Madison had a head start on us, but since Dinah had driven like a race car driver, I was hoping we were close behind them. I was out of the car before Dinah had pulled all the way into a spot. I took out my BlackBerry as I ran to the escalator. I was ruthless, pushing through shoppers and baby strollers as I headed toward the Santa setup, figuring that was where they'd go.

Santa had his own gingerbread cottage here with Raggedy Ann and Andy handling the photos. I pushed through the throng of parents and kids waiting, while I surveyed the crowd. Someone brushed against me and I automatically turned. My breath stopped when I found myself face-to-face with Emily.

"Molly, what are you doing here?" When I looked down both she and Madison were empty-handed and going in the opposite direction. I studied the crowd ahead, looking for a man with a jewelry bag, but it was impossible to pick out anyone in the crowd.

I swore under my breath. They had won.

CHAPTER 17

MRS. SHEDD WAS IN THE FRONT OF THE STORE when Adele and I walked in. Dinah had just dropped us off and headed home with the kids. She had evening plans with Commander—this time the kids were included—and she was nervous.

"Well, how did it go?" Mrs. Shedd asked. Adele stepped in front of me and took over answering.

"We didn't see the dead guy, but Pink thinks he's alive because of what some elf told her." Mrs. Shedd wasn't smiling when she looked around Adele and our eyes met. "Don't worry, I won't tell Mr. Royal about the money you lost in the investment scam," Adele said.

"How could you, Molly?" Mrs. Shedd said, her expression darkening. "I specifically told you I wanted to keep my situation a secret."

For once Adele's ego helped me. Adele insisted I hadn't told her anything, she'd figured it out all by herself. "Pink's not the only detective around here," Adele said. Mrs. Shedd muttered something about the afternoon being wasted, but Adele held out her shopping bag. "No, it wasn't. I got a new dress for the launch. I can't wait to show it to William." Adele kept giving me conspiratorial winks. Finally Mrs. Shedd asked her if she'd developed a twitch.

Adele looked horrified. "Of course not. Don't you know a wink when you see it? It was just my signal to Pink about some special information we have." Adele sighed. "And don't worry, I won't tell anyone who A. J. Kowalski really is and ruin the launch." Adele fingered the little vampire hanging off her sweater.

"You know who the author is?" Mrs. Shedd asked.

Adele waited a beat to build up the suspense. "It's William. My boyfriend." Mrs. Shedd looked toward me and I just put up my hands in a who-knows sort of way. The next moment Adele waved toward the parking lot and announced that William was driving by to pick her up and then she flew out the door.

With Adele gone, Mrs. Shedd and I discussed the afternoon. I didn't want her to feel hopeless, but at the same time I didn't want her to feel too hopeful, either, since there was no guarantee Bradley was even alive. And even if he was alive, after what the SEC people said about the checks to the casinos, it was doubtful there was any money to find.

"Just don't give up, Molly," Mrs. Shedd said in a tense voice. "No pressure, but the future of the bookstore is on your shoulders." She let the words sink in and then went back to her normal self and asked if everything was ready for the upcoming holiday event.

Thanks to CeeCee's effort to get everyone making snowflakes, I felt comfortable saying yes. Finally, Mrs. Shedd went back to her office.

I looked back at the activity table in the yarn area and was surprised to see Elise sitting by herself. Even from here I could tell by her body language that she was upset. She was slumped in a defensive posture over her yarn. She looked up when I approached the table. I almost expected her to put her hand in front of her face to deflect any blows. She had balls of black and white yarn and seemed to be starting another vampire scarf. I slid into the seat next to her.

"I couldn't stay home any longer. The phone keeps ringing. It's always the same thing. They want to talk to Logan. Why isn't he answering his cell phone? Why isn't he answering his business phone? Then they want to know what's going on with Bradley Perkins. Is it true he's dead? They called Bradley's office and all they did was take a message and refuse to give out any information. It ends with something frantic about wanting to know if their investments are okay."

Elise leaned back in the chair. "I was afraid to come to the Hookers meeting this morning. Everyone is so angry. They think Logan was making some kind of commission off the people he got to invest with Bradley." Her expression darkened. "I don't know how much more Logan can take. He seems pretty close to cracking."

I felt sorry for her, but at the same time wanted to know the truth. "Did Logan make money off his dealing with Bradley?"

Her face hardened. "Logan didn't make any commission on the clients he introduced to Bradley. The only gain he got was that Bradley tried to push real estate business his way." She said the line as if she'd said it many times before. She ended by staring at me and saying a defiant, "Okay?"

I reached out and touched her in support. I believed her

and felt sorry for her situation. "Would it make any difference if Bradley was alive?"

Her eyes focused and she straightened. "Did you see him? Where? When?" Her voice sounded frantic.

"No, I didn't see him," I said. "I just have reason to believe he might still be alive."

Elise held on to my arm. "Find him, please. If he is, he's the one who should pay for his crime. Not Logan."

I lightened the mood by asking her about her crocheting. As soon as I got her talking about Anthony and what we thought would happen with the vampire and the reporter in the next book, she went back to being her regular self. I asked her about the directions for the scarf and she apologized for forgetting she said she'd bring them in. She pulled out a piece of paper and began writing down how to make it. As I was leaving the yarn area, a woman had come up to the table and was admiring Elise's work. It was probably only temporary, but at least for the moment she seemed to have some peace.

Since I'd been gone all afternoon I stayed at the bookstore until eight. Most of my time was spent helping customers, but in between I went through my checklist for our So Many Traditions event, as we were calling it. The centerpiece was celebrating Santa Lucia Day, which it more or less coincided with. To many the Swedish holiday kicked off the holiday season. Mrs. Shedd was the Santa Lucia expert. It was part of her Swedish heritage and as a child she'd been the one to wear the white dress, red sash and crown of candles. In our version, Rayaad's daughters were going to wear the outfits, though our candles were going to be battery operated. Since part of the tradition of Santa Lucia had to do with feeding everybody, refreshments were on the house. I stopped in the café to check with Bob on the status of the ginger cookies, or *pepparkakor*, as Mrs. Shedd called them. He had taken advantage of the slowdown in customers and was leaning on the counter, typing on his laptop.

He startled when I stepped up to the counter and stood up abruptly.

"I tried two recipes. Tell me what you think." Bob was very serious as he handed me two cookies shaped like stars and a shot of milk to clear my palate between tastes.

"I thought so," he said when I pointed out the cookie I preferred. "Those are the ones with molasses."

He asked about the rolls we were serving. Technically, they were supposed to be saffron buns, but Mrs. Shedd's family had been renegades and served cardamom buns instead. Bob was the king of cookies, but he was nervous about doing anything with yeast, so I'd offered to make the buns.

"I'm making a test batch tonight," I said and promised to bring him a sample.

I MADE A STOP AT THE GROCERY STORE FOR SUP-plies and headed home. Shortly after Charlie died, I'd thought of selling the house and moving to a condo. It had really been more Peter's suggestion, telling me I should downsize. Now I was glad I hadn't done it. With two dogs, two cats, too much yarn and Samuel as a temporary resident, I needed the space. I was sure Samuel would make some other living arrangements in the near future. But I was willing to put money down that when the time came for him to move, the cats would stay with me.

I was looking forward to taking my time and enjoying making the rolls. Even if Samuel was home, he'd probably be in his room and not in my way.

It had become an automatic response to check the Perkins' house as I drove by. From the street it looked dark. Not even the porch light was on.

I shut off the motor and grabbed the grocery bag. Along with the baking supplies, I'd picked up a pint of ice cream. One of the things I'd said I liked about being on my own was being able to have an occasional ice-cream dinner and not have anybody look askance. No cars in front of my house and no cars in the driveway. I pulled into the garage and the automatic door shut with a rumble. I walked into the backyard and looked ahead to the back door. And no one ruffling through things in my house. The door was locked and any mess inside was strictly my fault.

Once inside I saw there was a note on the table. Barry had stopped by and given the dogs yard time along with feeding them and the cats. Feeling like a lady of leisure for the moment, I set the grocery bag down and took out the pint of ice cream. First things first. I'd have my Bordeaux and strawberry dinner and then begin baking.

I took a bowl of ice cream and settled in the middle of the couch and put my feet up. The dogs plumped down on either side of me and the cats jumped up and perched on the back of the couch. I let out a big satisfied *ah* as I took my first spoonful of my favorite ice cream.

The back wall of the den was all windows that looked out on the backyard. Something moving outside caught my eye, and I sat bolt upright and almost choked on my mouthful of ice cream. A moment later I heard someone fidgeting with the back door lock. Was it a key or someone with a hairpin?

I marched to the kitchen and grabbed a broom, ready to do battle as the door opened.

I raised the broom, ready to smack whoever entered.

Luckily I looked before I swatted. Barry and Mason walked in, talking about football. They both looked up at the same time.

"Oh, you're home," Barry said, giving the raised broom a strange look.

"Hey, Sunshine, what are you doing, trying to sweep the ceiling?" Mason said with a grin.

I set the broom down. "I got a little nervous when I heard someone fiddling with the back door." I glanced from one of them to the other. Something wasn't right. They were acting friendly toward each other. "What's up with you guys?"

"Sunshine, even with a BlackBerry you still have to answer it or look at your messages." When I didn't get what he was talking about, he asked to see it. I found it in my purse and handed it over. He hit some keys and displayed a list of messages, he'd left. He'd left voice mail messages, too.

"I stopped by the bookstore this afternoon and you weren't there, either. Finally I came by here. Greenberg was in the yard with the dogs. I hung around awhile to see if you were going to show up. When he finished with the animals and you still weren't here, we decided to get some dinner together."

I looked at Barry for confirmation and he smiled and nodded. "Yeah, we went to a sports bar and got some burgers. Some football game, huh, Mason?"

Hmm. I suddenly felt very left out.

"Molly, if you're not going to answer your phone or call anybody back, you can't expect us to sit here and starve waiting for you," Barry said.

"I was working," I protested.

"I know," Barry said. "And now I get how you feel when I make plans and then don't show up because I have to follow some lead." He turned to Mason and made some comment about some great football play, but there was something in his manner that implied that Mason could now leave. Mason played Mr. Dense and walked through the kitchen toward the living room.

I retrieved my ice cream, which was quickly turning into mush. Barry followed both of us.

"I have the dog sweater in the car," Mason said, gesturing toward outside. "I got to something that said decrease and I didn't know what to do."

I really wondered about that. It meant he was working on it on his own, and from what I'd seen, he only worked on Spike's future coat when I was around.

"Molly's had a long day. I don't think she's up for crochet lessons," Barry said, putting his arm around my shoulder.

I heard the front door open. "Is this door ever going to get fixed?" Samuel said. He looked at the three of us in the living room. "What's going on?" Ryder, the kid from down the street, came in behind him and waved a greeting with his video camera. At the same time Barry's cell went off. It was his son, Jeffrey. He was done with rehearsal and going to get dropped off. When he heard where Barry was, he said he'd get dropped off at my house.

Mason looked at the bowl in my hand. "Was that your dinner?"

I nodded and he chuckled. "And we ruined it for you, huh?"

"It doesn't matter," I said, going back to the kitchen. "Look guys, I have baking to do for work."

"Baking!" they all said together. So much for peace. Ryder had never seen anyone actually make something with yeast. Apparently, the best his mother did was a cake mix. He videoed the whole rising process and was going to do some time-lapse trick. He couldn't capture the smell though. The yeasty smell mixed with the spicy scent of the cardamom spread throughout the house as the dough rose.

The front doorbell rang and then I heard a key in the lock. The door opened and shut, and a moment later, my older son, Peter, came in the kitchen. "What's with the front door and do you know that a channel three news crew is out front?" he said. He looked at the flour-covered counter and Ryder videoing me shaping the rolls. It was hard to tell if Peter was coming from some event or just a long workday. Not a hair out of place or a wrinkle in his dress shirt. He certainly didn't get that perfection from my side. I hadn't realized at first that he wasn't alone. A slender woman in a dark suit and heels so tall my feet hurt in sympathy was with him.

Explaining the door was easy, but not the news crew. Peter and his companion followed me into the den, where Barry and Mason were watching ESPN. I flipped to channel three and had the eerie encounter of seeing my street on the screen. Kimberly Wang Diaz was doing a remote. It turned out there was nothing happening next door, it was just the news style now to have field reporters do their stories in the area where something had happened. The story was an update on Bradley and his apparent suicide and the investigation into his business.

"More investors are coming forward," Diaz said just before going to a tape of her standing in front of the building where Bradley had his office. An older woman I recognized as a bookstore customer came out holding her head down. Diaz asked her for a statement. The woman looked as if the wind had been knocked out of her. The reporter again asked her for a statement. The woman was probably too dazed to think about what she was doing and told the reporter she'd turned over her life savings to Bradley. "He was such a nice family man. And so helpful. I was trying to figure out my Medicare options and I was so confused. Bradley spent an afternoon helping me straighten it all out." She sighed. "How can he have left his business in such a mess? Those investigators are saying all the money is gone. It just can't be. It was all I had." The woman's eyes filled with water and, in a moment of humanness, Diaz touched her shoulder and said how sorry she was.

The tape cut to Diaz interviewing Nicholas in his store. He talked about how personable Bradley was. "But isn't that the way it works with con men?" Nicholas said. He was angry at being taken in, but not devastated. Diaz had tried to interview Logan coming out of Le Grande Fromage, but he put his hands up, blocking the camera, and hurried away. Diaz filled in why he was in such a hurry.

"A number of the investors told this reporter that they invested with Perkins based on the recommendation of Logan Belmont, a well-respected local real estate broker."

The tape ended with Diaz talking to the SEC investigator. "We still don't know the complete scope of the apparent Ponzi scheme. The records are a mess. We're trying to come up with a complete client list." He looked into the camera. "We'd like anyone with information to come forward." A number was flashed on the screen.

The story ended with a live shot of Diaz out front giving a list of tips people should think of before turning over their savings to anyone.

"She ought to add, 'don't do it,'" Peter said as if he thought he was being clever. I told him his comment was cold and how bad I felt for the woman who'd lost her life savings. Peter seemed grateful when the kitchen timer went off and ended our skirmish.

Everyone followed me to the kitchen, talking as they went. Peter made a big deal about introducing the woman to Mason. Not a surprise because he liked Mason and thought if I was going to be involved with any man it should be him. He introduced her to Barry, but it was perfunctory. I had finally acknowledged it wasn't going to get any better between Peter and Barry. No matter what Barry said, I couldn't ignore the friction. And I thought when you were as old as I was you got to do what you wanted.

Peter had stopped over to introduce Brooklyn to me, which I gathered meant he was serious about her. Though I think he regretted his decision. She was friendly enough, but I couldn't miss the way she focused on the flour all over my apron or the way she stared at Jeffrey sleeping on the couch with the dogs. I don't think Samuel and Ryder made the best impression, either. And to finish it off, Holstein jumped in her arms and got fur all over her immaculate suit.

She was still brushing the fur off as they went out the patched-up front door.

The rest of the crowd hung around while I finished making the rolls. And when I finally took them out of the oven and offered samples they all looked at me as if I was some kind of cooking goddess. Since this was just a run-through, I packed up to-go bags of rolls for all of them.

Samuel retired to his room. Ryder's mother called him and wondered where he was. Jeffrey was still asleep on the couch. Barry and Mason kept standing around. It was pretty obvious what was going on. Neither wanted to leave before the other one. They even offered to help me clean up the kitchen. Like I was going to turn that down.

"Your boss wouldn't say where you were this afternoon,"

Mason said, taking a spray bottle and some paper towels and cleaning up the flour around my mixer. I started to hand wash the mixer bowl and all the spatulas. Barry dried them and put them away. I considered for a moment what to say. Why not throw it out in front of both of them and see what they thought I ought to do with the information?

I went through the whole thing about how I'd begun to think that Bradley might not really be dead. I brought up the watch and seeing it in the car. I didn't mention the afghan. I was still having a problem figuring out why Bradley would want that anyway.

When I mentioned following Emily and Madison, I saw Barry's jaw clench. I explained both theories—that Bradley just wanted them to run all over the place or that he'd seen me following them. "I realize the woman who came up to them at the Topanga Mall must have been sent by Bradley," I said. I hesitated when I got to the second mall. Should I really tell them what happened or just say we followed them to The Grove? It wasn't the same without explaining about the elf. I mean, he had seen who was passing the message. Hoping for the best, I brought up the elf. I saw Barry's eyes roll up in his head. Mason skipped past a chuckle and went right to a laugh. "And when we got to The Grove, it was too late. The women didn't have their packages anymore and Bradley was nowhere to be seen."

"So?" Barry said.

"So, I'm wondering what I should do with the information. I'm sure those SEC investigators would like to know that Bradley might be alive."

"Molly, you don't know for a fact that he's alive. You didn't see him. And the description the elf gave you." Barry shook his head. "Am I seriously considering what a guy dressed as an elf said?" Barry went into his interrogator mode and wanted to know if I'd actually seen Emily with the watch at The Grove. When I said no, he pointed out that since I didn't see her with it, seeing her without it didn't necessarily mean anything. "You see my point. If you tell this story to any investigators, they're just going to stamp you as being a nutcase." He put a hand on my shoulder and started to repeat his stay-out-of-it speech. "And let's just say, for argument, Perkins is alive. He's not going to be hanging around here waiting for you to find him. He's probably halfway to somewhere already."

"Where?" I said.

"Someplace where's he's not going to get caught." I wasn't happy with what Barry said and looked to Mason for his opinion.

A smile lit up Mason's eyes. "Personally, I like the elf story. But as I said before, I wonder why he'd take a chance on getting caught just to pick up a watch, no matter how valuable it is."

"There was something else." I paused, getting ready for their reaction when I told them what the something else was.

"An afghan?" Barry rolled his eyes. He didn't have to say the *kook* word, I knew he was thinking it. "A valuable collectable watch, I might buy, but some crocheted blanket. No way would some guy take a chance on getting caught for that. They've been giving out big sentences for investment scams. One guy just got a hundred years. Remember what I said about seeming like a nutcase?" Barry shook his head again. Mason swept up the flour from the floor and the kitchen was done, though neither man made a move to leave.

My head was spinning now and I began to doubt myself.

Maybe there was another explanation. I just didn't know what it was. Finally Barry couldn't stall anymore and woke up Jeffrey. Mason hung back, but Barry grabbed him with his other arm and they all went to the door together. Mason looked over his shoulder and blew me a kiss.

CHAPTER 18

I THOUGHT ABOUT WHAT BARRY HAD SAID ABOUT seeming like a nutcase, and even though the SEC guy had urged people with information to come forward, I didn't. Not that I had time anyway. The next few days went by in a blur of snowflakes and preparations for the So Many Traditions event.

Luckily, CeeCee's snowflake pattern was simple and I was able to turn them out pretty quickly. My crochet partners came through, too. Sheila stopped by on her break from her receptionist job at the gym and gave me a handful. Eduardo brought in more that he'd made while he was waiting around a commercial shoot he was doing for fat-free sour cream. CeeCee dropped some off as she rushed off to a meeting with her agent. Rhoda sent her husband Harold in with the ones she'd made. Of course Adele insisted she'd done her share and I didn't even think about Elise. Dinah brought the ones she'd made when she came over to help me starch them all. She'd left the kids at home. "You got a babysitter," I said.

"Commander came over," she said with an uncertain flutter of her eyes. "This will either make or break things. He said he'd teach them how to play checkers."

I had stacks of cardboard pieces, rolls of wax paper, pushpins and a big jug of starch. When we'd laid out all the snowflakes, we took them outside and laid them on the lawn furniture to dry. It seemed almost like magic how they went from limp masses of tangled-looking thread to dainty things of beauty. Dinah turned up toward the night sky. "Good," she said. "Dark blue. No chance of rain." Maybe it wasn't going to rain, but it was cold. We could see our breath as we rushed back inside to the warm kitchen.

Dinah hung around while I mixed up the dough for the batch of cardamom rolls for the bookstore. I mentioned that I'd gotten several voice mail messages from Emily. "I haven't called her back," I said. "At first I felt sorry for her and thought she'd been left to deal with a terrible mess her husband made. But after the whole thing with the watch and the shopping malls, I'm not sure how much she's involved. And I don't have time to figure it out now," I said, putting the dough in a bowl and covering it to let it rise.

"THANK YOU, THEY'RE BEAUTIFUL," MRS. SHEDD said, taking one of the snowflakes and handing it to me so I could hang it on the window. She was on the ground, attaching small balls of quake wax to the flakes, and I was on a ladder doing the actual hanging. The bookstore had just opened and there were only a few customers browsing while drinking some of Bob's first brew of the day.

Mrs. Shedd was quiet for a moment, and when I reached

for the next piece to press against the window, I noticed her face had settled into a sad expression. She mentioned seeing the woman on the news the night before and it was obvious she related. "How could all the money he took from everybody be gone?"

By now I was becoming an expert on how Ponzi schemes worked, so I explained how he used the money he took in from new investors to pay the few people who wanted to take out the returns on their investments or who wanted to cash out of the whole venture. "The rest of it . . ." I said with a deep sigh. I reminded her of what I'd overheard the SEC investigator say about all the checks written to all the casinos. "It looks like Bradley lost it all gambling." I asked her if she was going to talk to the SEC people and give them details of her dealings with Bradley.

"Eventually I will," Mrs. Shedd said. "But right now I want to think about tonight's event and the launch party and the future. Just the thought of finding the paperwork to bring them is upsetting, and it's not as if it's going to change anything."

Adele came over to where we were working. She looked at the large stack of snowflakes and how many were already hung. "Where'd they all come from?" Her voice sounded surprised and maybe a little disappointed that I'd managed without any more help from her.

"Well, I have things to do," Adele said, flouncing off. "I have to tweak the setup in the kid's department and then I am the one in charge of the whole Santa Lucia procession."

Mrs. Shedd watched her go. "Do you really think the last part was such a good idea?" she said as I continued hanging the snowflakes.

I was having second thoughts myself. Adele had begged to be part of the event and I felt guilty about the yarn department even if she'd brought it on herself by being so anti-knitters. But it was too late to do anything about it anyway.

"What can go wrong?" I said. "All she has to do is help Rayaad's daughters into the white dresses and hit play on the CD machine."

Mrs. Shedd sighed. I knew that no matter what she'd said, she was having a hard time getting in the holiday spirit. How was she going to tell Mr. Royal about her losses? I knew she was worried he might be so disappointed in her judgment that their whole relationship would unravel.

By evening the windows had their blizzard of snowflakes and we'd cleared a space in the middle of the bookstore for the procession. The travel books had been cleared from their table and a white paper tablecloth had been put on it. Bob had brought in the trays of brown ginger cookies and I'd cut the buns into quarters and set them on a doily-covered platter. There was punch for the kids and coffee for the adults. We'd covered the whole table with a sheet to be unveiled after the Santa Lucia procession. Even with it covered, the spicy scent of the cardamom and ginger gave away that there was something good under the sheet.

People had begun to filter into the bookstore. I was glad to see them browsing the aisles as they waited for the event to begin. After Mrs. Shedd's comment, I tried to check on Adele and Rayaad's daughters, but Adele had them all barricaded in the office and wouldn't let me in.

Battery-operated candles flickered around the bookstore and we'd added a seven-candle candleholder for Kwanzaa to the table with the menorah. The trees out in front of the store had been strung with tiny white lights and looked very festive.

I was surprised to see Emily Perkins come in with her daughters. She got a lot of hostile stares as she worked through the crowd. Her determined stride in my direction made me think she was on some kind of mission. Whatever it was got aborted when Mrs. Shedd pulled me aside and said we ought to begin the festivities.

I knocked on the office door and told Adele it was time to start. I went back to the center of the store and cleared the customers from the path of the procession. Mrs. Shedd lowered the lights. The store holiday music went off and the familiar Santa Lucia song began. Personally it reminded me more of the singing gondoliers at the Venetian hotel in Las Vegas, but the look on Mrs. Shedd's face made me think it was all connected with Christmases past for her.

Everyone turned as Rayaad's daughters made their entrance. They wore the traditional white dresses with red sashes and had crowns of battery-operated flickering candles. I realized I'd been holding my breath in anticipation of disaster, and now that all seemed okay, I let it out in a gush. And then I saw Adele.

She had on a long dress, too, but instead of white, it was swirled with lime green, purple, rosy pink and sky blue. No red sash for her. She wore a purple one. Instead of the crown of candles, she had a crown of fiber-optic threads that kept changing colors.

The music lowered and Adele started prowling around the girls in white and playing to the crowd.

"Yo, yo," she said in rhythm, holding up two fingers on both hands and waving them rapper-style. She stopped and took a stance, waving her arms in a hip-hop dance mode.

"Santa Lucia comes from a long time ago.
She started out Italian, don't ya know, don't ya know.
Then somehow she got to Sweden, how we don't know,
Where they celebrate the day with white dresses and
    candles, yo, yo, yo, yo.

Her name means light and she comes bringing hope.
Her goodwill lasts throughout the holidays, so don't ya
   mope, don't ya mope."

Adele threw in some more "yo, yos" as she started clap-
ping her hands and dancing around Rayaad's daughters. I
looked at Mrs. Shedd. Her mouth was open in shock. The
crowd seemed unsure what to make of it. No one stopped
Adele and her holiday rap.

"We celebrate with cookies and rolls, don't ya know,
   don't ya know,
Because St. Lucia said bring those goodies to the table.
She wants to feed everyone as long as she's able, don't
   ya know."

Adele punctuated it with some more "yo, yos" as she
rocked back and forth toward and away from the crowd.
   "Give it up for the lady in white. But she's not the only
thing we celebrate tonight, yo, yo," Adele said, pointing
at the crowd. "Say 'yo, yo.'" She had to repeat it several
times before everyone got it that they were supposed to
join in. Once they did their repeat "yo, yos," they started
to clap in time to her rap. Mrs. Shedd closed her mouth
for a moment, but then it opened again as a noise went
through the crowd when Koo Koo in full clown outfit
joined Adele. Rayaad's daughters had moved out of view,
but nobody noticed as the colorful couple continued the
holiday rap.

"For Hanukkah, we have the dreidel game.
Some call it gambling, but it's fun all the same, don't
   ya know, don't ya know.

Kwanzaa has a candleholder, too, it's called a kinara,
    woo-hoo, woo-hoo.
We've got books for Hanukkah and Kwanzaa, don't ya
    know.
We've got them, too, for the man in the red suit who
    says, ho, ho, ho."

Both of them prowled around the cleared center, getting
the crowd to join them in their "yo, yos." With a flourish,
Adele pulled back the sheet on the table.

"Shop for books and stop for a treat, don't ya know.
Good words to read and good things to eat, yo, yo."

The music stopped and Adele and Koo Koo took their
bow. Okay maybe it hadn't been exactly traditional, but
everyone looked like they'd enjoyed it. I saw Ryder hiding behind a bookcase with his video camera going. Adele
would be thrilled to know she and Koo Koo were probably
going to end up on YouTube.

With the show over, the crowd moved toward the goodie
table. CeeCee and her guy (her title for him), Tony Bon-
nard, trailed the crowd. They were carrying shopping bags
and had obviously made several shopping stops at the other
stores on the street. CeeCee kept sniffing the air, seeming
to be carried forward by the scent of the treats. Not a surprise. Her sweet tooth was legendary, along with her battle
to keep it under control. She must have been reading my
thoughts.

"My character in the Anthony movie is known for her
soft curves," CeeCee said. "The director thought I looked a
little gaunt for the part."

I hated to admit it, but as soon as she made the gaunt

comment, I looked over her face and body. She'd kept the soft brown hair color and midlength style the stylist she'd hired a while back gave her, but she'd wavered from the woman's choice of clothing style. The brown corduroy jean-style pants and creamy-colored cable-knit sweater were more revealing than the long tops over slacks the stylist had chosen for her. Nowhere in any of this did I see anything remotely resembling gaunt.

"Is Elise coming?" CeeCee said, then turned to Tony and explained she was the Hooker she'd been telling him about who was so over the top about the Anthony books. "She's already asked me to get her on the set when we film."

I mentioned that Elise's mind seemed to be on other things now and described how she'd been hiding out in the yarn department.

"Poor dear," CeeCee said. It was a sincere comment. CeeCee hadn't forgotten what it was like to lose what you thought you had. Things were going well for her now that she had the successful reality series and even better with her movie role.

Adele bypassed the food table and headed into the children's department. Koo Koo followed her, not an easy feat in the big red shoes. He stopped next to me and I was about to compliment him on his performance when Emily stepped in front of me.

"I need that afghan back," she said. "Right away." The comment seemed to come from left field and it didn't register for a moment what she was talking about. Once I realized she was talking about the pretty green blanket with the multicolored flowers, I reminded her that she had told me to give it to some charity sale. I pulled CeeCee into the conversation to explain.

"You passed on that afghan, didn't you?" I asked. CeeCee

nodded and said she'd given it to the Hearts and Barks holiday sale.

"But the sale hasn't taken place yet, has it?" Emily said with desperation in her voice. She reached toward CeeCee and I thought she was going to grab her. I was struck by the change in my neighbor. The pleasant-looking suburban mom had been replaced by a wild-eyed woman. Now she looked gaunt.

"Well, no, dear," CeeCee said, edging out of Emily's reach. "It's in a few days, but the display has already been set up and the insiders have had a chance to look at everything. I think someone put a hold on it. It would really be bad form to take it back now."

"You have to get it back." Emily's voice had risen to almost hysterical. "I'll pay whatever price was put on it plus twenty bucks."

CeeCee shook her head and Emily made a move toward her, and this time it was clear she was going to grab the actress. I stepped in to protect CeeCee, assuring Emily I'd get the blanket back for her.

"What was that about?" Dinah said, coming in at the end of the exchange just before Emily and her daughters made a fast exit. Ashley-Angela and E. Conner were clutching my friend's sweater and taking in their surroundings. When they realized they were standing next to Koo Koo, they started jumping up and down. I thought they would faint with excitement when he offered to escort them into the children's area.

I brought Dinah up to speed, and then told CeeCee even if it was bad form, she had to get the blanket back.

"You're too nice," CeeCee said. "There's a name for what she's doing. I'd say it, but it's not politically correct these days." She looked around, no doubt checking for any paparazzi who might catch her in the faux pas. When I stood firm, CeeCee pulled out her cell and said she'd see what she could do.

"It's not totally about being nice," I said to Dinah. "Think about it. She didn't care about the afghan before—she didn't even like it. Now suddenly she has to have it back. There's something going on with it, and I am sure it has something to do with Bradley." I reminded Dinah that when we'd followed Emily to the malls, she'd had the watch and an afghan, and even if Barry had tried to convince me there was no proof she'd actually connected with her supposedly dead husband, I was sure she had.

Dinah and I headed toward the kid's department. She wanted to check on Ashley-Angela and E. Conner and I wanted to see what Adele had set up for the event.

"But if she already took him an afghan—why another one?" We crossed onto the carpet with the cows jumping over the moons. I was surprised at all that Adele had done. Handling story time had been the consolation prize Mrs. Shedd had given her when I was hired to arrange the bookstore's events. Adele had been less than thrilled with it and kids in general, but maybe being the girlfriend of an important children's author, as she referred to William, had changed her. Or maybe it was all about helping him sell more books. William as Koo Koo was standing adjacent to a display of the full Koo Koo library. Adele had also set up a table with a dreidel and was inviting the kids in the area to play.

She held up the four-sided top and showed the kids the Hebrew letters on the side. She let each of the kids take ten silver-wrapped chocolate candies. The way the game was played each of them put one of their chocolates in the pot, then someone got a turn to spin the dreidel. When it stopped and fell, depending on which letter showed on top, the player would get nothing, get to take all the candies in the middle, get to take only half of them or have to add one of their candies to the pot. Then the next person got their turn and so on around the table. At the end of the game whoever had the most candies was the winner.

Once the kids took their candies and began to play, we continued our conversation and Dinah repeated her question about why another afghan if she'd already taken him one.

"I've been thinking about that. When Emily first told me about Bradley being missing, she said one of the things they had argued about was that the afghan was missing. She had thought he was just angry about everything and had thrown in that comment." I mentioned how she had said she didn't even think he liked it. He had been the one to stick it in a drawer. "But suppose he really was upset she had lent the afghan to me." A thought struck me and it was one of those moments when I knew I had hit the truth. "Someone came into my house right after he disappeared. Suppose it was Bradley looking for the afghan?"

"What about the second time someone broke in?" Dinah asked in a low voice.

I thought it over a moment and realized it was the same night I'd seen the motorcycle in the Perkins' driveway. The motorcycle Emily denied was there. "That could have been Bradley, too."

"Obviously Emily didn't know whatever it is about the afghan that makes it so important or she wouldn't have lent it to you."

"Right. She said his sister had made it, so maybe she just thought he wanted another one made by her," I said. "Like it had some kind of sentimental value like the watch."

"But it wasn't about the sentiment," Dinah said. Her voice started to rise, but she forced it back to a whisper.

In the end we came up with two conclusions. There was something hidden in the afghan and once Emily had it back, she was going to get it to Bradley.

CHAPTER 19

CeeCee called me at the bookstore the next day. She wailed on about what a production it had been and how embarrassing for her, but she had gotten the afghan back. She said she would bring it to the next Hookers' meeting. I didn't want to wait and said Dinah and I would come to pick it up. CeeCee hesitated, at first anyway. It took a certain amount of bribery for her to agree.

"Did I mention I'd be bringing cookies?" I said. "Homemade butter cookies."

"Well, I wouldn't want those cookies to go to waste," CeeCee said before setting up a time.

I had already spent the morning clearing up the bookstore from the previous night's festivities and was going to take off for a while since I was working in the evening until closing. Ashley-Angela and E. Conner were at a play date with the neighbors and Dinah had come by to meet me for lunch.

We dropped our lunch plans and flew to my house to

make the offered cookies. It took no time as I had mixed the dough up a couple of days earlier and formed logs and put them in the refrigerator. It was the same recipe I used for my showstopper stained glass cookies. When I made those I rolled out the dough and used cookie cutters and mashed up hard candy to make them live up to their name. For CeeCee's, I just sliced them, sprinkled on some red sugar and baked them. Within a half an hour we were out the door with a plate of warm cookies minus a couple that Samuel had snatched.

I pulled the greenmobile to the side of the road in front of the wrought-iron fence surrounding CeeCee's property. I got the cookies and we went up to the intercom on one of the stone pillars on either side of the gate. In the old days, the gate was unlocked, but the price CeeCee paid for her renewed success was the need for security.

The pillars were beautifully decorated with pine fronds and red bows. Once we announced ourselves, the wrought-iron gate swung open and we walked onto a path lined with poinsettias. The pathway led through a small forest to the stone cottage–style house, which looked like something out of a fairy tale.

We heard the "girls," as she called her two Yorkies, before the door even opened. Once Talullah and Marlena got a whiff of the cookies, they ran over my feet and danced on their hind legs, looking up at the plate as I walked into the entrance hall. Two people were hanging more pine fronds on the archway that led into the living room. Even from the hall I could see the tree. It went up to the ceiling. Someone was on a ladder hanging the lights on it. For a moment I watched mesmerized. I knew celebrity-types hired people to decorate for the holidays, but it still seemed strange not to do it yourself.

CeeCee led us into the dining room, which seemed our usual place to meet. She'd already taken the plate of cookies from me and lifted the wax paper off the top. "Molly, these smell delicious." She had a cookie in her mouth before she set the plate on the table.

The housekeeper came in from the kitchen with a silver tray set up for tea and coffee. She put it on the table. "Rosa, will you get that Neiman's shopping bag on the service porch?" CeeCee said before taking another cookie and telling us to help ourselves to coffee and tea.

A moment later the woman returned and set the department store bag next to CeeCee.

The actress leaned toward us, not making a move toward the bag. "Okay, ladies, fess up. What's the big deal about this afghan?"

There was no point in lying, so I told her the truth. Or the reduced version. When I started at the beginning with Bradley disappearing and their argument about the crocheted piece, she waved her hand impatiently. "Too much information. Get to the point."

"I am sure there is something hidden in it."

"You know, dears, I played a guest spy in that TV show *Retail Espionage*. Of course, my character was only concerned about smuggling out the formula for a lipstick shade, but I learned a little about hiding things in plain sight." She took out the afghan and spread it on the end of the table and the three of us began to look it over.

Dinah fingered one of the white flowers that sat on top of the background. "I wonder how Madison did this?" She tugged at it to see if it had been sewn on, but it hadn't. "Somehow she crocheted it up from the green squares." I started to explain about surface crochet, but CeeCee interrupted me.

"Who cares how it was made?" CeeCee said, flipping though the tassel on one corner. "If I was going to stick in some microfilm, it would be here." She checked the two tassels hanging off another corner. When she came up empty she moved on to the next corner. "I think some of the tassels must have gotten knocked off in transit," she said, noting that corner only had one tassel and the other corners had none.

"Do you even know what microfilm looks like?" Dinah asked.

CeeCee glanced at the table and flicked off a crumb. "The script didn't exactly cover that," she said.

"Bradley isn't a spy anyway," I said.

"You have a point," CeeCee said. The three of us looked at the whole coverlet again, trying to figure out what could be hidden in it. Then we went over every inch and checked each flower, but in the end, we couldn't find anything.

"It really is pretty, but I think if I was making it, I'd drop the yellow flowers and just go with the violet, red and white ones," Dinah said. "And I think I'd space them better. It's kind of strange to have a bunch of flowers in one square and then none in the next one."

We stared at it until our eyes were blurry and all the cookies were gone.

"Molly, dear, no offense to your abilities as a sleuth, but maybe since her husband is dead and even with all the trouble he's caused, she really does want it for sentimental reasons." CeeCee mentioned her confused feeling when her husband died and she found out the financial mess she was in. She rolled up the coverlet and put it back in the bag. "Well, I don't want to keep you. I'm sure you have something you have to do," CeeCee said, walking us toward the door.

Dinah and I discussed the possibility of CeeCee being right about why Emily wanted the blanket as we drove to my house. The truth was we hadn't actually seen Bradley and the elf had only said a man talked to him. It could have been some other man. But who?

"Nicholas, maybe," Dinah said, mentioning the Luxe shop owner. "Remember she went there the day she told you Bradley was missing. Kind of an interesting time to go shopping for tea. And she was there again around the time Sheila dropped off the blankets."

I reminded her that she'd been returning things, trying to get cash. Dinah's red scarf blew across her face and she peeled it back. "Or so he said," she said as I pulled onto my street. "Until you see a living, breathing Bradley, you really can't be sure."

I stopped in front of my garage and got the afghan out of the shopping bag. There was no point in stalling its return. Dinah came along as we walked across my lawn and moved onto the Perkins' property. The Santa's sled had been knocked on its side and the half-done string of lights hung from the roof. It looked depressing and I wished she'd finish putting them up or put them away.

Emily ripped open the door before the bell even did its last chime. She glanced up and down the street and then at me. "Do you have it?" she said in a sharp whisper. In answer, I held out the Neiman's bag, but she pushed it back at me abruptly. "Not here."

She glanced past us toward the street and her eyes darted nervously. We started to turn our heads to see what she was looking at. "Don't turn around," she barked. "They're watching me."

"Who," I said, wishing I could turn to see if there was someone there or she was being paranoid.

"The FBI, the SEC, the state's attorney people. People who invested money with Bradley. Didn't you see the way they looked at me at the bookstore? Don't they get it—I'm a victim like everybody else. I'm hanging by a thread here. Any money I had is frozen until everything gets settled. And then they'll probably take it, saying it was ill-gotten gains. My credit cards are canceled. And everybody thinks I was part of Bradley's scheme."

We stood there a moment and I didn't know what to say since I'd sort of joined that last group. "Go home," she said in a impatient whisper, "and throw it over the fence into the backyard." She shut the door without waiting for a confirmation.

At least now I could check out the street as we walked back past the sideways Santa. Under the circumstances, I could see how she might not care about the decorations. The only vehicles on the street at this time of day were usually gardeners, pool cleaners and cleaning women, with an occasional plumber or pest-control truck thrown in. The assorted cars and vans seemed to fit those parameters. But were they what they seemed?

I watched a man sitting in one of the cars on the street. Was he eating his lunch or keeping an eye on Emily? I shuddered, thinking of being in her position.

Dinah and I went into my backyard. I knew just where to throw it over the fence, thanks to my adventure with Mason. I stepped up on the bench and leaned through the bushes to the chain-link fence. I took the bag and tossed it over. It landed with a *plop*. There were some rustling noises and I heard something that might have been "thank you" before receding footsteps and finally the sound of a sliding glass door closing.

"Now what?" Dinah said when I climbed down.

"Let's see what she does," I offered. Really what I meant was let's see if she goes anywhere. As if an answer, I heard the rumble of her garage door opening.

"C'mon," I said, running across the yard to the driveway. As soon as we got in the greenmobile, I backed down the driveway just far enough to see what was going on in hers. A moment later, Emily's SUV roared backward toward the street. She stopped and checked both ways before backing out. A moment later she was zooming away.

I didn't bother to look if anyone had pulled away from the curb. I just made the same move she had and took off after her. I was disappointed when I realized she was headed toward the few blocks of stores considered downtown Tarzana. She parked the SUV on the street next to the back parking lot behind the bookstore and the stores adjacent to it.

"Looks like we rushed for nothing," I said, pulling into the parking lot next to a car with a bike in a bike rack. Still, as soon as I'd stopped the motor, we jumped out and tried to catch up with her. "Geez," I said, "it really was for nothing." Ahead she'd just walked into the bookstore. We plastered ourselves against the wall and watched her through one of the big windows that faced the main street.

"The snowflakes look really nice from the outside," Dinah said. I stepped back to get a better view, then caught myself. We weren't there to admire the windows. Emily kept walking around, appearing to be looking at books, but every time she picked one up, she fluttered through the pages and replaced it. She spent about five minutes with the books and walked toward the door quickly. We tried to wish ourselves invisible as she came out of the bookstore.

If she saw us, she didn't seem to care. Her pace slowed and she walked down to Luxe.

"See, I told you," Dinah said, nudging me in the ribs. "She's got something going with him." We crept down the street, staying close to the buildings. When we got near Luxe's display window, we moved just far enough to look in. Emily was sitting by the waterfall, drinking a cup of tea. Every so often, she looked toward the counter where Nicholas was waiting on a customer. It was pretty clear after a couple of minutes that she wasn't going anywhere.

We slunk back to the bookstore. "There you are," Adele said, stopping us near the entrance. "Pink, someone wanted to buy some yarn as a gift. A knitter," Adele said, practically spitting out the word. "She wanted to see a knitted swatch, but there was nothing hanging on the bin. What's up with the swatches?"

I was impressed that Adele had actually waited on a knitter. I was always afraid if any came in while I wasn't there, Adele would ignore them until they left.

I explained that I wasn't really back to work, that I'd just stopped in. Adele's eye's narrowed. "What are you two up to? Some detective thing, Jessica Nancy Fletcher Holmes?" I didn't answer and she went on. "More about your neighbor?"

I said nothing and Adele stayed planted, saying she wanted to come with. She didn't even ask where we were going, she just wanted to be part of the action.

"Remember, we're musketeers," she said, referring again to a title she'd come up with during our last adventure. She started to pout but then saw that William had joined us and we were suddenly old news. I don't know what was harder to deal with, Adele trying to get in the middle of stuff or acting flirty with William as she explained to him the musketeer reference.

I told Adele there were some swatches in my tote bag in

the office, hoping she heard among all the eye batting and touching the lapel of his sports jacket. "I'll be back this evening," I said as Dinah and I headed for the door. Dinah's house was barely a block from the bookstore parking lot, and instead of going home, she'd suggested I come over. The area was called Walnut Acres because at one time it had been a walnut farm. One of the nutty trees still stood in Dinah's yard.

We walked around the corner off Ventura onto the side street. Emily's SUV was still parked where she'd left it. "Maybe I was wrong about everything," I said as we walked down the block almost completely past the parking lot. "Besides, what am I going to do—I can't keep trailing her." Instinctively I looked back toward the parking lot and the greenmobile, but something else caught my attention. Something moving. I elbowed Dinah and she watched with me. The back door of Luxe had opened and someone's head was sticking out and checking over the area.

"What the . . . My God, it's her," I said. Emily pulled the door shut behind her and sprinted across the parking lot. You didn't have to be a Mensa member to figure out she was headed for her Element.

"Where's your car?" I said. Dinah was already getting her keys out as we speed-walked across the small street toward her house.

Emily jumped in her SUV and made a sharp U-turn back toward us. Dinah's car was parked in the direction Emily was now going and a moment later we were inside the Honda with the motor running. Emily was already down the block when we took off after her. Even with the commonness of the car, we kept our distance so as not to be made, as the PIs called "being seen." I looked over at my friend as she hovered over the wheel, keeping the SUV in sight. Her smile was unmistakable. She was having a good time. I had to admit I was, too. Was it wrong to get caught up in the thrill of the chase when someone might be dead and lots of people had lost their money? I hoped not. We were on the side of good, I reminded myself.

The stop in the bookstore and Luxe must have been just to shake off anyone on her tail. I looked around to see if anyone was following us. There was just one car in the distance behind us that I figured was just traffic.

She had to be taking the crocheted piece to Bradley. I thought she would double back toward the freeway, thinking that she must have arranged to meet him in some crowded place again. Instead she zigzagged on side streets. When she got to the stop sign at Vanalden, I looked for her right turn signal to go on. Instead no turn signal flashed, but she turned anyway—onto Vanalden going left. She stayed on the street as it wound around and then began to go uphill. Ahead I could see the greenery on the side of the Santa Monica Mountains. The telephone poles marked the unpaved section of Mulholland that ran along the top.

She turned onto a side street that paralleled the mountain and zipped onto another steeper street. We stayed a safe distance behind her. The street was almost vertical and the houses were built on pads cut into the side of the hill. I knew where we were now.

"Park," I said to Dinah. I knew from coming up here before that the street dead-ended ahead. We waited a moment to see if the SUV would make an abrupt U-turn and head down the hill, but a few moments passed and it didn't drive by us. Dinah turned off the car and we got out and hid behind a bush. It was eerily quiet up here. For just a moment I looked back at the panoramic view of the Valley.

We peeked from behind the bush. The black SUV was

parked with its wheel curbed and Emily was just getting out. She pulled out a backpack, and as she slipped it on, I saw something green sticking out. She pushed the door shut and I heard the chirp of the lock as she was already walking toward the metal bumper and closed gate that marked the end of the street. She walked around the barrier and started up the sandy road.

I grabbed Dinah and we followed in Emily's footsteps. When my boys were young we came up here to walk and I was familiar with the area. The road Emily was on intersected with Dirt Mulholland, the name of the unpaved section of the road that ran from Encino to Woodland Hills. I knew once Emily reached Mulholland she could go left or right. The dirt road wound around the top of the mountains, and whichever way she chose, she'd disappear around a bend in moments and we'd have no idea which direction she'd gone.

The sky was overcast and the afternoon light was already beginning to fade. Damp cold air rose off the sandy road as we went up the hill. Emily neared the top and must have been confident she had eluded anyone following her because she never looked back. We'd stayed to the side of the road where we were less visible in case she turned around. Our clothes choices helped us blend in, too. We looked like the khaki twins in our slacks and similar-colored hoodies.

Emily paused a moment, probably to catch her breath after the steep walk.

"She went left," I whispered. Dinah was bent over, breathing heavily and swatting at a swarm of black flies. I worried that this might be too much for her, but she straightened and followed along up the rest of the way to Mulholland. We followed in the direction she'd gone even though the dip in the road had obscured her. She came back into view when we got a short way down the road.

We stayed back, hoping if she looked back she'd just think we were two walkers. It was never crowded up here, but today it seemed absolutely desolate.

There was a meadow on one side of us, though thanks to the winter rain, the grass had grown so tall it blocked any view of the Valley. On the other side of the road there was a large concrete pad. The ground around it had a scattering of green and then big stone boulders. I'd seen a helicopter land there once. I thought it was probably a staging area for fire trucks in the event of a forest fire. Either way, it seemed out of place in this area where everything else had been left to go natural. Ahead the ground rose on either side of the road and was covered with tall grasses, reedy bushes and low trees with thick foliage. Emily's footprints stood out in the damp sandy road.

When I looked around at all the wild growth, it was hard to imagine we were just minutes away from the traffic-clogged Ventura Boulevard. I heard a crunch behind us just before a mountain biker flew past.

"Usually, they at least call out some kind of warning, like 'on your right,'" I said, looking ahead at the figure on the bike as it whizzed toward Emily. The biker flew past her without even slowing and she was startled just as we'd been. She stopped and looked around.

I took Dinah's hand and pulled her into the growth on the side of the road before Emily saw us. When she started walking again, we went back on the road. My BlackBerry strained against my pocket and I took it out. It slithered from my hand and I made a fast save to grab it. There were so many gizmos on it, I knew I hit something by mistake.

When I looked up, Emily had turned off the road. We rushed ahead, trying to catch up.

We got to the spot where she'd disappeared, and an expanse of blacktop road ran up a steep hill next to a barbed-wire fence. Beyond it there was a huge water tank surrounded by a green lawn. The road looked like someone must have made plans that were long since forgotten. It ended abruptly at the edge of a cliff. Looking down, all you could see were mounds of green scrub and bushes that extended into the valley below. Beyond there were just more mountains. A white-tailed rabbit ran in front of us and disappeared in the brush. Where had Emily gone?

Some branches crackled and I turned toward the sound. In the distance, I saw that Emily had taken a path paralleling the cliff. We kept low as we followed her. The path was narrow and ran between bushes as tall as we were. She had picked up speed and we struggled to keep her in sight but not get too close.

She stopped next to a tree surrounded by a thicket of bushes. I pulled Dinah into the cover of a twiggy bush as someone stepped from inside the leafy tent.

"Bradley," I gasped. I spent some time just staring. After all the uncertainty if he was dead or alive, finally I was seeing him with my own eyes. He wore jeans and a leather jacket. His face looked florid, as if he'd been spending a lot of time outside. Emily rushed toward him and threw her arms around him.

Quickly my wonder at seeing a living, breathing Bradley turned to anger. Thanks to him the bookstore and my future were in jeopardy. People like that woman on the news had lost their life savings. All the nice stuff he'd done, like coach the girls' soccer team, had just been a way for him to get clients. He was a bad man and he shouldn't be able to walk away from what he'd done.

I still had the BlackBerry in my hand. But who to call? It was too convoluted a story to try to tell to a 911 dispatcher. Better to call Barry. I clicked on his number, but nothing happened. True we were only a few minutes from civilization, but there was no cell signal.

Dinah saw me fiddling with the phone and I showed her the screen. "We have to do something," she whispered.

"I have an idea," I said, holding up the BlackBerry. "I'll take some pictures of him. At least we'll have proof we saw him and I can send them to Barry."

I quickly took a number of photos before we slipped down the path and retraced our steps, checking my phone every few moments to see if I'd gotten service.

We were practically back to Dinah's car before I got a signal. As soon as I talked to Barry and sent the photos, despite his telling us to stay put, we rushed back toward where we'd seen Bradley.

"What are we going to do when we get there?" Dinah asked as we made our way back. "We can't make him stay there until the cops show up."

It turned out not to be a problem.

CHAPTER 20

WHEN WE GOT BACK TO OUR VANTAGE POINT, WE
looked over at the bushes and tree and the surrounding tall
grassy area. There was no Bradley and no Emily. The only
activity was a hawk flying overhead.

"Where'd they go?" I said, looking around. It was more
of a rhetorical question or at least that's how Dinah took
it and didn't answer. Brushing past sparse sage plants, we
kept moving closer until we ended up at the tree where
they'd been standing. The pungent-smelling bushes that
hugged the California oak formed an enclosure with an
opening at the front.

Dinah peeked in and pointed at the ground. "Look at
this." I looked over her shoulder. It was hard to see because
of the darkness, but there was a pile of dirt and a hole in
the ground.

"I wonder if there's anything in it?" I said. I was hopeful
Dinah would pick up on the question and offer to stick her

hand in. She didn't and I really wished I had the Pinchy-Winchy with me. The toy claw hand would have been perfect to stick down the hole. Finally curiosity overcame my concern over crawly and slithery things that might be in there and I knelt down and put my hand in. I'd reached all the way to my elbow before I hit the bottom. The dirt was cold and damp and empty. I sat back on my heels and examined the nearby area. The afternoon was fading and it seemed like the sun had come out just in time to go down. I noticed something dark in the tall grass. When I touched it, it felt slippery.

"It's a plastic garbage bag," Dinah said, bending next to me. We opened it with a fair amount of trepidation. Instead of reaching in, we decided to dump out the contents. We stood and I held the bottom at arm's length and shook. A couple of hundred-dollar bills fluttered out along with what looked like a small booklet. I gathered them off the ground where they'd fallen.

"It's a passport," I said, opening the booklet. The photo was Bradley, but the name was listed as Allen Richman. "I wonder what that's about." We stuck the money in the passport and kept examining the ground. Around the side of the tree we found a motorcycle helmet and a backpack. I opened the backpack and looked inside. A map of northern Mexico fell out. Below there just seemed to be some clothes and a bottle of water and some energy bars.

"I wonder why they left this stuff," Dinah said.

"And I wonder why we didn't pass them on Dirt Mulhol-land." I stood up and surveyed the area. The narrow path we'd been on continued up a hill. Dinah and I followed it up to the top, which was flat and mostly rocks with some short grass. From there we could see that the path contin-ued on down into a valley and roughly paralleled Dirt Mulholland. "I think that explains why we didn't see them," I said. The path was an alternative to the unpaved road and joined Mulholland in the vicinity of the short road we'd taken up from the street.

"Maybe we weren't as stealthy as we thought and they saw us," Dinah said. The hilltop gave a good view of the whole area. We could see the Dirt Mulholland as it passed the concrete pad, which from here seemed postage stamp–size, and continued on to the road that ran down to the street. Turning the other way, the water tank seemed far away and small, too. From here we got a different view of the area around the oak tree. As I looked down on it, my breath caught. There was something partially hidden by the wild growth.

I rushed down the narrow path so quickly I lost my footing and slid. Dinah came behind me and helped me get up. We pushed through the bushes and tall grass until we found what I'd seen. Bradley Perkins was sprawled on the ground. His pale blue tee shirt was spattered with blood and his eyes were wide open as if he'd been caught in surprise.

For a moment, I froze at the shock of the discovery. Then autopilot kicked in and I reached to touch his neck and check for a pulse. He was still warm.

I knelt down to get closer, but I didn't feel any sign of life. Dinah got down next to me as the reality began to sink in. I wanted to look away, but I felt compelled to do something. I had seen the new method of CPR on television. The directions were simple and there was no need to do mouth-to-mouth. I put my palms together and began to do the pumping motion on his breast bone. I tried for several minutes, but nothing was changing, and Dinah touched my arm.

"He's gone," she said.

I pulled away and looked at my hands. There was blood all over them, and I thought I was going to throw up. I started to frantically wipe my hands on my clothes.

"Whoever did this had to be very angry and able to get close to him," I said, noting the slashes in the shirt. I wasn't an expert, but they looked like they'd been made by a knife.

"Is there any doubt who did it?" Dinah said. "Emily was with him when we left and he was alive. We come back a little while later and he's dead." I couldn't deny her point.

Looking down his body, I saw a leather sheath hanging off his belt. The size and shape made it seem right for some kind of big knife. It was empty. Something about the sheath stirred a memory and I stared at it for a moment, but only a moment. The sound of a motor broke the quiet and I looked up as a helicopter approached. Within seconds it was overhead, circling low above us and I recognized the police markings. A voice over a loud speaker ordered us to step away from the body and put our hands on our heads.

Dinah and I looked at each other. "This doesn't look good for us, does it?" she said as we followed their orders.

I saw a cloud of dust when I looked back toward Dirt Mulholland. Traffic wasn't allowed on this section, but that didn't count cops. The tip of the black Crown Victoria showed as it stopped on the paved road near the water tank. A moment later, Barry came up the path, pushing through the twigs and foliage.

Barry must have walked into scenes like this countless times and kept his cool, but when he looked at me, he lost it.

"What happened? What did you do, try to stop him?" he said. He didn't wait for an answer. He went to check Bradley for a pulse. "Tell me you didn't do this," he said.

Dinah stepped in front of me. "What kind of question

is that? Are you out of your mind?" I calmed her down and said I could speak for myself.

"What kind of question is that? Are you out of your mind?" I said. "We came back here to keep an eye on him and this is what we found." Barry pointed at my hands and arms, which even with the wiping were still bloodstained. I explained the CPR.

Barry kept shaking his head.

Apparently the cops in the helicopter had called for the paramedics and backup. All of them stirred up the dirt road and pulled near the Crown Vic. Barry pulled us back as the paramedics checked over Bradley and a couple of uniforms took out yellow tape and started to wind it around a big perimeter. I looked back to where Bradley was sprawled and tried to make a mental note of as much as possible. One of the uniforms gave me an odd look. I recognized Officer James. He rocked his head from side to side. "What's with you and crime scenes?"

He'd been the one to find me standing over a body once before. "Don't say it," I said, cringing, but he did anyway.

"It's like you're some kind of crime-scene groupie." If Barry heard, he ignored it.

"I guess you know I won't be getting this case," Barry said. I nodded in understanding. He couldn't investigate anything where he knew someone who was involved.

He held on to both Dinah's and my arm. Partly it was for support since we were both rubber kneed and partly it was to move us away from the area. He led us back to the short expanse of paved road where all the cops had parked. "Okay, you two, stay put." He separated us and told us to wait to be questioned as if I didn't know the drill.

The police helicopter kept circling and was soon joined by news helicopters that stationed themselves in hover mode.

It was almost twilight now. I heard a uniform say something about sifting through the area looking for the murder weapon. Sift through the area? I glanced around. We were in the mountains with a cliff that led to green mounds of scrub oaks as far as the eye could see. I hoped they had a lifetime.

I had my fingers crossed on who would be doing the questioning, or more who I hoped wouldn't be doing it. It turned out to be a waste of twisted fingers. Detective Heather Gilmore got out of another Crown Vic and went to talk to one of the officers.

I called her Detective Heather in my head or when I was talking to Dinah about her. If there was a Barbie the homicide detective, she'd look like Detective Heather. We had a bit of a history. She'd questioned me a few times before when I had gotten in the middle of murders. The rest of our history had to do with Barry. She had wanted him and was annoyed that I had him. During the time Barry and I were broken up, they'd gone out enough times for him to figure that even with her hot body and hot looks, she wasn't for him. Did I mention she was really smart, too? She seemed to have come to terms with the fact that there was going to be nothing between them.

"Not you again," Detective Heather said, walking toward me. Her curve-hugging dark blue suit and heels seemed at odds with the surroundings. Barry had been hanging around, but when she arrived, he had left.

Detective Heather asked for my information as if she'd never heard it all before. It was only when she got to my age that she volunteered anything. "You're fifty, right?" she said, pen poised.

"No," I said, "not until next year." I knew it was her chance to make me feel old next to her late thirties. I thought she'd gotten over Barry, but maybe not.

"So, tell me what happened," she said, flipping her notebook to a new page. I glanced over to where her partner was talking to Dinah, who seemed very agitated and was pointing at her watch. The sky was translucent blue now and there was just a trace of lavender and pink near the horizon. In the distance coyotes were howling, announcing their dinnertime. It had been chilly to start with, but now was downright cold. I was glad for my sweatshirt hoodie, but could have done with a down vest over it. Some cops went by carrying big lights to set up around the crime scene.

I gave her all the basic information about who Bradley was. She looked at my arms and pants. "Thanks, but let's hear how you ended up with blood all over you."

I mentioned how it had seemed like Bradley was dead, then it seemed like he was alive, then dead again. "I was back to thinking he was alive and I thought his wife was meeting him."

"What made you think his wife was going to meet him?"

I was dreading this part, but I plowed ahead anyway and told her about the afghan. I even offered to show her the photos I'd taken of Bradley holding the afghan. Unfortunately I clicked the wrong thing and a photo of Holstein appeared. Detective Heather didn't seem amused.

In the midst of it I stopped as I remembered the passport and the cash. Without thinking, I'd stuck it in the back pocket of my khakis. I pulled it out and handed it to her. To say the look she gave me was hopeless was an understatement. "Tampering with evidence," she said as she made a note.

I didn't wait for her to ask but offered to be fingerprinted and give up a sample of my hair so they could eliminate them.

Detective Heather wanted to know about Emily, but she

made sure to tell me I was still a person of interest. It didn't matter that I pointed out I had no motive.

Down the way, Dinah finished with her questioner and, seeming agitated, took off. A uniform came over and said my friend apologized for leaving, but she had to pick up some kids.

"If the wife left, why didn't you pass her on the road?" Detective Heather said.

I pointed out the other path. "You should check to see if her SUV is still parked on the street." I described the location and the stickers on the back window. Detective Heather seemed less than pleased with me telling her what to do. She paused for a beat, then like it was her idea, took out her cell phone and punched in a number. Lucky her, she got a signal. She turned to me. "What kind of car is it? You don't happen to know the license number?" I told her what I knew and she relayed the information.

"Well?" I said when she hung up.

"No black Element is parked on the street." She began to ask me more questions about Emily. No matter what she'd said about me being a person of interest, it was obvious she'd now decided Emily was the guy.

The lab people arrived and started processing the crime scene. I gave my samples and I was free to leave. There was only one problem. Dinah was my ride. Detective Heather was heading for her car. I had a pretty good idea where she was headed. I swallowed my pride and asked for a lift.

She hesitated, but finally agreed and I followed her to the car. She let me out in front of my house before she pulled in front of the Perkins' house. Ryder was walking down the street but stopped when he saw me. The look on his face, and the way he picked up his camera when he saw me, made me look down. It was the first time I noticed the front of my white shirt was splattered with blood. Ryder saw me checking out my shirt and gestured toward my pants. Blood was smeared around the pockets and the front had dirt and grass stains. He nodded toward my hair and I put my hands up to feel it. I could tell it was messy and clumped together. He made a face and I figured there was blood in my hair, too. I must look like an escapee from a horror movie. Now I understood Barry's reaction.

Ryder didn't let up until I'd given him all the details. We stood at the end of my driveway and watched as Detective Heather walked up to the Perkins' front door. I could only see body language as Emily stepped outside. The news about Bradley wasn't something you said on the front porch, but Emily didn't seem to want to invite her in.

As I was watching the scene, something surfaced in my mind. When Dinah and I had looked at all of Bradley's things, there was something we hadn't seen. Where was the afghan?

CHAPTER 21

"SO, YOU FINALLY SHOWED UP." ADELE CAUGHT
me at the door when I finally got to the bookstore. I'd taken
a long hot shower and scrubbed away any traces of blood,
but I couldn't scrub away the image of leaning over Bradley
Perkins. Barry had said the first dead body you encountered
was the worst, implying it got easier as you went along. I
hadn't planned on ever seeing another body after my first
one, but that wasn't how it worked out. I could speak from
experience: It didn't get easier, and if I saw a hundred, I'd
never get immune. I'd taken my clothes, even the things
that had no sign of blood, and put them all in a trash bag. I
was glad for the cheerful atmosphere of Shedd & Royal and
the sense of normalcy.

Adele trailed along behind me, reminding me again how
late I was and how she'd had to stay and cover for me even
though she had plans. As self-absorbed as she was, she noticed I seemed a little off.

"Pink, what's up?" I muttered something about needing to talk to Mrs. Shedd. I felt obligated to tell her what happened. Adele pointed toward the table we'd set up for gift wrap. Mrs. Shedd was talking to some customers while she tore off a sheet of decorated paper. I had to give her credit for keeping her spirits up, despite her loss, and joining us down in the trenches for the holidays. She cashiered, helped customers find books and now was even wrapping them.

I waited until she handed the gift item back to the customer and they'd walked away before approaching her. Adele was still trailing me. "I need to talk to you," I said.

"It's okay, you can go now," Mrs. Shedd said to Adele. "I know you have plans."

Adele leaned against the best-seller table in a leisurely manner. "It doesn't matter now. My boyfriend called and said he can't make dinner." Inside I was groaning. So her comment must have been to hassle me. What else was new?

I told Mrs. Shedd maybe we ought to go in the office. It didn't seem like a good idea to tell her about my afternoon where anyone might hear. Adele tagged along as we went to the room in the back. "It has to do with your sleuthing stuff, doesn't it?" Adele said. She fingered one of the yarn candy canes hanging on her necklace. "Since I almost went along, I ought to hear what happened, too."

"Is it about Bradley Perkins?" Mrs. Shedd asked. "I told Joshua all about handing over the money to Bradley." She looked down and added she'd mentioned using the bookstore's line of credit, too.

I swallowed and told Mrs. Shedd that I knew for sure that Bradley's suicide had been a fake and I'd seen him alive. Her eyes brightened, but only for a moment. Once I told her the rest of it, her face fell.

"How awful for you," she said. Then she sighed. "Well, I

suppose that really closes the door on the whole situation."
She explained Mr. Royal had convinced her she ought to
go to the SEC investigators and show them her paperwork
in the event they did recover any of the money. "Joshua
was very understanding. He said, thick or thin, we were
in it together," she said. Just mentioning Mr. Royal's name
brought a flush to her face. I was glad that she'd straightened things out with him since there seemed to be a strong
bond between them.

"It sounds like a pretty open-and-shut case that his wife
did it," Mrs. Shedd said.

"No question that Detective Hea—Gilmore thinks she's
the guy. But I'm not completely sure. Maybe it's because I
know her, but I just can't imagine her stabbing him. There
must be a lot of people angry enough to kill him." I prepared to offer a list, but Adele cut me off.

"Nancy Sherlock Fletcher Drew, I think you're losing your
touch." Adele gave me a disparaging look. "You said yourself
that it was empty up there except for the four of you. It wasn't
you or Dinah, was it? That leaves the wife."

Mrs. Shedd ended the line of conversation by saying she
appreciated what I'd done, but at this point, who did what
to Bradley wasn't my responsibility anyway. She opened the
door. "We need to focus on the Anthony launch party. It's
probably going to be the biggest event in the bookstore's
history. The eyes of the world will be on us, ladies. Whatever happens after, let's make this a shining moment for
Shedd and Royal Books and More. Not to mention helping
our holiday shoppers in the meantime." She waved us back
into the main part of the store.

The store was busy for a night with no event. Forcing myself to shut out all thoughts of what I had witnessed, I paused
and surveyed the main area. The two young men hired for

the holidays were at the help table aiding customers. Ray-aad was at her station at the cashier stand. In addition to the young men, Mrs. Shedd had hired Rayaad's older daughter and she was manning a second cashier stand. The café alcove was busy, too. I looked over the customers. "Isn't Mr. Royal here?" I said to Adele before she went to the kids' department.

She turned back just long enough to say, "He left around the same time you did this afternoon. I don't know where he was going. Nobody tells me anything."

I supposed Mr. Royal was entitled to some time off. Besides it was none of my business.

The exhausted feeling I had from the afternoon's events began to go away and I got a second wind. I was glad to occupy my mind with looking over the list of news people covering the vampire book launch. The local TV stations, CNN and all the entertainment shows were supposed to be sending someone to cover the midnight signing of *Caught Under the Mistletoe, Blood and Yarn #3*. I knew it was all theater, but I loved the drama of it all. And I couldn't wait to find out if William really was A. J. Kowalski. I still needed to get some confirmations, but it was too late in the day now, so I set the folder away and checked to see if any customers needed help.

Everyone seemed to be doing okay, so I went back to the yarn department. I'd finally gotten the owl's head right and wanted to start the body, but the swatches were work related. I took out the knitting needles and a ball of red mohair and started casting on. I was getting a little better at it. Once I had enough stitches I began to knit. I was using large needles and the rows came out loose and lacy.

"When did you start knitting?" Detective Heather said, walking into the yarn department. She stopped at the table and fingered my work.

I mentioned my being in charge of the department and our intention of having swatches on all the bins. I put down my work and offered to help her with yarn. Not that I thought shopping was the real reason she was here. I was right. She'd barely picked up a skein of multicolored sock yarn before she brought up Bradley.

"You haven't decided that I'm the guy, have you?" I said.

"No, Molly. I don't see you as the stabbing type. You're too wishy-washy. Stabbing takes decisive action. You'd think about it too long."

I wasn't sure if I should thank her or not, but I was glad not to be a suspect. Been there, done that and didn't like it.

"Your neighbor brought up an afghan," Detective Heather said, hesitantly. Her manner instantly got my attention since it was not her usual assertive self. I got it. She felt awkward bringing up the afghan after she'd practically laughed at me when I'd told her about it when she was questioning me.

"Did Emily Perkins tell you what was so important about it?" I said.

"I'll ask the questions," she said curtly. "You saw her giving it to him?"

I thought back to watching them and remembered the photos on the BlackBerry. I pulled it out and flitted through them. "Here," I said, holding it out. I think Detective Heather was expecting another cat picture by mistake and barely glanced at it. But her eyes moved back and stayed on the small pictures. She took the BlackBerry and held the screen closer.

I had captured the moment when Emily handed Bradley the backpack. After the last time, I suppose he wasn't taking any chances. I told her to scroll forward. The next pictures showed Bradley holding up the unfolded afghan.

"That's what the fuss is about," she said, disappointed. On the small screen the flowers didn't show up well.

"It's much prettier in person."

Detective Heather rolled her eyes at me. For a moment I thought she wasn't going to give the BlackBerry back, saying it was evidence, but she gave it back and told me to e-mail her the photos. She stood over me while I did it. Her presence was making me tense and I was glad that I didn't screw it up.

"I'm sure you noticed that both the backpack and afghan were missing," I said. Her answer was a withering sigh.

"I think Emily Perkins took them with her. The backpack and afghan must have traces of her DNA, and after she stabbed him, probably his blood." The detective looked at me to see if I was following what she said.

"Right, so they would tie her to the crime," I said. Detective Heather walked around the yarn department.

"I can't believe I'm actually asking for your help, but I really need to find that backpack and afghan. The murder weapon would help, too," she muttered. "She let me look around her place, which makes me think she knew I wouldn't find anything. Any ideas?"

We threw ideas back and forth for a moment. I suggested she might have thrown the knife by the side of the road or in a trash can. But Detective Heather nixed the idea. "I don't think she'd take the chance of dumping it. I think she has it stashed somewhere. Keep your eyes open."

She had stopped in front of a bin of rust-colored mohair. She picked up a skein and turned it around in her hand.

"That color would look good on you," I said. She turned toward me and seemed surprised. My comment was personal—girlfriendish—and all of our dealings had always been on the adversarial side. For a moment she let down her guard and held the skein up near her face.

"You really think so?" I nodded and she gathered two more skeins.

"There's a lot of tension in my job and knitting helps." She caught herself and went back into professional mode and finished up our interview. After she left, I saw her take the yarn up to the cashier stand. The color really did look good on her.

Even though it was late when I left the bookstore, I went over to Dinah's. I was pretty sure the news media was parked in front of the Perkins' now that he was dead. I wasn't up for dealing with trying to sneak past them. Besides I needed to sort out everything that had happened.

I expected Dinah was having some kind of aftermath from the day, too. I knew I was right as soon as she opened the door. She had a frozen, stunned look on her face. I hadn't realized it until now, but this was her first body.

We hugged each other and just stood there for a few moments. Then we collapsed on her couch and leaned against each other for support. With the kids there, she'd decorated and the house seemed festive with the lighted tree. The kids had made another chain from construction paper and it hung over the windows. The usually clear dining room table had crayons and art supplies spread over the top. There was a foam dreidel and a jar of gold glitter. For a moment I forgot my heavy heart and thought back to the fun of making holiday decorations with kids.

"It didn't hit me at first," Dinah said. "I just kept going through the motions. I picked up the kids and apologized for being late. I ordered pizza and let them watch a video. Somewhere around then I started to fall apart. I kept seeing

Bradley lying there." She shook her head as if trying to get rid of the image.

I told her about Detective Heather's little visit. "She's decided Emily Perkins is the guy," I said.

"Well, she is, isn't she? We saw her with him. And then he was dead." Dinah said.

"I agree she had motive. The man left her with a mess. And she had means. His knife provided that. And as for opportunity, she get's points for that, too."

Dinah noticed me hesitating. "But you don't think it was her, do you?"

"I agree all arrows point to her, but I don't want it to be her," I said.

Dinah got it. I had helped Emily get the afghan. If she had killed him, I was somehow involved. "If Emily didn't kill him, then who did?" Dinah said, bringing up the obvious question.

I had been thinking about it. "There's no shortage of people angry enough to want to do him in. The very top of the list is Logan Belmont. He not only lost his money but his reputation as well. Nicholas said he'd lost some money. He didn't seem that upset, but it could have just been a cover. And what about Bradley's sister? Who knows what's going on with her. And you could throw in a bunch of other people." I mentioned the woman on the news who'd lost her life savings.

"Okay, but you might have noticed there was no one up there but the four of us," Dinah said.

I thought a moment and was about to say she had a point when I remembered something. "There was someone else," I said excitedly. Dinah seemed surprised and wanted to know who. "I forgot all about it until now. Remember the person on a mountain bike who rode past us?" I said.

Dinah processed the information and her face lit up with recognition. "You're right. Was it a man or a woman?"

I admitted I hadn't really noticed. They'd been moving fast and from the back all I remembered was a helmet and dark clothes. We discussed the fact that the biker had seemed to have gone past us, but we realized they could have left the road ahead and doubled back on a trail without us seeing them. "Suppose they waited until we left, and Emily left and then made their move?" I said. Dinah nodded in agreement. I commented that it was pointless to mention any of this to Detective Heather. She had settled on Emily being the killer and nothing was going to change her mind.

"All Detective Heather cares about is gathering evidence and building a case against Emily. I bet she keeps working on her, trying to get her to confess," I said. Dinah agreed and said something about Detective Heather being relentless.

I mentioned the girlfriend moment with Detective Heather and Dinah chuckled. I got up to leave. "It's been a killer day," I said.

"You can say that again." Dinah stood and walked me to the door. She seemed to have something else on her mind. Dinah was a direct person; that was how she dealt with her students, by just confronting the problem and telling them to knock it off. Her hesitancy to speak seemed odd. Finally she sighed.

"I don't think it's going to work out with Commander." She sounded wistful. I shut the door and we sat down again and I asked what the problem was.

"He was supposed to come over tonight. It wouldn't have been the best night anyway, but he canceled. He can't seem to understand why I am involved with my ex-husband's kids with another woman." Dinah leaned back and looked at her hands. "Who their parents are isn't the point anymore. I care about the kids for themselves." Dinah left the rest hanging, but I knew what she was thinking. We weren't teenage girls anymore, where you dumped anything or anyone that got in the way of your boyfriend. No more pretending to like anchovy pizza, even if it made you gag, just because he did. No more changing to suit someone else. "Maybe he'll come around," I said. I had an idea and presented it to her. "What about this?" I said. "Maybe he's upset because he feels like he's getting pushed off to the side. Why don't I babysit for you one evening and you go out with Commander—just the two of you."

My friend's face brightened as she accepted my offer and I finally left. All the way home I kept thinking about Emily and Bradley. Everything did point toward her being the murderer, didn't it?

CHAPTER 22

STOPPING AT DINAH'S HAD ONLY PUT OFF THE INevitable. No quiet street tonight. The news vans were out in force and a clog of people were in the street in front of the Perkins' house. As I got closer I saw the lights trained on each of the reporters. Obviously Bradley's death had hit the news and they were preparing for live reports for the late broadcast. As I pulled in my driveway, the attention turned in my direction and I saw several of the reporters rush over. I drove up quickly and parked in the garage, ending their pursuit. Ryder was probably out there in the midst of all the excitement.

It was a relief to get inside. The dogs made a fast trip outside before I called them in and fed them. The light was flashing on my phone, and when I checked, there were messages from Barry and Mason. Both messages were pretty much the same—they'd called my cell and I hadn't answered. Please call.

I was talked out, exhausted and worn down from my day. I needed a little peace before I was ready to talk to anybody—even Barry and Mason. The phone rang and I thought about not answering it but finally gave in. Emily sounded frantic when I answered.

"I need to talk to you," she said. "Some homicide detective thinks I killed Bradley. It's nonsense. Of course I didn't do it." She let out a yelp of consternation. "Those reporters keep ringing the bell. Can't they leave me alone?"

I didn't know what to say. It wasn't just Detective Heather who thought she'd killed Bradley. Everyone I'd talked to thought she was the guy. Even though I'd expressed some doubts, it was hard for me to believe it was anyone else. Did I want to invite a possible murderer over, particularly since it was because of me that Detective Heather knew that she'd been up there with Bradley? His body might not have been found for days. In other words she might have a grudge against me. And if you've killed one person . . .

I told her I was sorry for all of her trouble, but right now was a bad time. Maybe tomorrow. I figured by then I'd have thought of some way out of it. She breathed heavily a few times and clearly wasn't pleased with my answer and hung up.

I made myself a cup of camomile tea and the sweet flowery scent filled the air as I took it to the kitchen table. It was supposed to be relaxing and I hoped it would work its magic. I took a sip and closed my eyes. I hadn't realized how hunched my shoulders were and I made a conscious effort to lower them. Just when I was beginning to feel a little better, I heard someone pounding on the window of the back door. When I looked up, Emily was looking in on me. Before I had a chance to think of what to do, the door pushed open and she came inside.

Her eyes had a crazed look and I swallowed hard, glancing around the kitchen. The block with the knives was on the counter in plain sight.

I mumbled something about wondering how she'd gotten past all the reporters. She stood in front of the large windows facing my backyard and pointed toward the white bench Mason and I had used to climb over. She'd noticed me standing on it when I'd thrown the afghan over the fence. She'd been able to step on her hose holder and then hold on to the shed in her yard while she stepped over the fence and onto the bench. She'd done exactly what Mason and I had in reverse. I suddenly felt very alone in the big house. Blondie had gone back to her chair. Only Cosmo had responded to the sound of the door opening. He seemed confused. He knew her, but something about the way she was acting seemed strange. The small black dog sat down across the kitchen and watched her.

I jumped up from the table, wanting to put some space between me and Emily. I grabbed the broom and started sweeping the floor, thinking of its potential as a weapon.

"I need to talk to you," she said. Her short choppy breath was a sure sign of anxiety.

"What about your girls? You didn't leave them home alone?" I said. She took a step closer to me and said Bradley's sister, Madison, was with them next door.

"I was trying to figure out how that police detective even knew I was with Bradley. I was so careful to make sure none of the people investigating Bradley's business followed me, I knew it couldn't be any of them. Then I realized it was right after you'd given me the afghan. It was you, wasn't it?" Emily looked at me intently.

I clutched the broom a little tighter. It didn't matter that I didn't answer, she repeated that it was me.

My heart was pounding and I considered what to do. She started talking, the words tumbling out of her mouth.

She had believed the suicide note and thought Bradley was dead until the night I'd seen the motorcycle. "I heard some noise, and when I went out in the driveway, Bradley was coming out of the bushes. He didn't see me at first and I'm pretty sure he would have just gotten on the motorcycle and left if I hadn't moved, triggering the motion-sensor light. As soon as he heard the police helicopter in the distance, he begged me to hide the motorcycle and him.

"He admitted he'd gambled away all the investors' money. All his supposed business trips to Vegas weren't to see clients. He kept thinking he'd win it back." She looked disgusted. "Like that ever happens."

Someone had complained to the Securities and Exchange Commission and Bradley knew that once they looked at his books, they'd figure out what he'd done. "He said he wasn't going to go to prison," she said. He told her the fake suicide had been a hasty plan. Mason and I had been right. Bradley had put a newly purchased motorcycle in the back of the SUV. He parked the Suburban in the Long Beach Terminal parking lot and put the motorcycle in the spot next to it. He used a credit card to buy a one-way ticket on the Catalina Express. Midway on the trip he planted his wallet and cell phone on a bench. It's a slow time of year and there were plenty of empty spots on the boat so nobody noticed what he did. Just before the boat reached Catalina, he alerted a crew member about the wallet and phone. "I didn't recognize him in the crowd getting off the boat because he put on a thick coat and a baseball cap," Emily said.

She explained that he'd merely bought a return ticket with cash, gone back to Long Beach and left on the motorcycle. He'd dropped the suicide letter in the mail. His plan was to ride across the border into Mexico and disappear. "He said it was better for me if I thought he was dead."

"Why'd he come back?" I asked.

"It was for his watch and the afghan. With all that he'd done, who would figure that he was sentimental. He said it wasn't about the value of the Rolex Bond watch, but because his father had given it to him. His sister had made the afghan for him. I didn't have either. The watch was still at the shop for cleaning and I had given you the afghan. He insisted he had to have them. He had kept some traveling money and if I could get those items for him, he'd share some of the money." Emily tried to read my face to see if I was judging her. "I was up against a wall. Everything was frozen or canceled. I have children," she wailed. Getting the watch had been no problem, but after telling me that she didn't like the afghan and never wanted to see it again, she thought it would look suspicious if she asked for it back. Since she just thought he wanted it as something from his sister, she had asked her to make another one for Bradley. There wasn't a lot of time and Madison had whipped up something on a big hook with bulky yarn.

By now Madison knew what her brother had done, but when she heard how he felt about the afghan, she wanted to see him one last time.

Emily detailed the convoluted plan to meet Bradley, and how she'd given him the two items. I asked why she didn't turn him in.

"He was my husband and I loved him," she said as if it was an of course. "Bradley assured me that once they got investigating they'd realize I had nothing to do with any of it and leave me alone."

Then everything had gotten weird. "He hadn't looked at the afghan until after we left. He called and yelled that he didn't just want an afghan his sister made, he had to have the original one. I told him it was gone and I couldn't get it. But he kept calling me and started offering more and more money for it and I was feeling desperate."

I was feeling a little desperate myself. It had been my experience that when people did a whole lot of confessing like this, they planned to kill you. I clutched the broom tighter, ready to start swatting.

She kept on talking, describing how she and Bradley used to walk in the mountains and he'd arranged for them to meet at a familiar spot. He'd checked the afghan that time, and when it was the right one, he'd handed over the promised money. She slouched in despair. "That police detective kept hammering away at me. 'You'll feel better if you tell the truth. Just tell me what happened and we can work something out.' On and on," Emily said, getting agitated. She walked to the counter. I knew what was coming next. Any second she'd start telling me she had killed Bradley and all the reasons why. Then she'd say she was really sorry, but now that I knew, she'd have to get rid of me, and she'd grab one of my knives and stab me. But I was ready for her. I'd clock her with the broom as soon as her hand even got near a knife.

She was looking down at the counter and I had come up behind her and raised the broom, ready to strike. The back door made a noise as it opened and Emily turned toward it just as Mason came in, fussing about me not returning calls. She took in my raised broom and her mouth fell open. "Are you crazy?" she yelled as she pushed past me and Mason and took off without a word. She rushed across the yard, jumped on the bench and launched herself over the fence.

"Was it something I said?" Mason said, deadpan.

I didn't react to Mason's comment. I was a little zoned

out by what had just happened. I'd been so geared up for Emily to make a move, it seemed anticlimactic that she'd run off. Finally Mason waved his hand in front of my face to get my attention and asked what had just happened.

"I'm not sure," I said. I started to tell him everything about Bradley from the beginning, but he already knew.

"That's why I'm here," he said. "Greenberg got in touch with me. He was worried you might need a lawyer. Something about you being found hovering over Perkins' body, covered in his blood. I left you a bunch of messages." I still had the broom poised for action and Mason took it out of my hands and put it in the corner.

"Detective Heather said I was a person of interest, but I think that was just to bug me. She seems to have focused on Emily being the killer." I shuddered when I said that, thinking she'd been in my kitchen with close access to knives a few minutes ago. Still there was something that didn't seem right. I'd noticed it when she was running across my yard. I mentioned to Mason that she had on the same clothes she had on in the photos. "If she'd stabbed Bradley, you'd think she would have gotten blood on her clothes or been worried that she had and she would have changed them," I said.

"It's too bad the detective didn't arrest her," Mason said, glancing out the window toward the fence. "I don't like leaving you here. Come to my place." When I looked askance, he quickly added there was no hidden agenda in his offer.

I assured him I'd be okay, though I still startled when I heard a key in the front door lock. Samuel came into the kitchen a moment later. He'd been picking up a lot of work at holiday parties and I'd barely seen him even though we were sharing the same roof. He nodded at Mason and asked why there was a media frenzy going on out front. I was glad to let Mason tell the story since I'd repeated it so many times. Samuel's eyes widened at what he was hearing and then he seemed upset.

"Mother, are you nuts?" Samuel said, before launching into a lecture about me staying out of trouble. Mason offered to stay, but Samuel said it wasn't necessary. Nobody listened to me when I said I thought I might have been wrong about Emily's intent, now that I'd realized the thing about her clothes.

"Please take care of your mother," Mason said. "And for God's sake, Molly, keep your doors locked."

After all that had happened, I expected to have a hard time sleeping but surprised myself by falling into a deep sleep. True I had a lot of strange dreams, but by morning I felt normal. It was a little creepy at how well I was adjusting to finding dead bodies and possibly being threatened by neighbors.

Even with the holidays, the Hookers had decided to keep our regular crochet sessions. After everything with Bradley, the cops and Emily, I really needed a little crochet and talk time right now.

Most of the group was already assembled at the table when I got to the bookstore. I almost laughed when I got toward the back and saw what everyone was working on. Adele, CeeCee, Sheila, Eduardo and even Rhoda were making vampire scarves. Elise had returned to the group and was displaying her finished scarf on the table. I picked it up and looked it over. I had to give her credit, everything about it did say vampire.

Dinah came in from the café with the kids in tow. When they got to the table, Ashley-Angela and E. Conner sat down near Adele. In keeping with her seasonal attire, Adele had worn the sweater with all the holiday symbols hanging off. The kids were as entranced this time as when they'd seen it first in the car. I was afraid of a scene and went to move them away from her before they started touching the sweater and she went berserk. I wasn't fast enough and Ashley-Angela touched the dreidel near Adele's shoulder.

"We're making our own dreidels," the little girl said. "Only ours are going to have glitter."

Adele twisted her head to see what Ashley-Angela was looking at. "I bet yours aren't crocheted," Adele said.

The little girl shook her head so her curls bobbled around. "I don't know how to crochet. Aunt Dinah said she'll teach me someday. I don't know when someday is."

Adele did one of her grand gestures and threw her head back in disbelief at the comment.

She pulled out a hook and some cotton yarn from her bag and offered it to Ashley-Angela, along with a lesson on how to crochet. Okay, the rest of the table was all watching with their mouths open. Adele never ceased to surprise. E. Conner watched for a while then pulled out the coloring he'd brought along.

I took out the owl head and glanced at the pattern. I picked up some black yarn with a sparkle in it and connected it to the finished head and began to work on the body.

When Elise looked up, I gave her a reassuring nod. I was glad she had rejoined the group.

"What's with this neighbor of yours, Bradley Perkins? He's dead, he's not dead, he's really dead," Rhoda said to me. "I saw on the news they found his body up in the mountains. I think even that Kimberly Wang Diaz called it a strange case with twists and turns." Elise looked up at the comment. Her face seemed to tighten and she glanced around to see if anyone was staring at her.

"They're saying his wife did it," Rhoda continued. "You know her, don't you, Molly?"

I nodded in acknowledgment and then explained why I wasn't so sure she'd done it. All eyes were on me, particularly Dinah's. Adele stopped with her lesson and got in the middle of the conversation.

"Okay, Sherlock Fletcher, then who did it?" Adele informed the table that Dinah and I had been following Emily when she went to meet her husband.

CeeCee seemed troubled. "Why were you following her?"

"You certainly get in the middle of things, Molly," Eduardo said.

It was obvious at this point that there was a gap in information. If we were going to talk about it, it made no sense not to share the whole story so we'd all be on the same page.

"Good for you for trying to trap him," Elise said when I'd gotten to the end.

"It's kind of beside the point now," CeeCee said. "The man's dead."

"Maybe somebody else saw Emily coming out of Luxe and followed her, too," Sheila said.

"Yeah, like Nicholas. It's his store so he must have known what she was doing," Rhoda offered.

"Nicholas wouldn't do anything like kill somebody," Sheila said. Her comment got everyone's attention.

"I didn't know you were so chummy with him, dear," CeeCee said.

Sheila stumbled over her words. She wasn't chummy with him, but she'd been selling her blankets and other accessories in his store for a while and she thought that gave her some insight into him.

"Nicholas lost some money with the Perkins guy?" Eduardo said.

I said he appeared not to be that upset by it, but several other people threw out comments that it might have been an act. "Someone could have overheard me," I said. "The bookstore was crowded. I thought I kept my voice down, but who knows?"

"What did the person on the mountain bike look like, Pink? Isn't that the most obvious question?" Adele said.

"We didn't get a good look. Whoever it was flew past us," Dinah said, finally joining in. "They flew past Emily, too."

Rhoda threw out a question about the bike. Did we know what it looked like or at least what color it was? Both Dinah and I had noticed only that it had wheels.

"If you want to know about mountain bikes, you can ask Logan. He knows all about them. He goes riding up in the mountains all the time," Elise said. She didn't seem to have any sense about what she'd just said. Everyone focused on her and I knew what they were thinking. If you wanted a suspect, Logan was a good choice. He'd lost money, his reputation and probably a lot of his real estate business. The implication of what she'd said finally sunk in and Elise looked horrified. "It couldn't have been him. He wouldn't do anything like that. Besides, he was . . ." Her voice trailed off and then she muttered something about her being at Christmas bazaar all afternoon. She cut herself off abruptly.

Suddenly the big question was where had Logan been yesterday afternoon?

CHAPTER 23

DINAH AND I DIDN'T EVEN HAVE TO SAY IT; AS
soon as the group broke up, we checked the bookstore café
for Logan. When he wasn't there, we headed to Le Grande
Fromage. Though I wondered if Logan would still be using
a table as his portable office. Those two men had been pretty
hostile to him and I was sure there must be others just as
angry. I wanted to get there quickly, before Elise warned
him to come up with an alibi. She'd rushed off to a hair ap-
pointment, so there was a chance she hadn't talked to him.

The sun was burning off the clouds and shining in the
window of the French café. The fragrant wreath wrapped
in tiny white lights made it seem festive. The lunch crowd
was clogging the place and the line at the counter went all
the way to the back of the restaurant and blocked my view
of the tables.

Dinah was trying to keep the kids from getting jostled
by the crowd. Finally the line moved up and I got a clear

view of the area where Logan always sat. To my surprise it appeared to be business as usual for him. He had his laptop on the table and seemed to be reading something. I pulled Dinah and the kids with me and we made our way across the small restaurant.

"Mind if we join you?" I said, pulling out a chair. Logan did a double take as his empty table suddenly filled up. He stammered something about expecting someone, but I countered by saying we'd leave when they showed up. Dinah went to join the line to get food and the kids and I stayed behind. I made some small talk about the weather and the book launch party. It was to soften him up before I started asking the real questions and it was a stall while I tried to figure out exactly how to put it. I couldn't very well just ask him where he'd been the afternoon before. I kept looking at him, trying to picture him on a bike with a helmet to see if it matched my slip of a memory. If only the rider hadn't been wearing a helmet, I would have recognized Logan's odd hairline if it had gone past.

One of the things Dinah had done was teach the kids how to take part in the conversation. Ashley-Angela pulled out the little crochet swatch Adele had taught her to make and showed it to Logan. The kids might have been accustomed to being included with adults, but Logan didn't seem to feel the same about kids. He blew out his breath a few times and I knew he was wishing we'd leave.

"I have a bike, too," E. Conner said. Logan didn't seem to be listening, and I suddenly realized the kids were like loose cannons. Dinah was coming back with a tray of drinks and I was trying to get up from the table and take the kids. "What's an alibi?" E. Conner said. I turned to Logan, hoping he was still tuning out as I tried to grab the kids and make a fast exit. "I can get up myself, Aunt Molly. That's what Aunt Molly wanted to know if you had in case you were the one who killed that man on the mountain," E. Conner continued.

Let's just say we didn't have to leave the table. Logan grabbed his stuff and pulled his jacket off the back of the chair and was out the door before Dinah even arrived with the drinks.

"Did I miss something?" she said, looking at the empty chair.

Dinah apologized for the kids a bunch of times and I told her not to worry. We'd just have to come up with another way to figure out if Logan was the killer. In the meantime, why not branch out and check up on the other list of possibles. I gestured toward Luxe, but Dinah looked at the kids. "After what just happened maybe you'd rather go alone," Dinah said.

I wasn't worried since we hadn't said anything about Nicholas being the possible murderer in front of them; besides, they were good cover. Who would think we were investigating anything with a couple of kids in tow? There were a few customers in Luxe and I noticed that Nicholas had some additional sales help. "He could have left the store and followed Emily," I said in a low voice.

A smile lit up Nicholas's dark eyes as he came over to us. He pointed the kids to a low table with drawing supplies and cookies. Dinah seemed relieved to get the kids out of the way before they could say anything. "What can I show you, ladies?" he said. "Christmas is just around the corner and so is Hanukkah. Books are nice, but so is a silver bowl."

Nobody could say I didn't think fast on my feet. "Well, actually I was looking for some accessories for a mountain bike. I don't know anything about them, so I'm not sure what kind of accessories there are."

Nicholas seemed surprised. "The only accessory I can offer is a weatherproof jacket." He took us over to a rack on the wall and pulled out a forest green one. "I think you'd be better off at a sporting goods store," he said. Dinah gave me a tiny nod of approval as she saw what I was doing.

"Do you know anything about mountain bikes? I realize you might not have anything here, but maybe you could give me an idea of what to look for when I go to a sporting goods store."

"A bike store would be even better," he said. "I have a mountain bike, but I'm not really an expert in the accessory department." I tried to hide my excitement.

"Really. Do you ride a lot?" I said, feigning polite interest.

He gave me a quizzical look. "Frankly, I don't use it very often. I didn't know you were so interested in bicycling." The door opened and Eduardo walked in. He nodded in greeting to Dinah and me, and then gestured to Nicholas and headed to the back of the store. "If you need any other help, just talk to one of my assistants," Nicholas said, walking away from us.

"That was a little abrupt," I said to Dinah. "It was almost like he didn't want to talk about his bicycle. Great. We're two for two washouts now." I went with Dinah as she got the kids. They got up from the table quickly and showed us their drawings. Ashley-Angela's slipped from her hand and sailed to the floor and E. Conner accidentally stepped on it. She started crying when she saw the footprint on her picture of fairies. He started crying when she socked him. Dinah was a firm believer in kids behaving well in public—so we hustled them out fast.

Back on the street, Dinah tried to smooth things over. I took Ashley-Angela's picture and tried to give the footprint a positive spin, which wasn't easy. The tread of his sneaker pretty much took over the paper. I kept looking at it and it stirred something in my mind.

And then suddenly it came to me. I told Dinah we had to go somewhere quickly. Once we got in her car, I directed her back to the dead-end street. As she drove, I explained my sudden inspiration. "I looked at E. Conner's footprint and it reminded me of the footprints on the dirt road. A mountain bike would leave an impression, too. An impression that could identify that particular bike," I said. "We can't very well make a plaster cast, but I could take a photo." I held up my smart phone and sent a silent thank-you to Mason for giving it to me.

"I get it, I get it," Dinah said in an excited voice. Dinah parked and we got out. The kids were excited at the prospect of an adventure.

We walked around the gate, past the sign marking it as part of the Santa Monica Mountain conservancy, and the kids ran ahead. As soon as I looked down at the short stretch of dirt road, my beautiful plan fell apart. Maybe if it had been a regular day at this time of year when the road was damp and the area quiet, the track of a mountain bike might not have been disturbed for a day or so. But yesterday had turned out to be anything but regular. "I forgot about the police cars and ambulance," I said as we looked down at churned-up sandy dirt.

"It was a good idea," Dinah said.

"Yeah, a good idea that didn't work," I said. I didn't have the heart to ruin the kids' moment, so we took them on a short walk—going in the opposite direction on Dirt Mulholland, while I tried to come up with plan B.

IT SEEMED LIKE I'D JUST COME BACK FROM MY lunch break/side trip to the mountains and then it was closing time at Shedd & Royal. The store was getting busier and busier as the holidays got closer and closer and time flew by. I'd just sent my last customer up to the cashier stand with an armload of books when I passed Mr. Royal standing by the travel section bookcase while a customer picked up a book on Burma. As Mr. Royal bent to point out another book, I noticed the leather sheath hanging from his belt. The image of Mr. Royal slashing open the boxers of Anthony accessories floated into my mind's eye. More things surfaced. He'd been absent from the bookstore during the crucial time, and since Mrs. Shedd had told him about her loss putting the bookstore on shaky ground, Mr. Royal could have been very, very angry at Bradley.

Mrs. Shedd had already started turning off the lights as the last customers checked out. There was no time to talk to Mr. Royal now, but it was definitely on my to-do list.

As I was walking to my car, my BlackBerry rang and I pulled it out.

"You answered," Mason said, sounding surprised and pleased when I said hello.

"This time I heard it," I said with a little chuckle. He claimed he'd reached an insurmountable snag in Spike's sweater. Could he come over? He'd asked me if there'd been any more incidents with Emily after he'd left, which made me wonder how much his coming over had to do with the sweater and how much a desire to protect me in case Emily came over again.

As an antidote to the recent events, I had planned to get snuggy in old sweatpants and a tee shirt and actually have the ice-cream dinner I'd planned before while I watched a romantic comedy. But I was good at changing plans in midstream.

Barry had only been able to call the previous night.

He'd picked up a homicide. The call was short and I knew there were ears around listening, so it was very business-like. I had told him about Emily's visit and he lectured me on leaving the door unlocked. I thanked him for calling Mason.

"I didn't know what else to do. My hands were tied and I knew he'd be able to handle things, just in case," he said. Then his voice got low, as if he didn't want anyone around to hear. "He didn't take advantage of the situation, did he?"

I laughed. So much for the nice gesture.

The reporters were camped out in front of the Perkins' house again and the pools of their lighting seemed strange on the dark street. The hoard ignored me, instead descend-ing on Mason as he got out of his car. He parked on the street and was an easy target. I came across the lawn with the idea of rescuing him. When I got closer, I had to laugh at myself. What was I thinking? Mason was always giv-ing out some kind of statement about some high-powered celebrity client who'd gotten in trouble. It usually went something like, when the full story came out, his client's innocence would be confirmed.

Maybe I was a little bothered by how easily he lied on camera. Maybe it concerned me that stuff he said to me was more about winning—me being the prize—than about the truth.

By the same token, it was impossible not to like him. He was thoughtful—the kind of person who if he couldn't per-sonally bring you chicken soup when you were sick, would get it delivered. He was always willing to help with my sleuthing activities. He thought I was fun and cute. I liked the me I saw reflected in his eyes.

There was something else, too. Mason was closer to the world I was used to. High-profile lawyers and public-relations people like my late husband Charlie traveled in the same circles.

And the bonus was he didn't want to corral me. For the first time, I was dealing with being in charge of my life—as much as anyone ever really is. I liked having my own identity.

For now, I liked having both Barry and Mason in my life. Maybe it was nice being regarded as the prize.

Mason made quick work of the reporters. Easy because they all knew him.

"Molly Pink always thought the Perkins were great neighbors. She's in shock about Bradley Perkins' death and the alleged issues about his financial business."

Someone asked if it was true that I'd been one of the hikers who discovered his body and if I was a suspect.

Mason addressed the group with a warm chuckle and assured them I wasn't a suspect. A gush of questions followed. Did I think Emily had killed Bradley? Had I invested money with him? Mason charmed them with his smile and answers that sounded good, but really said nothing. Ryder somehow got in the middle of it.

"If you want to know about the Perkins, check out my YouTube piece 'Life and Death in Tarzana,'" he said. Mason made points with him by actually paying attention to him.

Mason ended the media encounter by wishing them all happy holidays and walking across my lawn to meet me. "That should keep them satisfied and they ought to leave you alone." He held up his leather tote. "Thanks for helping at the last minute. I've done something wrong, but I can't figure out what."

It was a relief to get inside away from the circus. Though hardly quiet inside. Cosmo was parked in the window barking at the reporters. The cats were stationed on either side throwing in an occasional weird meow. Blondie was silently watching from across the room. I closed the shutter on the big window and Cosmo gave up. I asked Mason why he'd deflected the question about me being one of the hikers.

Mason's smile evaporated. "It's information they don't need to have." Then he gestured his head toward the Perkins'. "Any more visits?"

"No," I said. "The more I think about it, I might have overreacted. It wasn't as if she actually picked up a knife and when I realized there wasn't any blood on her clothes . . ."

"Molly, you're looking at her the way all these people who gave Bradley money looked at him. It's the idea that someone you know couldn't have done something bad. It works with my celeb clients, at least most of the time. They're familiar faces so people find it hard to believe they did something awful." Mason made a point of locking the door after I'd let the dogs have their yard run. "It's better to be safe than sorry," Mason said.

Mason made some comment about missing dinner and wondered if I had as well. I let go of my plans for ice cream and a movie and said I'd cook something. He followed me into the kitchen. I'd heard of being able to feel someone's eyes staring at your back, but I could feel his smile. I'd never cooked anything just for Mason.

I suggested he get Spike's sweater-in-progress and show me where he was stuck. When he showed me, I wanted to laugh. He'd made a mistake and was trying to rip out a row, but the yarn had snagged and stopped coming free. Fixing it amounted to a little tugging and separating two pieces of yarn. I handed it back to him and suggested he sit in the built-in booth and work on it while I cooked dinner. If he ran into another problem, I'd be there to help. He looked too pleased as he slid onto the wooden bench.

"You ought to keep your cell phone out," Mason said. My tote bag was sitting on the bench where I'd left it when I came in. Mason reached for it but plucked the owl-in-progress out instead. "What's this?" he asked. I mentioned the elephant I'd made and how I wanted to make another toy to add to the things we were sending to the shelter.

"A snow owl?" Mason said, holding it up. For the first time it registered that the head was sparkly white and the body sparkly black. I pulled out the pamphlet with the pattern and looked at the photo of the snow owl on the cover. It was all white. When I went to check the pattern I realized the pages between the snow owl and penguin had gotten stuck together and in essence I had put a white head on a black body. I said something about having to unravel it, but Mason stopped me with a grin. "Keep it. I think you might have come up with something. You know it almost looks like a vampire."

I started to protest but then realized he was right. I was as bad as the rest of them with vampires on the brain. I set it down, deciding I'd figure out what to do with it later.

"The BlackBerry isn't in there anyway," I said as I took out some dry penne noodles and put water on to boil. I poured a bag of cut-up vegetables in the olive oil and garlic I'd been heating on the stove. As they began to cook I poured in some bottled marinara sauce and the kitchen filled with tasty scents.

"I want to thank you again for it," I said. As soon as I'd added the pasta to the churning water, I pulled out the smart phone from my purse. "I'd really never hear it ring if it was buried in all that yarn. The camera function sure came in handy." I looked at the screen and began to scroll through the pictures on it to show Mason. I got to the beginning of the photos I'd taken of Bradley. I meant to scroll back over them, but I hit the wrong button—like that was anything new—and a strange photo filled the screen. One I didn't remember taking. I couldn't even tell what it was at first. The whole frame was sand colored. I kept trying to make sense of it, and suddenly I remembered how I'd fumbled with the phone while Dinah and I were trailing Emily. In all my accidental button pushing, I'd done something right. I'd ended up taking a photo of the sandy road and captured the freshly made track of the mountain bike that had just whipped past us. I smiled and actually jumped up and down.

"Let's see the picture that's making you so excited," Mason said. He reached for the phone, but I held on to it.

"It won't mean anything unless I explain." I described the mysterious biker and my idea of being able to identify him or her by the impressions of the wheels. "For once my lack of nimble fingers paid off," I said after telling him about our trip back up to Dirt Mulholland.

The pasta bounced around in the boiling water, sending a spray on the stove. The sputtering sound got my attention and I went back to check on dinner. The penne was done, so I drained it and poured it into a bowl. A little toss with olive oil and I mixed in the sauce. While I told Mason my thought that the biker could be the murderer, I made a quick salad. He helped me bring the food and plates to the table and we sat down to eat.

Mason liked my idea about matching the tire impressions and wanted to know if I'd come up with any suspects.

"I know that both Logan and Nicholas have mountain bikes and both had reason to be angry with Bradley, though Logan seems to have a lot more reason. I'd include Joshua Royal if I find out he has a mountain bike. I think he might have done it to avenge Mrs. Shedd's big loss. And then there's anyone else with a mountain bike that lost money with Bradley."

"It sounds like it could be a lot of people. I don't mean to rain on your parade, but how are you going to get a look at all these mountain-bike tires?" Mason said. He began eating and barely had finished a bite before he said how good it was. Mason ate in the finest restaurants, but sometimes there was nothing that matched a home-cooked meal.

I heard a noise in the front door lock before it opened and closed. A moment later Barry walked in the kitchen, pulling his tie loose. He was sniffing the air. No way could you miss the garlic smell. He froze when he saw Mason and me at the table.

I didn't like this part of being the prize. Both men glared at each other. I got the feeling things were a lot different when the two of them had dinner together. I pointed to Mason's dog sweater and said he was in a hurry to finish because of the cold weather.

"I'll just say two words," Barry said, clenching his jaw. "Pet store." Mason totally ignored Barry's comment.

"I hope your people are keeping an eye on our girl," Mason said, using his shoulder to point in the direction of the Perkins'.

Barry flinched at me being referred to as "our girl." I think the only one who liked it was Mason. "I was hoping Heather would arrest the Perkins woman," Barry said. "But the photographs of her with Perkins that Molly took aren't enough to build a case on." He directed his next comment at me. "Has she been over here again?"

"I already asked Molly, and she said the answer was no," Mason said. Barry glowered at Mason.

"I don't think it matters." I brought up my doubts again that Emily had killed her husband.

Barry didn't seem impressed with my reasoning about Emily's clothes. "Don't let your guard down, babe. Heather's a good detective. She's got good instincts. If she thinks Emily Perkins is the guy, you better believe she is."

"Can't you get some kind of protection for Molly," Mason asked. Barry took off his jacket and hung it on the back door handle after checking that it was locked.

"I did. Me. I had to make some arrangements, but I can stay the night." He set down the small satchel he brought when he stayed over. There was a moment of awkward silence, then Barry took out a plate and helped himself to some food and sat down at the end of the table. The next minute they started talking about who they thought was going to be in the Super Bowl.

Apparently, I was only a prize sometimes.

We all had ice cream for dessert. As we were finishing, Barry put a travel brochure on the table.

"I know you don't like things being pushed on you," Barry said. In the past, in what he thought was a romantic gesture, he'd planned a trip to Hawaii. I mean really planned, almost to the point of packing my bag. He'd just neglected to check with me first. We'd had a fight and spent some time apart over it. Barry seemed pretty stubborn and set in his ways, so it was encouraging to see that he could change. I picked up the pamphlet and thumbed through it. It featured a cruise with stops in lots of places with white beaches and clear blue water. On the back were a list of dates.

"You can think about it," Barry said. I could only see Mason out of the corner of my eye. He didn't look pleased.

"You should tell Barry about your theory that the biker is the real murderer," Mason said before turning to Barry. "She has a picture of the tire tracks and everything." I gave

Mason an annoyed look. I knew it was useless to mention it to Barry and wasn't going to. Barry lived up to my expectations.

"What?" he said. "I told you Heather is sure it's your neighbor. You can't go around asking people to see their mountain bikes."

Mason packed up his dog sweater and I walked him to the door. "Let me know if you need any help checking tire tracks." He chuckled and gave me a soft kiss on the cheek and thanked me for dinner.

Samuel came home a short time later as I was cleaning up the kitchen. My son heard the TV in the den and wanted to know who was there. It was hard to read his reaction when I told him it was Barry. He said he was tired and got himself a snack and poured out some cat food before going off to his room.

When Barry shut off the TV, he insisted on going through the whole house and checking every window and door. When he headed for Samuel's room, I prepared for a scene. Barry stopped at the door and knocked. To my relief, he didn't insist on physically seeing that all the windows in Samuel's room were locked. Even better, he explained why he was concerned about everything being secure and left it at that.

Maybe there was hope we could all just get along after all.

CHAPTER 24

"COME IN, COME IN," DINAH SAID IN AN EXCITED voice. I'd called her as soon as Barry left in the morning to tell her about finding the photo of the tire impressions and said I'd stop over on my way to work. Barry had sensed something was up and had been all cuddly and affectionate, trying to find out what it was. After his reaction I wasn't about to tell him that I was going to pursue the mountain-bike idea. He gave up when his cell phone rang and he had to take off. Now that I was at her place, Dinah shut the door and we went into her living room. I had e-mailed myself the picture of the tire track and then printed it up. I laid the sheet of paper on the coffee table, and we both leaned over it. Seeing it enlarged made the imprint very clear.

"How lucky that you're such a klutz with your phone," Dinah said with a throaty laugh. The kids came in and wanted to know what we were looking at but lost interest when they saw the picture. It was only exciting if you knew what it meant.

The plan we came up with was we'd keep trying to find out who had a mountain bike, and then we'd try to charm our way into checking their tires. My cover story was that I wanted to buy a mountain bike for my son and needed recommendations from people who owned them.

We agreed we'd work as a team.

But sometimes opportunities just present themselves.

As was becoming the norm, the bookstore was buzzing when I got there. The store seemed very festive with the background holiday music and the scents of fresh pine and hot cinnamon cookies. After I dropped off my things in my cubby, I noticed that Elise was at the table in the yarn department. I was going to see how she was doing, but a commotion around the display of the Anthony books and paraphernalia grabbed my attention.

What was going on? So many people were crushed around the table, I couldn't even see the display. Using my bookstore-worker authority, I pushed through enough to see what was up. In the center on the upper level was a copy of *Caught Under the Mistletoe*. It must have just come in from the publisher and it was the first chance anyone was getting to see the cover. One of Elise's scarves was below it. Did I mention that the book and scarf were in a sealed Lucite box that was chained to the table? The cover was a winner. Looking pale and sexy, Anthony held up a piece of mistletoe and gazed longingly toward Colleen.

Mr. Royal neared the table carrying something and the crowd parted. He set a sign down that read "Exclusive to Shedd & Royal" before he put out a handful of plastic bags. A strip of paper in gothic type said "Vampire Scarf Kit."

Before I could take one to look at it, five hands had reached out and snatched them.

"What are those and where did they come from?" I asked Mr. Royal. He began by apologizing that they hadn't talked to me first since they were really a yarn item. Elise had made them up and brought them in. Each bag had yarn, a crochet hook and Elise's pattern for the scarf.

"We decided to put them out as a test," he said.

"Looks like they scored a hit," I said. Someone pushed between us and wanted to know if there were any more in the back. Joshua Royal explained that was all they had for now, but we hoped to be getting more in. The woman wanted to put a hold on three sets.

"Do crochet lessons come with the set?" she asked, and Mr. Royal looked toward me.

I quickly explained about our group and said we'd be happy to help her learn. Mr. Royal took her information and promised to set aside three sets when they came in. She walked away, saying something about how having the scarf would be like having a piece of Anthony.

Mr. Royal handed me the paper with her order, saying, "The kits are your baby now." He started to rearrange the books on the table and I realized this was my chance to question him. But how was I going to go from the scarves and the Blood and Yarn books to mountain bikes?

Luckily, he was preoccupied with the display. As fast as he'd stand a copy of the book on top of the stack, someone would come and take it. He turned to me. "I never would have guessed a vampire would be so successful," he said while I struggled for the words to find out if he had a mountain bike. Finally I just started to babble.

"Those people are lucky they know what they want to buy," I said. Mr. Royal pulled out a box of books from under the table and started to add to the stacks. "Me, I'm stuck. My son Samuel wants a mountain bike." Joshua Royal nodded and made the right kind of noises to show he was listening. "It's just there are so many kinds. I don't want to get the wrong one. I wish I knew more about them." I stopped to see if he'd respond.

"Why don't you ask your son? He probably knows what kind he wants," Mr. Royal said.

I struggled to come up with a response. "You're right, that's a good idea, but I wanted it to be a surprise. If I ask him, I'll be tipping my hand."

He suggested I might want to check online. It sounded like he didn't have a mountain bike and I was going to write him off but gave it one last shot. "Mr. Royal, you've been everywhere and done everything. Somewhere in all that you must have ridden a mountain bike."

He ran his hand through his shaggy multicolored hair. He had been everywhere and done everything. I'd heard he worked his way across the Atlantic on a freighter, operated the carousel at Tivoli Gardens, been a beer taster in Germany and a dogsled driver in Alaska. "I could tell you the kind I have, but it might not be right for your son at all. Where does he want to ride?"

My breath came out in a gush of surprise. So he did own a mountain bike after all. "He'd like to ride around here. Up in the Santa Monica Mountains."

I hoped I didn't sound as excited as I felt.

"Well, then one like mine should do fine. I'll write down the make and model and leave it in your cubby."

Now that he'd admitted to having a mountain bike, I almost wished he hadn't. Mrs. Shedd had waited a long time for the happiness she'd found with him. I hated to think it might be over and that *murderer in Tarzana* might be added to his been-everywhere, done-everything list. The next step would be to figure out how to get a look at it. I decided to press my luck.

"I know this would be something of an imposition, but I've never actually seen a mountain bike up close. Do you suppose I could have a look at yours?" He thought a moment.

"Sure. I'll stick it on the bike rack and bring it in later in the week," he said. I thanked him profusely but felt awful at the same time. I had just set him up.

I headed to the yarn area to talk to Elise. She was almost teary eyed when I told her how the kits had flown off the table and thrilled when I said we'd like more. "And as soon as possible. They make a nice gift item," I said.

Elise was overjoyed. It was a bright spot for her when everything else around her had been going down the tubes. When I asked her if she had more of the kits, she said she'd only made up a few but had everything she needed to make up more sets at her house. Suddenly I had an idea of how to get a look at Logan's bike.

It seemed like I was leaving the bookstore in the middle of working, but Mrs. Shedd was agreeable when I explained there were more scarf kits involved. She'd seen them fly off the table and recognized a good source of revenue when she saw one.

"Molly, thank you for coming to help me," Elise said. For the first time since everything had started with Bradley, there was a light in her eyes. She led the way to her car.

The Belmont's house was in a development called Brae-mar and the houses were built on the lower part of the Santa Monica Mountains. Elise was chatting a mile a min-ute. Making the kits had made her feel a part of the whole Anthony phenomena. "I should present a finished scarf to the author at the launch party," she said, almost in a swoon. "You know what they say about writers writing about what they know," she said with a wink.

She went on and on and I had a nervous stomach. I felt terrible using Elise, but I couldn't ignore what I knew. I had to see if Logan's bike tire matched my picture. I felt around in my purse to make sure the print of the photo was there.

Elise hit a button on the sun visor and the garage door lifted and she drove in. Between thanking me and telling me how this was a new start for her, she hadn't stopped talking since we'd gotten in the car.

I had formulated a plan. It wasn't very sophisticated, but I thought it would work. Elise got out of the car and led me through the door into the house. The garage door rumbled shut behind us. Like most tracts, the houses in Braemar all had similar designs when they were first built. But over time people had remodeled and added on. I noted that the exterior of the Belmont's still had its original look and, as expected, the door in the garage went to the service porch. Elise led me in through the kitchen. This was the room Logan had raved about redoing with the first money he'd made from Bradley's supposed investments. When Bradley handed over a large profit in a short amount of time, Logan had believed Bradley really did have some special method of buying and selling securities. It was the old proof-was-in-the-pudding thing. Who could blame him for believing in Bradley?

I had a hard time not shaking my head at how things had turned out as we passed the industrial-size built-in stainless-steel refrigerator and restaurant-quality stove. The counters were all rosy-toned granite and there was a center island with its own small sink. The rosy tone was picked up in the tiled floor. A greenhouse window featured glass shelves with an herb garden. Elise barely looked at the room.

I was doing my best to appear calm, but the farther into the house we went, the more tense I got. In my mind, I kept practicing the lines I'd come up with, hoping they would sound natural.

The house was quiet and I was relieved that Logan didn't seem to be there. After the encounter in Le Grande Fromage, who knew how he would react to seeing me. Particularly if he had killed Bradley. Once somebody had killed one person, would it be so hard to kill another?

Elise took me upstairs to their second den. She'd taken the chance that the kits would sell and had gotten enough supplies to make more. She showed me the long table laid out with black, white and crimson yarn, hooks, plastic bags and directions. At the end she had sheets of labels printed with *Vampire Scarf Kit*.

"How many do you think we should make?" she said, pulling another chair up to the table. Here was my dilemma. I really did want to help her make up some kits, but I wanted to check on the bike and get it over with. I made a quick decision and as I pretended to be getting ready to sit down, I felt my shoulder and acted as though something was missing.

"My purse," I said as if chiding myself for my forgetfulness. "I must have left it in the car." I let go of the chair. "I'll just go get it."

"You can leave it there. The garage door is shut. Nobody's going to bother it." Elise said. She pushed the chair out for me. "Maybe we can make an assembly line."

I hesitated. "My cell phone," I said in a voice that was a little too excited. "That's it. I need my phone. I'm expecting a call. It'll just take a minute." I was out the doorway and to the stairs before she had time to stop me. I backtracked across the house and pulled open the door on the service porch and went into the garage. With the garage door shut, it was completely dark. I felt along the wall until I located a switch and, hoping it was a light, flipped it.

An overhead light came on and illuminated the interior. My first move was to get my purse and the sheet with the print of the photo. The garage was perfectly organized. Elise had parked on her side of the line painted in the floor, leaving space for another car. Unlike my garage that had stuff all over, this one had a wall of cabinets and closets. I began opening the larger doors. This was taking too long and I was afraid Elise would come in at any second and wonder what I was doing. The third door I opened was the charm. The bike was hanging on the wall. The front tire was easy to see. I unfolded the photograph and was holding it up to compare to the tire when I heard a rumble as the garage door began to open.

CHAPTER 25

"OH MY GOD," DINAH SAID. THEN SHE SAID IT again. "Molly, are you okay? Logan didn't hurt you, did he?" Dinah had been my first call when I got back to the bookstore.

"All I can say is I'm glad they put all their money into a fancy kitchen instead of replacing their slow-moving garage door. I had managed to shut the closet door while the door was still going up. Logan started to pull in, then hit the brakes. Even through the windshield, I could see he was glaring at me. When he got out of the car, he eyed me suspiciously and glanced around the inside of the garage as if he was looking for something amiss."

"I'd have made a run for it," Dinah said.

"That would have been the worst thing to do. It would be like admitting you were doing something you weren't supposed to," I said.

"Yeah, but I'd be safe," Dinah offered and I said I saw her point.

"My heart was in overdrive, but I tried to put on a carefree smile. Before he could ask me what I was doing there, I held up my purse and said I'd left it in Elise's car. I said wasn't it wonderful about the scarves. I ignored his blank expression and went on and on about what a big success they were at the bookstore. By now it was pretty obvious he didn't know what I was talking about and the scarf enterprise was solely Elise's idea. A moment later Elise joined us, wondering what had happened to me." I stopped like it was the end of the story.

"And then . . ." Dinah prompted.

"I went back and helped her make up some more kits and she drove me back to Shedd and Royal."

"So then you never got a chance to compare his bike tires to the photo of the imprint," Dinah said with a sigh.

"Oh, but I did."

"Well?" Dinah said.

"He's not the guy. His tires were narrower than the photo." I added that I had talked to Mr. Royal and that he had admitted to having a mountain bike and he offered to bring it in to show me.

"I thought you were going to wait for me and we'd check out the tire-picture connection together." Dinah sounded disappointed, but I explained I couldn't pass up the opportunity.

"I promise—you're in on the next bike that gets checked," I said, trying to soothe her. "The only other mountain-bike owner slash person cheated by Bradley we know of is Nicholas," I said. Dinah mentioned the obvious problem. We didn't know Nicholas very well, so how we could we invite ourselves over to check out his bike. We agreed we'd both try to come up with a solution and meet later at Dinah's house to discuss.

I called the woman who put the hold on the three kits and she came in within a half an hour and bought them. She said she'd definitely be joining the Hookers. In the midst of the cheerful holiday shoppers, Adele came in out of sorts. Her eyes bulged when she saw the action with the vampire scarves. "I could have done that," she said. "I could have made the exact same pattern."

"But you didn't," I said. "Be happy for Elise; with all the downs she's had lately, she finally has a bright spot. She's already thinking of coming up with other vampire-related crochet kits."

"She's not the only one with a down," Adele grumbled. She really didn't seem to be her usual self. Even her clothes weren't normal. I'd never seen Adele look so plain. The only holiday decoration that adorned the white turtleneck she wore over blue jeans was a little crocheted wreath with two red balls hanging down.

Finally I couldn't take it anymore and asked what the problem was, hoping she wouldn't give me too much information. "I'm afraid William might not be the author of the Anthony books," she said.

I couldn't help myself and asked what had changed her mind. "He told me he has to go out of town in a couple of days. The launch party is just around the corner. The author wouldn't be going on a trip right before the biggest night of his life."

"Where's he going?" I asked, hoping I could find something reassuring in his destination. Adele was always difficult, but a depressed Adele was even worse. She tended to walk around making very loud plaintive sighs.

"It's research for his next book. He said something about there being only a small window of time to see an exhibit in Miami. He said he wanted me to come with, but he knew I couldn't take the time off because of the holidays and all."

"He could still be A. J. Kowalski," I said. "He's going to be back by the launch party, isn't he?" Adele nodded. "Well, there you go." Adele suddenly brightened at my words and hugged me a little too tight.

"Pink, thanks. That's what best friends are for." She instantly straightened and took some more holiday decorations out of her pocket and began pinning them on her top.

Sheila must have been on a break from her job as receptionist at the gym. She was at the back working on something. Even from a distance I could see she was working in a different palette. Everything she'd made to sell before was in blues combined with greens and lavenders. Whatever she was working on today was all about red. I had a few finished swatches that needed to be hung and I went back there.

I fingered the ball of rusty red fuzzy yarn in front of her. "What's up with the new colors?" It looked like she was working on a shawl and I could see where she'd mixed in some fun fur yarn that was red flecked with gold.

"Nicholas suggested I do something in warmer colors," she said, continuing to crochet. "I think it's turning out nicely." She held it up and draped it over her shoulder.

"I think he's onto something. At this time of year it's nice to have bright and warm colors." I glanced out the window. The colors of the shawl did seem to cheer up the cold gray day. Because we usually had so much sun, the dark days seemed even more dreary.

It was a pleasure to see how Sheila's confidence had surged. She still had plenty of tense moments, but she seemed to handle them much better.

I didn't think talking to Sheila about Nicholas interfered with my promise to Dinah to include her in my next caper. This was just about getting background.

I realized I really knew very little about him. Sure, I'd seen him a lot and had snippets of conversations, but I didn't even know if he lived in Tarzana. It wasn't hard to get Sheila to talk about him. After the experience she'd had selling her creations by consignment at another store, she appreciated Nicholas.

"He's a gentleman in every sense of the word," Sheila said. It wasn't just that he'd been complimentary of her work and very fair about what he paid her—it was his whole manner. "Did you ever notice how he really listens to people?" she asked.

"It sounds like you have a thing for him," I said. I'd never heard her say as much about anybody before. I regretted the comment almost as soon as I'd said it. Sheila stiffened and the color rose in her face. Her breath changed, too, and I recognized she'd gone into anxiety mode.

"It's not like that," she stammered. She took a deep breath and let her stomach balloon out before she expelled the breath slowly. She reached in her purse and took out a sandwich-size plastic bag she always carried with her emergency crochet kit. It held a size J hook and some cotton yarn that had been crocheted and ripped a bunch of times. She made a slipknot and began a chain. She made the loops big and loose and went back over them with single crochet stitches.

"I didn't realize I was coming across that way," she said with a worried look. "I hope Nicholas doesn't think I'm coming on to him." She kept crocheting and her stitches were all over the place, but since it didn't matter, it began to have a calming effect. "I don't want to mess things up with him. He's really paying me well for my pieces." She took some more deep breaths and moved on to another row. "I don't think Nicholas would ever think of me that way. He doesn't have a girlfriend, or at least he's never mentioned one to me. I don't know if there's room for anything besides that store in his life. He's there practically all the time."

I asked her if she knew where he lived. By now she'd stopped crocheting with the cotton and ripped out all the stitches and put it away. She answered without hesitation. "He has a small apartment, but I think he barely spends any time there. He's always at the store. I called his cell the other night about bringing over some more pieces and he had me bring them to the store. It was hours after it had closed."

"Really?" I said. The bookstore was always open later than Luxe and I'd gone past the store lots of time after its closing and it always looked dark and deserted. When I mentioned that, she said he'd told her to knock on the glass door. She'd seen him come from the back.

"Did you ever see what was back there?" I asked, remembering how Dinah and I had wondered about the walled-off area. She shook her head.

Eduardo stepped up to the table. "Ladies," he said in his rich deep voice. He took out several plain wool scarves to leave for the collection we were making. CeeCee and her companion, Tony, were going to bring them to a shelter on Christmas Eve. A vampire scarf in progress had gotten twisted with one of the scarves and landed on the table.

He picked it up quickly and put it back in his leather tote. "It's for my girlfriend. She's a big Anthony fan," he said. "A vampire who crochets," he said with a low laugh.

Even in jeans and a black sweater Eduardo looked like he'd stepped off the cover of some romance novel with a title like *Kiss Me, Touch Me, Thrill Me.* It occurred to me he probably knew more about Nicholas than I did, too. I recalled the way Nicholas had greeted him when Eduardo came into Luxe. They seemed to be friends.

I commented that we'd just been talking about Nicholas. Eduardo was generally quiet during the Hookers' meetings. So I was surprised at how much he opened up about Nicholas. Apparently after years in advertising, Nicholas had left it behind and opened the store. It had cost him all his friends and his wife, who thought he was crazy to give up a big job to take a chance on a long shot. "The guy's had some hard times. It's not easy when you take a chance on something."

"Is the store doing okay?" I asked, thinking Eduardo might know.

"It's more about his passion than profit," Eduardo said. "He's always upbeat when there are customers around, but I've seen him when he was pretty dark."

Mrs. Shedd interrupted and seemed frantic about me helping in the front with customers. I didn't have a chance to think about Nicholas again until I'd left the store and gone to Dinah's. The girl across the street was going to stay with the kids while we did some holiday shopping. I had hoped to crochet presents for everyone, but I'd finally accepted time was running out. Maybe next year. Lucky for us the mall was staying open until midnight.

On the way there, I told her about the whole discussion about Nicholas.

"I think Emily does have something going on with Nicholas," Dinah said. She reminded me that when Bradley had first gone missing, Emily's first stop had been at Luxe. "Remember the tea she offered us?"

"Right, and she went to the store to return things when she needed money," I said.

Dinah reminded me that Nicholas had said she was returning things. "How do we know he didn't just give her some money?"

"And when she was trying to avoid being followed, she slipped out through the back door of Luxe." I stopped as another thought surfaced. "Suppose she told Nicholas she was going to meet Bradley? She could have even told him where she was meeting him," I said.

"He had motive. There's the money he lost, and if there was something going on between him and Emily—" I stopped myself and shrugged hopelessly. "But none of it means anything if we can't tie him to the murder. Sheila said he practically lives at the store, so I'm guessing the mountain bike is there. Maybe the afghan and knife, too."

We'd gotten to the mall and the only investigating we did for the next couple of hours was to find a store that hadn't sold out of the electronic juggling bear the kids wanted. Several hours and a lot of packages later, Dinah drove into the back parking lot that serviced the bookstore and the other strip of stores along Ventura. She had pulled next to the greenmobile and I started to gather my packages. I glanced up at the back of the building. It was easy to figure out what windows went with Luxe.

It was late enough that everything was closed and I wondered if Nicholas was in the back section of his shop. I pointed toward the window next to the door we'd seen Emily come out of. There seemed to be some light coming from it. Dinah turned off the motor. Our minds were so in tune, we didn't even have to discuss it.

We got out and approached the back of the building

and moved along the wall until we got to the edge of the deep-set window. My heart was pounding in anticipation as I leaned in just enough to get a peek. I leaned back quickly and Dinah nudged me.

"What did you see?" she whispered.

"Nothing. The window's frosted." We stepped straight back and looked up at the window. The bottom might be frosted, but it looked like the top part was clear glass. Again, no discussion was needed. Without a word, we both started looking for something in the parking lot to climb on.

Dinah pointed out one of the Tarzana trash cans under a light pole. The square-shaped tall bins were part of the Safari Walk, as the stretch of Ventura Boulevard that passed through Tarzana was designated, and were supposed to add to the character of the area. Each side had the silhouette of a wild animal. The important thing was the flat top made it easy to climb on, and it was empty and moveable. The trash bin made a scratching noise as we started to drag it over the pavement. Dinah held up her hand and came back with one of the unfolded gift boxes she'd gotten at Macy's. We slipped it under the can and were able to pull it without noise. We stopped and gave each other a high-five at our cleverness when we got the can under the window. Dinah had wound her scarf around her neck so there were no long ties to catch on anything. I boosted myself on the top of the receptacle and then twisted around until I was on my knees. I figured I could balance against the sides of the window as I stood up. Dinah's job was to make sure I didn't step off the can.

I went from kneeling to crouching and began to ease my way to standing. Dinah and I had done things like this before, but it still sent my heart into flutter mode.

I had my hands on either side of the window as I moved up past the frosted area. Just a little more and I'd be in the clear area.

And then I felt two hands grab the back of my legs.

This was one of the problems of having a car that stood out. Maybe if I'd parked in the shadow instead of right under a light pole, he wouldn't have seen the greenmobile.

"Do you want to tell me what you're doing?" Barry said after he'd gotten me off the trash can.

"No," I said. He surprised me by laughing. He replaced the decorated can, while telling me I was lucky he, instead of a patrol car, had found me.

I told Dinah it was okay and to go on home, so she could let the babysitter go. Barry followed me back to my house.

He helped me take in the packages and looked around the inside of the house, making a few jokes about expecting Mason to pop up with his dog sweater.

"Okay, Sherlock, what were you up to this time?" Barry asked. It was late and I was tired so I just told him. I showed him the pictures of the tire impressions and said Nicholas had admitted to having a mountain bike.

After being down on the idea before, Barry's reaction totally surprised me. I wasn't sure if it was real or just because Mason was so willing to be my cohort in investigating.

"Interesting idea. I checked and there are a lot of different kinds of mountain-bike tires, and I suppose each person's would wear differently," he said, examining the print, which by now was getting a little worse for wear. He wanted to know what I would have done if I'd seen a mountain bike parked in the back room of Luxe.

"You don't want to know," I said in a teasing voice.

"You're right," he said in a light tone as he put his arm around my shoulder. We flopped on the couch. "Just remember, all arrows point toward your neighbor. Heather thinks there was no blood on her clothes because she was wearing some kind of covering like a rain poncho and had on gloves. She hasn't bothered you again, has she?"

Samuel came in later and the noise of him rummaging around the kitchen woke me up with a start. I was sitting up on the couch nestled next to Barry. We must have fallen asleep in midconversation. After thinking my bike tread idea was good, Barry'd gone back to telling me to let it go. When I said nothing, I think he'd smiled, thinking it meant I was agreeing.

Not exactly.

CHAPTER 26

I MET DINAH OUT IN FRONT OF LUXE THE NEXT day. She was taking the kids to a holiday program at the library, and I was on my way to the bookstore. I had come up with a quick plan I thought would get me into Nicholas's secret back area.

"We could just ask to see his mountain bike," Dinah said. "You could give him the same story you gave Mr. Royal about wanting to get one for Samuel."

"I already told Nicholas I was shopping for bike accessories. By the way, Mr. Royal hasn't shown me his bike yet. He might have just said yes to end the subject and had no plan to follow through. He could know why I'm so anxious to see his bike. Remember the biker might have recognized us as he zipped by." I looked at the kids. My idea was better. Who could turn down children?

There were several customers browsing in Luxe who I recognized from the bookstore and I nodded a greeting.

The kids wanted to leave and Ashley-Angela was getting dangerously close to a meltdown so I figured it was time to put the plan into action.

Nicholas was waiting on someone and I realized it was William. I tried to calm Ashley-Angela by pointing out William was Koo Koo the clown. For a moment she stopped fussing as she watched Nicholas hand him a shoe box. But as soon as she saw the shoes were some kind of brown wool-lined ankle boots instead of the red clown shoes she expected, she started fussing again.

My window of opportunity hadn't even opened and already it was shutting. I went up to the counter and didn't even wait for Nicholas to finish wishing William a nice trip before I interrupted.

"I'm sorry, but it's kind of an emergency," I said, pointing at Ashley-Angela. "She needs to use the restroom." I gestured toward the door to the back area.

Nicholas glanced toward the kids. Ashley-Angela's fidgeting gave credibility to my request. I knew he was going to go for it. He started to step away from the counter and I waved for Ashley-Angela to come. She broke free of Dinah's hand and ran up to me.

"Aunt Molly, why did you say I have to go potty? I don't have to go," she said. She looked up at Nicholas. "I didn't tell her I had to go." She rushed back toward the front door. "C'mon, I want to see the puppet show at the library. We're going to miss it."

How could I have forgotten that kids were loose cannons?

Dinah went on up the street toward the library and I headed to the bookstore. She said they'd be back in time for the Hookers' gathering. Dinah looked a little worn. As much as she liked the kids, having a pair of almost five-year-old fraternal twins 24/7 was getting to her. I was glad

I'd said I would take care of them for her evening out with Commander.

As soon as I walked in, Mrs. Shedd and Mr. Royal were in my face. There were all kinds of logistics to go over about the launch party. It was the biggest event the bookstore had ever been involved with and there was even more riding on its success. Though I wondered if selling a bunch of books in one night would be enough to save the bookstore. "The eyes of the world are going to be on us," Mrs. Shedd said. "We don't even know who we're dealing with. Suppose it's some high-strung person who freaks out when faced with a bunch of people. There has to be a reason they've been keeping their identity secret." Obviously, Mrs. Shedd had discounted what Adele said about it being her boyfriend.

"Molly, all your events turn out off center," Mrs. Shedd continued. "They're interesting and people seem to like them. But this one is different. This one can't end up in a riot."

We had a summit meeting in the café and by the end I think I'd calmed them both. I reminded them this wasn't going to be an event where an author gave a talk. It was just going to be a long line of people getting their books signed. The key was how to handle the line and how to make sure it kept moving. We decided to have a meeting with everybody working the event later and we'd have sort of a dress rehearsal.

When we dispersed, I went back in the bookstore and headed for the worktable. The Hookers were having their own little holiday gathering, and it was going to be our last meeting until after Christmas. We were celebrating with food and wrapping the scarves and other items we'd collected for the shelter. Everyone had nice comments about the elephant when I'd set it with the other things to be wrapped. The response to my other project was a little different.

I'd made the most of the vampire look of the sparkly white head and sparkly black body by altering the penguin wings to look like arms and adding feet. I'd embroidered on happy-looking eyes and a smiling mouth with a drop of red dangling from a fang. Finally, I'd added puffy black hair. When I had set him down, Elise had squealed and named him Anthony. Then everyone, including Rhoda, said they wanted to make one, too.

The store was busy for morning and now that our table was surrounded by the yarn display, we had shoppers around us looking at yarn and accessories while we had our get-together. I had to straddle being at the Hookers' meeting and trying to help customers at the same time. Adele was doing the same thing, but I had to be on the lookout for any knitters. Though Adele had been okay with them once, who knew how she'd be the next time.

I was surprised to see Madison Perkins come into the area. I hadn't seen Bradley's sister since the mall event. I wasn't sure if I should offer my condolences again, now that Bradley was really dead. I think everyone else was thinking the same thing. Madison helped end the awkward moment by asking what we were all working on. While she looked over the collection of warm things for the shelter and admired my toy creations, I asked her if she'd seen Emily. Her face grew stern.

"Under the circumstances I don't want to see her," Madison said. The circumstances being that at least Detective Heather was certain Emily had killed Bradley. "I wasn't close to my brother, but still . . ." She paused a beat and then added she'd had nothing to do with his business dealings. I looked at Dinah and nodded. We were on the same page. Could it have been Madison on the mountain bike?

Madison walked over to the bins of yarn, saying she needed more of the royal blue yarn she'd gotten before. I hadn't realized it, but it must have been pretty popular yarn because the bin was empty. I asked Madison for her phone number, assuring her I'd call her when some more came in. Really I just wanted a way to contact her.

By the end of the day, I was beginning to rethink my offer to babysit the kids. Sitting on my couch and crocheting sounded better than trying to entertain Ashley-Angela and E. Conner. But I knew Dinah was looking forward to the evening with Commander.

Mason was about to walk into the bookstore as I was coming out. He had his crochet bag with him, and when he saw me, he pulled out the half-done dog coat and said he needed help.

When I told him about my babysitting gig, he wasn't dissuaded and said he'd come along. We walked up the block to Dinah's. She was all done up for her evening and so happy about going out she hugged both me and Mason while thanking us. Commander's reaction was similar without all the hugs. When I saw how he looked at Dinah, I was extra glad I'd made the offer.

His eyes really did light up.

Once they left, Mason asked how it was going with my mountain-bike investigation.

"Not well," I said, mentioning that I'd only been able to check one set of tires against the photo. I hadn't told Dinah, but I was having second and third thoughts about the whole line of investigation. "And even if I find the right tires, what am I going to do?"

Mason nodded in agreement. "Just because someone was riding up there doesn't automatically tie them to the murder. Sorry, Sunshine."

"We want to play dreidel," E. Conner said, coming up next to us as we sat on Dinah's chartreuse couch. He disappeared and a moment later came back with the one they'd decorated. It wasn't enough for just the two of them to play with the top, so Mason and I got looped into joining. Mason didn't remember how to play and E. Conner explained the gambling game. He'd added some of his own rules. Instead of everyone having the same kind of candy to bet with, E. Conner's rules had everyone beginning with something different. E. Conner got chocolate kisses, Ashley-Angela got little candy bars, Mason got raisins and I got chocolate coins. Mason and I weren't exactly into it and we went back to talking about the whole situation with Bradley Perkins.

We went back to the beginning and Mason brought up how the SEC investigator had based his belief that Bradley had taken his own life on the hunk of money left in the checking account. "What did you say the guy said?" Mason said, "Something about someone running off would never do that. They'd clean out everything." Mason looked up at me as he absently fiddled with the holiday top. "Obviously the investigator was wrong and Perkins was clever enough to figure out that was what the SEC people would think."

I thought about it for a moment as E. Conner put one of his chocolate kisses into the pot. When no one else made a move to put their bet in, he took one of Mason's raisins from his pile, a chocolate coin from mine and then reached for a candy bar from his sister's. Ashley-Angela started to

fuss because her brother hadn't let her do it herself. I tried
to calm her down and told her she could spin first.

I turned to Mason. "Does it make sense that somebody
who'd be calculating enough to leave money in an account
to validate his suicide would also gamble away millions
of dollars?" I said. Mason asked me how they figured out
Bradley had lost the money by gambling. "I overheard the
SEC investigator say that there were piles of checks written
to different casinos and no money besides the amount in the
checking account."

Ashley-Angela's spin came up with the Hebrew letter
Shin that meant she had to put one of her pieces into the
pot. E. Conner went to add it for her and she went into
a tantrum and said she didn't want to play anymore. She
went to take back her pieces, but instead she took all of
her brother's candy kisses. While I tried to keep them from
socking each other, E. Conner said, according to the rules
you couldn't start with one kind of candy and then when
you quit, take something else out. Mason made a joke that
it was candy laundering.

"I wonder . . ." I was staring at the candies and thinking.
"What if that's what Bradley did—like Ashley-Angela, he
put in one thing and came out with something else?"

Mason's face lit with understanding. "Good thinking,
Sunshine, but in his case the stakes were a little higher,"
Mason said with a chuckle. "He could have been putting
in checks and coming out with cash." Mason reached for
his BlackBerry and started scrolling through numbers.
"There's a way to find out."

Mason said he had a contact in Vegas, which was no
surprise. He seemed to have contacts everywhere. He made
a call, and when he hung up, he was smiling and nodding.
Mason's contact was someone who acted as a concierge for

big gamblers. He worked for one of the major hotels and it was his job to keep them happy. He knew who Bradley was right away.

"He said the guy would change a big check into chips, he'd hang around and play a few hands of blackjack or something and then start turning in the chips for cash. He knew that as long as he turned in less than three thousand dollars worth at a shot, there was no paperwork. The guy I talked to said he thought Bradley spread money around and had some help with cashing in the chips and did the same thing at a lot of casinos. So now the question is, what happened to all that cash?" Mason said. He was standing now and walking back and forth thinking. "I'm guessing he stashed it somewhere offshore."

"So he didn't lose all of Mrs. Shedd's money after all," I said.

He put up his hand to temper my excitement. "Don't rush and tell her. The money is probably in an account somewhere, but only the dead guy knows where." He was right and I felt my initial enthusiasm drain out. The money might be stashed somewhere, but for all intents and purposes it was still gone.

The kids had long since stopped arguing and had fallen asleep on the couch. We carried them into the bedroom and put them to bed.

Dinah came home glowing. She pulled me aside and said Commander had accepted the kids no matter who their parents were. He realized her involvement with them showed what a big heart she had. Her smile dimmed when I told her what Mason and I had figured out. "But what's the point if nobody knows where the money is?" Dinah said and I agreed.

CHAPTER 27

TWO DAYS WENT BY AND WE WERE NO CLOSER TO finding Bradley's stash. It was down to the wire for the Anthony launch, and with the holidays filling the store with customers, *frantic* was the word of the day. I barely noticed that Mr. Royal hadn't brought in his mountain bike as promised. Maybe it was as I'd thought: He'd just agreed to end my questions.

I'd gotten wrapping-desk duty, which it turned out also meant I was the chief question answerer. Most of the questions involved the book launch. Was Anthony going to be there in person? No, because he was a fictional character. Was it true that Mrs. Shedd was the author? I didn't think so, but who knew for sure? Was it safe to come to the launch since the bad vampires might show up and make trouble? See the answer to question one.

I was so busy I didn't notice that Adele wasn't around until Mrs. Shedd came by the wrapping table looking for her. My boss seemed very agitated and I asked if there was anything I could do.

"Adele talked me into having a display of Koo Koo books for the launch. She seemed to think that people would be particularly interested in them. I agreed to the display, but said the books needed to be signed in advance. She was supposed to put up the display today. Now I can't find Adele or the books."

Rayaad overheard our conversation and told us Adele had left, saying it was some kind of emergency and she had to drive her boyfriend to the airport. Rayaad remembered that Adele had taken the box of Koo Koo books to be signed with her the night before.

"Those books weren't hers to take," Mrs. Shedd said, seeming even more agitated. "Molly, please see what you can do. I better not walk in the kids' department and see an empty display."

I had never seen Mrs. Shedd so upset about something as small as a box of books. But I was sure it was just a cover for what was really bothering her. I hadn't told her that I thought Bradley's ill-gotten money was hidden somewhere. There was no point in giving her hope unless I could deliver the goods.

I called Adele's cell phone to read her the riot act. "I can't bring the books in right now," Adele said in an irritated tone and made some comment about Mrs. Shedd making a fuss about nothing. She explained William was filling the gas tank and then they were stopping for snacks on the way to the airport. She wasn't supposed to be back at the bookstore until the evening anyway. When I said Mrs. Shedd was really upset about the books leaving the store and implied this might be the swan song for Adele's job, she finally got that she was in trouble with our boss.

"Pink, you have to help me," she said. "The books are at William's." She sounded desperate. "I left the keys to his place in my cubby." She asked me to get them and actually added a *please.* I must have really gotten through to her.

On the way to the parking lot I ran into Ryder making a video of a woman in a Santa hat sitting on the curb. He saw me rushing and wanted to know what was up. When I told him, he asked if he could tag along. Dinah was just turning the corner. The kids were helping Commander at the mail-it center. When she heard I was on a mission, she said she'd come along, too.

Ryder had his mother's Mercedes SUV and offered to drive. We all piled in and headed for William's house. It was late afternoon as we drove onto his street. In the time since I'd been there, the rest of his neighbors had put up their holiday decorations, though for now the lights weren't on and the street looked normal.

We passed the giant Koo Koo on the lawn as we walked to the front door. Adele had told me she thought the books were in the living room. I was going to get the box and go, but Dinah wanted to see what had made Adele think William was the real A. J. Kowalski. The three of us went into his writer's room and I cautioned everyone to keep their hands to themselves. I pointed out the worktable. The crochet books were still on it.

Ryder had picked up that William might be the vampire author and was filming the room and adding his commentary. I put my hand in front of his camera and ordered him to stop. No way was he going to post anything to YouTube and ruin the bookstore's thunder. In my haste I knocked into the table and books and papers fell off. I explained about William's eye for detail and the three of us went to try to replace all the things on the table just as they had been.

I set down the crochet book William had borrowed from Adele where I thought it had been. A piece of green paper had fallen down with the book. I recognized it as the sheet I'd seen when I'd been there with Adele. I had only gotten a glimpse of it then and remembered she'd said it was notes she'd made when she was figuring out the pattern of the afghan for me. This time I looked at her scribbles. There were all kinds of notes, and in the middle she'd drawn a rectangle and divided it into rows of boxes. The first couple of squares had Xs that probably were meant to stand for the flowers in them. Then she'd changed to just writing in numbers in a couple of the boxes. She'd just drawn one flower with a question mark in each of the rest of the squares. Across the top, in big letters, she'd written a note about the tassel situation stating that there should be one tassel on each corner or just one tassel on one corner, but not one tassel on one corner and two tassels on the next one and then none. I studied the sheet and showed it to Dinah and said William must have been really hard up for a bookmark to have kept the paper.

"Or maybe he was planning to have Anthony make the afghan in the next book," Dinah joked.

"He'd have a hard time using this for a pattern unless he understood Adele's secret code," I said. As I said it my eye went to a book on the floor.

"*Ciphers and Codes?*" Ryder said, noticing what I'd focused on. I stared at it for a long moment and then suddenly I had a thought.

We all gazed at the paper as I pointed out the afghan drawing. "What if the flowers really were some kind of code?" I said. Before anyone could answer, I pulled out my BlackBerry and scrolled through the contacts until I found Madison's number.

I called and asked her how she'd come up with the pattern of flowers for the afghan she'd given her brother as a wedding present.

"Not that afghan again," she said with annoyance in her voice. "I don't know who told you it was a wedding present. Bradley paid me to make it for him. He wanted it to be some kind of numerology thing. He gave me several long numbers and said they represented important dates for him and Emily and her kids and he wanted them incorporated in the coverlet. They had to be in the right order," she said. As she said it, I thought of Adele's note about the tassels and something clicked in my mind.

"And so that's why you put a tassel on one corner and two tassels on the next. You were showing where the numbers started, weren't you?" I said.

"Right. It made it weird looking, but Bradley didn't seem to care," she said. She said she'd given him the paper with the numbers when she gave him the blanket and forgotten all about it. She faltered and I said I knew she'd made another crocheted blanket for her brother. She admitted that Emily had contacted her with some confused message that Bradley wanted another afghan like it. She'd made up something quickly, but the only thing it had in common with the first one was that the background was green and it had some flowers incorporated in it.

When I repeated what Madison had said, Dinah got a skeptical expression. "Important dates? I don't think so. I bet all that fuss Bradley made about getting the afghan had nothing to do with sentiment."

"Exactly," I said. "More likely it had to do with where he stashed all the money."

"Numbers, stashed money, huh?" Ryder said. "Like maybe he had one of those Swiss accounts. There was this show on the Crooks and Spies channel called *Dude, Where's the Money?* It was all about those accounts that don't use names, just numbers."

Ryder's words hung in the air for a moment, and then everything really made sense. "Of course, that has to be it. Talk about hiding something in plain sight. What a way to keep track of the account number so no one would know. That's why Bradley wanted the afghan before his faked suicide. And why he took the risk of breaking into my house twice. Now it makes sense why he kept upping his offer to Emily to get it to him. And now I understand why whoever killed Bradley took the afghan with them."

"Right," Dinah said. "They had to understand what the flowers meant."

Ryder held the sheet of paper. "Do you think the clown figured it out?"

I suddenly had a strong urge to look in the garage.

Dinah and Ryder followed me. When I turned on the light, I saw it. The mountain bike was leaning against the wall, and when I took out my print of the photo, it was a perfect match to the size of the tire and the tread.

"Oh my God, William is the killer," I said. And something else popped forward in my mind. The image of William buying the wool-lined boots for his trip. "He's not going to Miami, he's going someplace cold, like maybe to Switzerland.

"We have to stop him," I said, rushing toward the front door. We got outside, hopped into Ryder's mother's Mercedes and he put the car in gear. By now it had gotten dark and all the holiday displays in all the front yards were illuminated. Ryder started to back out but stopped with a start. He hadn't seen that the street was clogged with cars because they had all turned out their headlights so they could see the lights of Candy Cane Lane.

He finally was able to pull out, but now we were part of the procession of slow-moving cars. I tried Barry's cell and got his voice mail. I began leaving a message, but it was so convoluted that it didn't make sense even to me. I took a deep breath and called Detective Heather. I got her voice mail, too. I cut to the chase with her message and just gave her the facts that I thought William was the killer and that he was on his way to the airport, and I bet he had the afghan. I had no idea if she would believe me.

"Adele is going to have to keep him from leaving," I said as I called her cell.

I heard Dinah snort from the backseat. I admitted it was going to be a challenge.

I got Adele in the car. She cut me off before I'd even finished hello. "Pink, just tell Mrs. Shedd I'm dropping William off at American Airlines and then I'll come back to the bookstore and straighten everything out about the books. I cut her off and told her I had to tell her something very important and that she should just listen and say nothing.

"Pink, if it's some of your detec—"

"Hush," I yelled at her. "I said just listen. You're not going to be happy with what I'm going to ask you to do. I need you to keep William from getting on the plane." She made a sputtering sound, but I quieted her again. I told her he wasn't going to Miami. I took a deep breath and told her that he had killed Bradley and I could prove it. I heard her gasp and then tell me I was nuts.

I told her to check his ticket and she'd see that he wasn't really going to Miami.

"You're ridiculous and I'm not going to do anything," Adele said. I made one more attempt to get through to her.

"I know you don't want to believe me because he's your boyfriend and what I told you is a total shock. I hate that it's true, but it is. I always thought you were too good for him, anyway." She didn't say anything else, and when we hung up, I figured the last thing she'd said still stood. She was in total denial and was going to let him leave.

By now Ryder had gotten out of the clog of cars and hit the gas as we headed for the freeway. The freeway wasn't moving, but Ryder said not to worry, he knew all the short-cuts.

I tried Barry again, thinking we were never going to make it in time. Ryder did know every back road. We went up steep streets and along the paved part of Mulholland before getting onto Sepulveda as it paralleled the freeway. I was leaning forward, willing the SUV to go faster. Ryder was a typical young adult male driver. He wove through traffic like he was braiding a ribbon. I finally closed my eyes and hoped for the best.

"Hey, MP, here we are," he said, finally pulling up to the white curb in front of American Airlines. I got out and he started to follow me, but the recording playing over a loudspeaker reminded us it was for loading and unloading only. Dinah came around to the front seat and said she'd park the car.

We looked in through the glass door at the line waiting to check in, but there was no Adele or William in sight. We took the elevator up a level to the area just outside the restricted zone on the slim chance William was up there.

There was just a small area before the first checkpoint for last good-byes. I didn't see Adele at first. She was hidden behind a post. When I checked the screening area, William was just putting his shoes, jacket and carry-on in plastic bins to go through the X-ray machine. He took off the vam-pire scarf around his neck and added it to one of the bins. Ryder was right behind me with his video camera going.

What was he going to call this YouTube piece—"Murderer Escapes"?

What could I do? It only took a moment to realize the answer was nothing. If I made some kind of fuss, the only one who'd get detained would be me. All I could do was watch him go. He was pushing the bins with his stuff onto the conveyer belt and the TSA guy said something to him and pointed. William nodded and reached into his pockets. As he pulled his hand out, he looked down and his face registered surprise as his hand came up.

Suddenly it was like everything went into slow motion. The TSA guy pointed at William's hand and yelled, "Gun," just as I saw it. All the people waiting in line screamed and dove for the floor as another TSA guy jumped over the row of metal tables and tackled William, before two uniformed officers ran from their station and joined the fray.

"Is it over yet?" Adele said, stepping from behind the post.

As they led William away, he caught sight of Adele and his usually placid face twisted in a grimace. "You," he spit out in anger. "I should have known that you'd ruin everything. The only thing you were good for was pushing the Koo Koo books." He grunted at her. "You and your ridiculous clothes, you're nothing but a big—"

Before he could finish, I stepped in. "Shut up," I shouted at him. "You should have been grateful to have a girlfriend like Adele. She's one of a kind and special. You're not good enough to kiss the hem of her colorful clothes."

William snarled at all of us before being led away.

A SHORT TIME LATER, DINAH, RYDER, ADELE AND I were sitting on the curb outside the terminal. The message about the area being set aside for loading and unloading kept playing, but we didn't care. We all needed to regroup.

"Did you really mean all that, Pink?" Adele said, leaning against my side.

I had to ask myself the same question. Yes, I did mean it, particularly the part about her being one of kind. Nobody could argue with that.

"I didn't want to listen to you, Pink," Adele said. "But when I went to get his carry-on out of the backseat, I finally checked his ticket and saw that he was only changing planes in Miami for one to Geneva. His passport was there, too. When I realized everything he'd said to me was probably a lie, I got angry."

"How'd you plant the gun on him?" I asked.

"It isn't real," she said, reminding me of the kid who'd brought the cap gun to story time and how I'd made her stick it in her car. "I found it under the seat of the car. I made a big deal of saying good-bye to him and insisted on him taking the vampire scarf I made for him. I had wrapped the gun in it and when I tried to stuff the scarf in his pocket, put the gun in instead. Then I said it was better to put the scarf around his neck. I was so smooth, he didn't know what was going on," she said, beginning to turn back into the Adele we all knew and were annoyed by.

A black Crown Victoria pulled up as we were sitting there and Detective Heather got out.

"You came," I said, surprised. "How'd you find us?"

"I just followed the ruckus," she said, rolling her eyes.

They wouldn't have been able to hold William for long since the gun was a toy, but Detective Heather was able to look in his carry-on and found the afghan. There were traces of blood and no doubt tests would confirm it was Bradley's.

She figured the knife was probably hidden someplace at William's, which she'd find when she got a search warrant.

We all had to go back to the station to give our statements. To my surprise Detective Heather even mumbled a thank-you for what my friends and I had done to stop him. That was as far as she went, though. She didn't mention that me and my friends basically solved the whole thing for her.

Then Detective Heather did something else, which totally surprised me. She didn't say anything in explanation, but she let me watch her question William. I suppose it was her way of showing off what she could do.

I didn't get to sit in one of those rooms with the window that looks like a mirror on one side like you see on TV. I had to watch on a grainy monitor with a bunch of her colleagues just outside the interview room.

I thought for sure William would clam up and ask for a lawyer as soon as she read him his Miranda rights. But no, William insisted it was all a misunderstanding and he was sure once she understood everything, she'd let him go. Detective Heather never did get a chance to show off her skill at interrogating. In fact, she barely got a word in. William insisted he wasn't like the others who invested money with Bradley. "I wasn't after fancy cars or mansions. I was going to use the profit to devote myself full time to the Koo Koo book series and the legacy I would be creating.

"Bradley Perkins not only stole my money, he stole my dream," William said, looking Detective Heather right in the eye. "I'd committed to buying a house, and set up the perfect writer's studio for myself."

But when he had told Bradley he wanted to cash out, Bradley had stalled him. William had become more insistent. He needed the money to pay for the house and he'd given notice at his job. Finally William became suspicious and called the SEC and instigated an investigation.

"I believed Bradley had killed himself at first. If it was true he'd lost everybody's money and the SEC was after him, it made sense. But then I overheard things at the bookstore and began to think Bradley had faked the whole thing. It made me wonder if he'd really lost all the money after all." By chance William said he'd been paying attention when Adele was ranting about the afghan pattern and when he heard Emily demanding it back at the holiday event, he figured there was more to it than crochet. It had taken a little while, but he'd figured out what was hidden in the afghan. The problem was Adele had changed the tassels and messed with the numbers of flowers, so that there was no way he could get the correct sequence of numbers.

"All I wanted was the money he owed me," William insisted. He'd been in the bookstore when we'd been following Emily. Adele was glad to tell him about all our theories and crazy sleuthing. He'd realized we might know something and followed us. He'd been planning to ride his mountain bike anyway and it was in a rack on his car.

As he said that, I remembered that when I'd parked behind the bookstore, the car next to me had had a bike in a rack on it. It must have been William's.

"I passed the three of them and hid in the bushes until I saw where they were headed. I know all the trails up there. It was easy for me to go another way and not be seen. I waited until his wife gave him the crocheted thing and left. I saw Molly Pink and her friend take off. This was my chance; I was going to make a deal with him. I'd keep quiet about everything. All I wanted was what he owed me."

William claimed he tried to reason with Bradley, but he kept insisting the money was all gone, that he'd lost it gambling. When William tried to grab the afghan, Bradley had pulled out the knife.

"I held on to the afghan and tried to make a run for it. Bradley wouldn't let go and neither would I. He stepped back and tripped over a branch. When he fell, he pulled me and the afghan with him. He was going to stab me. We struggled over the knife and I got hold of it. I was just defending myself when I stabbed him."

But that didn't explain why he'd stabbed Bradley so many times and then left him there to die. And why did he say he was going to Switzerland with the afghan? "I was going to get the money and then share it with all the investors."

Right. Like any of us believed that. I think William was truly surprised when Detective Heather didn't agree with him about it all being a misunderstanding and didn't let him go.

Detective Heather told me William would most likely be charged with second-degree murder and tampering with evidence, but under the circumstance, the incident with the toy gun would probably be let go. Detective Heather said it would be up to a jury to decide whether they believed the self-defense story, but she was betting they wouldn't.

And was William A. J. Kowalski? No. He really had been planning to write *Koo Koo Learns to Crochet*. But it looked as though it was more likely he'd be writing *Koo Koo Goes to Prison*.

Barry was a little awkward when he came by the next day to finally help install my new front door. "What can I say?" he said, looking at me with a sheepish smile in his eyes. "You done good."

Meanwhile Ryder's video of the episode at the airport made it to the news, and when he intercut it with William in his clown attire doing the holiday rap, it was number three on the YouTube top ten for the day. He came over just as Barry was finishing the door and, with a flourish, bowed to me.

"M, thank you for letting me ride along." Then he straightened and asked me if I would explain to his mother why her SUV was gone so long, when he was just supposed to be getting gas for it.

Mr. Royal kept his word and showed me his mountain bike in the bike rack on the back of his Prius. Nicholas came by with a brochure from the bike store. I was glad neither of them knew why I'd wanted to see the bikes.

Emily came across the lawn and thanked me. She wasn't off the hook exactly. She was still trying to convince everyone that she had no knowledge of Bradley's fraudulent activities, but it didn't look like she was going to get charged because they didn't have a case. It seemed likely she would lose the house and she was broke. She had talked to her mother in South Carolina, and as soon as she could, she was going there to try and make a fresh start.

The SEC investigators were embarrassed about not figuring out what Mason and I had about the money not being lost. When the numbers of flowers were written out, they identified the bank and the account number. Word spread quickly among the investors that all was not lost. Not that they'd get the big profits on their investments they'd hoped for, but they'd get back at least a hunk of their original investment. The SEC investigator said what had thrown him off was Bradley's lifestyle. Most swindlers were flamboyant and lived high. Bradley was the first one they'd encountered who'd been frugal. They figured he looked at the money he was taking as savings for his retirement.

Mrs. Shedd thanked me deeply. She knew her share of

the money wouldn't cover all that she'd borrowed to invest, but she hoped it would cover a lot of it. In the meantime, Mr. Royal was going to keep the bookstore afloat with his own money. It turned out all those years of adventuring, he'd lived very cheaply and banked the rest.

By now Adele was telling everyone that she'd figured there was something fishy with William all along and had really been planning to break up with him.

And then all thoughts turned to the midnight launch party and the unveiling of Tarzana's own vampire author.

CHAPTER 28

THE NIGHT OF THE BIG EVENT, WE CLOSED THE bookstore at 9 and said we'd reopen at 11 P.M. There were already people gathering, so we junked the idea and unlocked the door. I had the plan down. We gave out different-colored wristbands that corresponded to when their group would get their book signed, then we let them shop. Under the circumstances, Mrs. Shedd had removed the display of the Koo Koo books. Adele was still in shock about William and said she was going to skip the big night, but she showed up anyway, saying she'd come to support me.

"We're musketeers," she said, grabbing me. "I couldn't let my musketeer sister down." She instantly became lord of the wristbands and corralled the people by the color of their band and started ordering them around.

The parking lot was filled with TV trucks, with their satellite dishes extended. The crowd was overflowing the bookstore. It was cold outside, but nobody seemed to care. The excitement generated warmth. We'd rearranged the café and hired extra help. Some of the people were wearing vampire scarves they'd made from the kits, though by now they were calling them Anthony scarves. Logan had come with Elise. They had put together a bunch of kits, which sold out quickly. The dust hadn't settled on the whole affair with Bradley, but now that it was clear that Logan hadn't been in cahoots with Bradley, people were talking to them again. Still it was going to take a long time to regain their trust. In the meantime he had ideas for the vampire-accessory business working with his wife. He wanted to talk to A. J. about endorsing the scarf.

The excitement level kept building and by eleven thirty we'd given out all the wrist bands. Mason had come by, not for a wristband, but because of his curiosity about who the author was. Barry came by, as well.

"Vampire shampire," Barry said, shaking his head.

"You're out of touch, Greenberg. Vampires are hot." Mason smiled and I saw that he'd put on wax fangs.

I had set aside a spot for the Hookers. Maybe it wasn't fair, but they were part of the bookstore family. And Anthony was a crocheter and so were they. Sheila was the most dressed up I'd ever seen. I was surprised to see Rhoda elbowing through the crowd.

"No way was I going to miss this. Who knows, maybe this A. J. Kowalski looks like Quentin Tarantino," she said. She looked at Elise with her vampire scarf wound around her neck. "You know that she still thinks A. J. is a real vampire," Rhoda said. Dinah slipped in and announced that Commander was home with the kids. Instead of her trade-mark long bright-colored scarves, she was wearing a long vampire scarf. CeeCee and Tony arrived and got caught up with the media people. I noticed some other local actors in the crowd. Most were recognized more from the movies or TV shows they'd been in rather than their names. The media people grabbed them anyway. Mrs. Shedd was watching the whole thing in amazement. Nicholas came over and we let him in the VIP Hookers area. I noticed Sheila's whole being lit up when she saw him.

"Wow," he said, admiring the crowd.

We had set up a big clock in the front of the store. It felt like New Year's Eve as I watched the last five minutes tick down. When it got to the last sixty seconds, the people began chanting the countdown. On the dot of midnight, three plain-sided trucks pulled into the parking lot followed by a stretch limo. The trucks stopped in front of the bookstore and the drivers and their help rolled up the back, loaded their dollies with boxes and began to wheel them in. Mr. Royal used his knife to cut them open and we began handing out books and taking payment.

A few minutes ticked by and everyone kept looking toward the limo parked out front. At last the door opened and a woman stepped out. All heads craned in her direction. A man got out after her and they came in the bookstore. A writing team? I'd never seen either of them before but I pushed through the crowd to get to them and lead them to the platform.

I introduced myself and thanked them for coming and took them up the steps.

"I hope you have a pen," I said in a joking manner. They looked at each other and then at me. When they finally introduced themselves it turned out they were the publicists the publisher had sent.

"Where's A. J. Kowalski?" I said. The door to the bookstore opened and Eduardo walked in. A surprised gasp went through the crowd and he seemed confused. Then he got it.

"Hey, folks, it's not me."

We had the first group ready to file past the author, but no author for them to file past. Mrs. Shedd gave me a dark look. Could she think this was my fault? I looked skyward. "Please, A. J., wherever you are, please show up." I felt movement in the people next to me and the crowd parted as someone walked through toward the platform.

Nicholas!

Eduardo gave him a high-five as he passed and Sheila's mouth fell open. The media people with their cameras focused on him and stuck microphones in his face. Questions came from everywhere. He looked overwhelmed for a moment, then the Nicholas we knew clicked in and he was all charm, explaining why he'd never revealed his identity until now. At first it was because he didn't know how the books would do and if the first one bombed no one would know he'd written it. And when the books took off, the mystery of who he was caught on and he'd let it be. But now he felt it was only fair to the fans to let them know who he was. I'd heard parts of the story before, about how he'd worked in advertising, but it never felt like his passion. When he got divorced, he decided to take a chance and become authentic. The store and the vampire books were always a dream and he'd made both come true. He wrote at night in the store. What better time to write a vampire book? The crowd ate it up.

He seemed suddenly shy and waved to the crowd. He held up a copy of his marked-up manuscript as proof of who he was. Elise got to be first in the line. She held the book to her heart after he signed it and gave him one of the scarves, pointing out the vampire features. He laughed and thanked her. Sheila was right behind. She struggled to say something, but nothing came out. With a warm smile, Nicholas told her to relax. He was just the same person she'd known all along. He signed her book and hugged her. Then everything fell into place and the lines started moving. Nicholas was wonderful. He talked to each person as he signed their book.

It was the first time we'd ever kept the bookstore open all night. The agreement was that he would sign copies of just the new book, but when we ran out and there were still people left he signed copies of the first two books in the series. He signed vampire scarves, pieces of paper, coffee cups, whatever, until the last person in line was satisfied.

"Luxe won't be open today," he said, putting his head down on the table as dawn was peeking through the big windows that faced Ventura.

I asked about the mysterious back room and he laughed. "I can show it to you now."

He took me down the hall that led to the back exit. On one side there was a door that opened on the space behind the store. His desk and computer were in the middle of the large room. Along with a table full of yarn and partially done projects, there was a coffin, though a Hollywood prop sort of thing. One wall was covered in pictures he said acted as his inspiration. He had an easy chair with a lamp on one side and a table stacked with books he used for references. It was the antithesis of the stylish store. "My creative den," he said with a flourish. Eduardo came in and Nicholas gave him a man hug and thanked him again. Eduardo was his crochet consultant.

One thing did seem a little strange. The kitchen area in the corner appeared as though it was never used. When I looked inside the small refrigerator, it was empty except for a carafe of scarlet liquid. Tomato juice, perhaps?

EVERYBODY RECOVERED FROM THE ALL-NIGHT SESsion at Shedd & Royal. The event showed up on newscasts as far away as Australia. The last few days before Christmas went by in a flurry of vampire fans who wanted to buy an Anthony book from the store where the author shopped and last-minute shoppers who just wanted to buy something for the people still on their list.

And then it was the night before Christmas and all through my house there was lots going on, but thankfully not a mouse. For the first time since Charlie died I'd reinstated our traditional holiday party. I felt a tear well up as I looked around at all the people I had in my life. The dining room table was full of food, with everything from blintzes and potato pancakes to lasagna and salad and my showstopper stained glass cookies.

"Dear, these are almost too pretty to eat," CeeCee said, holding up the cookie so the light shone through the windowlike red candy center. "But just almost." She popped the buttery cookie in her mouth. She and Tony had just come from dropping off our crocheted gifts at the shelter. It had been an emotional experience. "Molly, I felt like I was the one getting the gifts," she said. "To see how much the packages meant to them and the fact that we'd taken the time to make something for them . . ." Just telling me made her eyes well up and made her reach for another cookie for sustenance.

I had wondered about sending the owl/penguin that had turned into a vampire, afraid it might be too scary for a kid's gift. When I asked about it, CeeCee rolled her eyes and laughed. "Scared of it? Are you kidding? Everybody was trying to trade for it."

Rhoda and Elise flanked Nicholas as he helped himself to food. Both women were still awestruck that he was the vampire author. Rhoda hadn't called him foofie once. Sheila brought in a pot of coffee and set it on the dining room table. Nicholas glanced up at her and smiled broadly.

"Now that everything is out in the open," he began, "my life is going to change. I'm going to need help for Luxe. More than help, I need someone I can depend on to manage things."

The whole time he'd been talking, his gaze had stayed on Sheila. "Is it something you'd be interested in?" he asked. When she didn't reply, he added that the job came with full benefits and she could continue with her costume design classes.

"Oh my," Sheila said at last as her breathing became choppy. "Oh my," she said again as she reached in her pocket for her hook and string. She began to make a length of chain stitches without even being aware of what she was doing. Her breathing calmed when she began a row of single crochets and she had a beautiful smile. "Yes," she said, finally. "I would like that very much."

Mason brought Spike, who was wearing his crocheted red sweater. I'd finally taken pity on Mason and, once the murder was settled and the launch party over, I'd finished it for him. Peter had brought his girlfriend for another chance to meet me. Samuel had invited some of his musician friends, who had set up in the corner of the living room and started to play. Jeffrey was following him around like a shadow. Ryder had come, too. I heard him working the crowd, telling everyone to check out his YouTube piece. Dinah and Commander had come with the kids. I was glad things seemed to be working out for them. It was nice having some little ones for the holidays. In between everything, I'd managed to crochet a little monkey for Ashley-Angela and an elephant for E. Conner. I'd gotten a stocking for each of them and, along with the toys, had filled them with candy canes, maple candy and art supplies. Dinah was going to hang them up when the kids went to bed so they would have a surprise in the morning.

Adele was still recovering from the shock about William and behaved in true diva fashion with a lot of sighs and faraway looks. I must have needed my head examined, but I'd talked Barry into trying to fix her up with a motorcycle cop he knew.

As I stood in the dining room, Barry came and put his arm around me. We looked out at the backyard full of orange trees and then something happened.

It started with a few white swirls and I thought I was seeing things. But then there were more spots of white twirling around the orange trees before landing softly on the ground. Barry and I watched as a thin layer of snow began to cover the grass. It wouldn't last and would probably be gone by morning, but for now it was pure magic. He pulled me closer as we shared the moment.

"Hmm, snow in Tarzana. Maybe Santa will show up, too," he said with a smile. "Merry Christmas." He reached in his pocket and pulled out a small blue velvet box.

Simple Snowflake

Materials: 1 ball of J&P Coats Royale Metallic crochet thread—white/pearl (enough to make a number of snowflakes)
Size 00 (3.50 mm) hook
Tapestry needle
Liquid starch
Wax paper
Cardboard
Rustproof pushpins
Clear transparent thread (for hanging)

Finished size: About 7 inches across

Chain 8 and join with a slip stitch.

Round 1: Chain 14 (first 6 chains count as first triple crochet), single crochet in the sixth chain from hook, chain 2, *triple crochet in the ring, chain 8, single crochet in the sixth chain from hook, chain 2.* Repeat from * to * 4 times. Join with a slip stitch to sixth chain of the beginning chain 14.

Round 2: *Chain 6, single crochet in the third chain from hook, chain 6, single crochet in the third chain from hook, chain 9, single crochet in sixth chain from hook, chain 6, single crochet in sixth chain from hook, chain 6, single crochet in sixth chain from hook, chain 6, single crochet in third chain from hook, chain 6, single crochet in third chain from hook, chain 3. Join with a slip stitch to top of first triple crochet in the preceding round.* Repeat from * to * 5 times. Fasten off and weave in ends.

Finishing: Dip the completed snowflake in a small amount of liquid starch (a sandwich-size plastic bag works well). Squeeze out the excess starch and lay on a piece of wax paper on top of a piece of cardboard. Shape the snowflake and, starting in the middle, hold in place with rustproof pushpins. When it's dry, remove the pushpins and carefully pull off the wax paper. Attach clear thread and hang.

Vampire Scarf

Materials: 1 skein white Bernat Satin Sport yarn (about 221 yards or 202 meters)

2 skeins black Bernat Satin Sport yarn (about 221 yards or 202 meters)

About 4 yards of rouge Bernat Satin Sport yarn (for tassel)

Size H 8 (5.00 mm) hook

Tapestry needle

2-inch piece of cardboard (for tassel)

Finished size: About 5½ by 88 inches

Gauge: 15 half double crochet stitches and 12 rows = 4 inches

Note: When changing colors, you can carry the yarn along the side of the scarf. The edging will cover the carried-along yarn.

With white, chain 22.

Row 1: Half double crochet in third chain from hook and in each chain across—20 stitches made. Chain 2 and turn.

Row 2: Half double crochet in each half double crochet across. Change to color in the last stitch. (Change color by working last stitch until there are 3 loops on hook; yarn over with new color and pull yarn through all 3 loops to complete the stitch.) Chain 2 in new color and turn. Repeat rows 1 and 2, alternating between white and black until the ball of white and ball of black are used up. End with white. Fasten off and weave in ends.

EDGING

Attach black yarn and single crochet evenly around the whole scarf, making 3 single crochets in each of the corners. Fasten off. To make the fang trim, attach black yarn to the edging on one end of the scarf, *single crochet, double crochet, triple crochet, double crochet, single crochet,* repeat from * to * 3 more times. Fasten off. Repeat on the other end. Weave in ends.

TASSEL

Wrap about 3 yards of the red yarn around a 2-inch piece of cardboard. Take a 6-inch piece of red yarn and thread it through the tapesty needle. Slip the needle under all strands of the yarn at the top of the cardboard. Pull it tight and tie it around the wrapped yarn. (Keep the ends separate from the tassel and use later for tying the tassel to the scarf.) Cut the loops of yarn at the opposite end of the cardboard. With an 8-inch piece of red yarn, wind it tightly around the loops and tie securely. Trim the yarn so the loose ends are all about the same length. Tie the tassel to a corner of the scarf.

Mrs. Shedd's
Santa Lucia Buns

1 cup milk
1 package dry yeast
¼ cup lukewarm water
1 tsp. sugar
²/₃ cup sugar
5½ cups sifted all-purpose flour
½ cup softened butter
2 eggs
1 tsp. salt
1 tsp. ground cardamom
1 egg white, slightly beaten
1 tbsp. cold water
¼ cup slivered almonds

Scald milk and cool to lukewarm. Proof yeast by stirring it into the lukewarm water and teaspoon of sugar. Cover and set aside. After 5 minutes it should begin to bubble. Pour the proofed yeast into the mixing bowl. Stir in the luke-warm milk and $^2/_3$ cup sugar.

Gradually add 2 cups of flour and beat until smooth. Add the butter, eggs, salt and cardamom and beat until well mixed. Add the remaining flour and mix. Turn the dough out onto a lightly floured pastry cloth, board or piece of wax paper and knead until smooth and elastic.

Place the dough in a greased bowl and cover. Let rise until doubled in bulk (about 1½ hours). Punch the dough down, cover and let rise until double in bulk again (about ¾ hour).

Divide the dough into about 26 equal pieces. Roll each piece between hands and coil the rope into a circle. Cover and let rise until double in bulk. Brush with egg white and cold water and sprinkle with almonds. Bake at 350 degrees for about 23 minutes.

Showstopper Stained Glass Cookies

1 bag of fruit-flavored roll candy or other hard candy
1 cup softened butter
2/3 cup sugar
1 egg
2½ cups sifted all-purpose flour
½ tsp. salt
2 tsp. vanilla

Separate candies by color; put each color in a plastic bag. Cover the bag with a towel and crush candies with a hammer. Set aside.

Cream butter and sugar. Add egg and beat until well mixed. Gradually add flour and mix until well blended. Add salt and vanilla and mix well. Chill the dough for at least 3 hours before rolling out. Roll out the dough to about ¼-inch thickness and cut out cookies. Cut out a hole in the center, leaving at least a ½-inch border. Place cutout cookies on parchment-lined cookie sheets. Fill cutout space with crushed candy. Bake at 350 degrees for 8–10 minutes. Candy should be melted and cookies lightly browned. Let the cookies cool before removing them from the cookie sheet.

An alternative: The dough can also be shaped into logs before chilling and then sliced and decorated with colored sugar or sliced almonds or a few chocolate chips and baked at 350 degrees for 8–10 minutes.